BUILDING EDEN

This, above all: to thine own self be true,
And it must follow, as the night the day,
Thou canst not then be false to any man.

— Hamlet, Act I, Scene 3; William Shakespeare

BUILDING EDEN

A Novel

Matthys Levy

Upper Access Books
Hinesburg, Vermont
www.upperaccess.com

Published by Upper Access Books
87 Upper Access Road, Hinesburg, VT 05461
802-482-2988 · *https://upperaccess.com/*

Design of cover and interior layout by Kitty Werner.

Upper Access titles are available at special discounts for bulk purchases.
Please contact the publisher to inquire. For such inquiries, email Steve
Carlson, *steve@upperaccess.com*, or call 802-482-2988

Library of Congress Cataloging-in-Publication Data

Names: Levy, Matthys author.
Title: Building Eden : a novel / Matthys Levy.
Description: Hinesburg, Vermont : Upper Access Books, 2018. |
Identifiers: LCCN 2018002034 (print) | LCCN 2018005904 (ebook) | ISBN
    9780942679458 () | ISBN 9780942679441 (trade pbk. : alk. paper)
Subjects: LCSH: Architects--Fiction. | Skyscrapers--New York (State)--New
    York--Fiction. | Construction industry--New York (State)--New
    York--Fiction.
Classification: LCC PS3612.E93735 (ebook) | LCC PS3612.E93735 B85 2018
    (print) | DDC 813/.6--dc23
LC record available at https://lccn.loc.gov/2018002034

ISBN 978-0-942679-44-1

Printed on acid-free paper in the United States of American
18/ 10 9 8 7 6 5 4 3 2 1

Acknowledgments

This tale is drawn from my many years of experience in the construction industry and the many architects, engineers, developers and contractors that I met, worked with and admired. The work is fictional and is not meant to represent any particular character among those I knew. Nevertheless, the reader might find similarities to some personages in the news. This is strictly coincidental.

As I labored to develop this story, many people helped me along the way. One of my first readers was Helen Goddard, who provided an early critique that guided me. Other readers from whom I gained valuable insights include David Robinson, Richard Porter, Bill Dodge and Amy Cherry. Steve Carlson, Kitty Werner and Sarah Antonick provided the needed editorial and artistic guidance to bring the book to publication. Of course, my wife Julie Simpson deserves all the credit for giving me continual moral support that I needed along the way.

Dedication

To Monica, Jennifer and Alex

Contents

ONE
The Groundbreaking
September 4, 2000; Monday Morning

THE COLD, EARLY MORNING LIGHT cast long shadows ahead of the blue-jean-clad men and a few women passing through the wood and wire mesh gate, wearing hooded sweatshirts in muted colors with imprints emblazoned with the crests of local unions. Hands in their pockets, hoods pulled tight obscuring their faces, shoulders hunched forward to ward off the chill of this early fall day, the workers looked down to avoid tripping on some haphazardly tossed timber or stone. Beyond the gate they peeled left and right with a nod toward friends. "Later," said one. "Yeh" was the response lost in the general din.

Spread out before them was a construction site that encompassed over two full city blocks between the confining steel and concrete of Manhattan Island and the expansive Hudson River waterfront. The outlines of a large excavation were barely definable, obscured by apparently randomly placed mounds of earth. It seemed a disorganized, ravaged, lunar landscape with workers meandering through the maze, each directed by some unseen force toward their assigned station.

A few men climbed onto earth-moving machines, heaving themselves up over rusty crawler tracks partially buried in the wet clay. Within minutes, puffs of smoke rose as engines from bulldozers, trucks, and pile drivers awoke from their nightly sleep. Giant buckets anchored to their mechanical arms reared upward, like the trunks of snorting elephants, and then dropped hard into the ground with steel claws, scraping earth and rocks into their gaping mouths. As the buckets filled, they were raised once more and simultaneously rotated until they hung precipitously over the injured beds of dump trucks before dropping their loads of earth and rocks, causing the trucks to shiver from the impact. Then, like a monster ballet, the cycle was repeated over and over again until a truck was full and roared off toward a remote New Jersey landfill where it would disgorge its detritus. On another part of the site were tall pile drivers with hammers rhythmically pounding steel H-shaped piles into the resisting ground. The mixed sounds of the construction site were deafening.

To the right of the gate, with workers hammering and slowly assembling a hastily built wooden platform, a man with a camel-hair coat casually draped over his shoulders angrily faced a round-faced bear of a man with unruly thinning white hair who was wearing a stained yellow parka and clutching a notebook under his left arm.

"I don't give a fuck what you have to do to finish this podium but I want it done long before the politicians and guests arrive for the groundbreaking in two hours. I gave you the position of site manager for this project because you did a good job on the midtown office building. This project is a million times more complicated and if you can't even organize the construction of this simple viewing platform, maybe I've made a mistake."

Trying to control his explosive temper, Patrick Connolly turned red in the face as he said, "Look, Alex, we've had rain for days and I had to bring in clean gravel to stabilize the soil before we could even start work on the platform."

"I thought I made it clear that I don't accept excuses." Alex Grant paused for a minute and, with an accusing finger rising from under the front of his coat, pointed down toward an older worker who was sipping the last of his morning coffee. "In fact, I want this man out of here. Get me a carpenter who can do the work. Is that clear?" Without waiting for an answer, Grant turned and walked briskly toward a waiting limousine, his tan coat ballooning out behind him, the empty sleeves flapping like a drunken bird. Grant was of medium height and build, an altogether average looking man, except for his fierce intimidating blue eyes shielded by thick chestnut eyebrows. He was a man who was clearly used to getting his way.

Patrick Connolly turned toward the carpenter who had just been summarily dismissed and brusquely said, "You heard the man. Get your tools together and collect your pay at the office trailer… and tell Sam … never mind." While grumbling under his breath the carpenter gathered his belongings and moved away. With his somewhat stocky, muscular, almost six-foot frame, Connolly was physically superior to Grant in every way, but recognized that Alex was the boss and had to be respected even though he was often irrational and impulsive. Feeling frustrated, Patrick lifted the field phone brusquely to his lips and tensely said, "Sam."

After a moment of crackled sounds, the answer came back, "What's up?"

"We've had another blowup here. Alex is in one of his moods. I've had to sack one of your carpenters and I need another one NOW."

Sam Ruth was the contractor's job superintendent responsible for managing the labor force and scheduling sub-contractors. "OK, Pat. I know Alex can be a ball buster but please, don't order my guys around. You know that's not the way it works. We're the contractors and the workers on the site are my responsibility. You're the owner's rep and it's up to you to deal with Grant."

"Sorry Sam, I know he's my boss but some days," taking a deep breath, "Grant just pisses me off. Help me out this time. I really need another carpenter to finish this platform in the next hour before the bigwigs arrive." After a moment he added, "You know the score. After all, we're both cut from the same cloth."

Sam broke in, "That's a bit of a stretch don't you think? Our backgrounds may be similar but you're cut from white cloth and mine was black."

"Okay," chuckled Pat with a smile on his face. "So, your family came from Harlem and mine from Hell's Kitchen, but we both worked our way out of.... but, look, let's talk later. In the meantime, I really need another carpenter."

"You've got it."

Patrick Connolly was in his early sixties with a ruddy complexion resulting from too much exposure to the sun. He had graduated from New York's City College with a degree in engineering but quickly discovered that construction was both more remunerative and offered him greater opportunities. He enjoyed the challenge of juggling the many disparate needs of a construction project, organizing the players to move smoothly from one task to the next and watching a building take shape, knowing that his leadership provided the linkages that made it happen. For many years, he worked for contractors as a site superintendent, a position he held on Alex's earlier project. When he was offered the position of site manager for the Eden project he did not hesitate in accepting the challenge, knowing full well that working for Grant would not be easy.

AFTER LEAVING CONNOLLY FUMING ON the unfinished platform, Alex retreated to his limousine, which was parked just outside the gate, and threw his coat onto the backbench. Surrounded by an enclosing structure of steel and glass, he felt protected for the first time since arriving at the site, although his heart continued to pulse rapidly.

He opened a drawer of the desk that faced the bench and pulled out an envelope, carefully spreading the white powder onto the table into two tracks forming little ridges a few inches apart; his pleasure hills, he called them. Taking a short straw and leaning over the desk, he rapidly inhaled from one nostril and then the other while drawing the straw along the white ridges. He closed his eyes and wiped his nose with the back of his right hand, leaned back against the bench as the muffled sounds of engine-driven hammers began fading slowly from his consciousness and his mood changed from insecurity to a sense of supremacy and increased energy. He was ready to conquer the world.

He could, at long last, feel the joy of taking full responsibility for a major project. When the elder Mr. Grant had died five years earlier, Alex Grant inherited the firm that his father had grown into one of New York's major real-estate development groups. During all the years Alex had worked for his father, he suffered constant criticism. Nothing he did was ever good enough to earn praise or even an acknowledgment of a job moderately well done. All he could do was to suppress the hurt, the frustration and the anger that constantly burned within him, knowing that one day the firm would be his and he could mold it in any way he desired. The anger never left, even as he coveted the power and authority he now held.

The sun rose higher in the sky, seeking open passageways between densely packed Manhattan buildings to spread its warmth onto the site. Participants in the anticipated ceremony began arriving; the politicians in their chauffeur-driven limousines, the engineers and architects on foot from the nearest subway station, and a few invited guests on a bus that had been chartered for the occasion. All milled around on the newly completed platform, talking and shaking hands until, precisely at ten in the morning, Alex stepped out of his limousine, smiling, and walked briskly across the gravel-strewn ground, jumped onto the platform, stood at the podium and raised both hands to calm the assembled crowd.

"Friends," he started, "fellow New Yorkers, thank you for coming on such a cool, gray fall day to what I'm sure many of you see only as a muddy field. Imagine that three years from today, instead of a naked site, you will see behind me three spiraling towers with offices, residences and a hotel. Surrounding them will be a nature complex with a cavernous lower-level pool fed by a wall of water cascading against an exterior glass wall. Above this, and originating from an underground shopping arcade, will be a gently rising hill with a meandering path lined with plants and multicolored flowers bathed by the warm sun penetrating through a crystalline skylight. What a thrill it would be to take an elevator down from your apartment for a morning walk through this temperature-controlled magic forest and then be whisked up to your office, feeling relaxed and ready to tackle the challenges of the day. This will be a self-contained city within a city. Nothing this ambitious has ever been attempted before, not even in Tokyo or Paris. It will be a veritable Garden of Eden in the middle of this bustling city, which is why I've named it *Eden Center.*

"Now, let me introduce the project team that is going to create the most spectacular complex ever conceived by man," hesitating as he looked across the crowd… "or woman. Sorry, Claire, I didn't see you behind Patrick. Construction men always seem to stand up front, hiding important team members, and…" Alex paused to emphasize his next thought, "it is a team that will accomplish the dream of this project. I'd like to take all the credit, but I can't. Since he is in front, I'll start with Patrick Connolly; he's my right-hand man and the one responsible for the platform you're all standing on, keeping your polished shoes out of this muddy site. He's also the person I will rely upon to keep the construction on schedule and see to it that every feature of the design is built correctly."

Patrick shifted his muscular frame uncomfortably from one foot to the other and smiled nervously, suppressing the anger he still felt from his morning encounter with Alex. When dealing with construction people he was direct, often crude, staring them down with his deep-set green eyes and arguing forcefully until they acceded to his position. But, among softies, as he viewed this group of politicians, bankers, architects and engineers, he felt uncomfortable. It was not clear to him why.

Alex continued: "You might not see Claire Fletcher too often, but without her there might never have been a project. She shepherded it through the political minefield, wangling approvals from all the government agencies. It's to her credit that most of the people she had dealt with are still talking to her. Of course, not all of them!"

Careful what you say, big boy, thought Claire as she absentmindedly combed a hand through her short blond hair. Even in a coat covering a black jacket and skirt fitted to her trim body, she was clearly the most beautiful woman in the group standing on the platform.

"Seriously, folks, I will be forever grateful to Claire for her critical role in bringing us to this day. Of course, there was the grand architectural idea conceived by the man now looking out at this virgin site. Philip Corta, turn around so we can all see you. I've admired this man ever since I first failed his architectural design course, but hired him on Claire's recommendation and I haven't regretted it for a moment. Phil's the most imaginative designer I ever met. He's created an architectural masterpiece, a complex of buildings strongly rooted in this earth but yet light and soaring toward the clouds. I love the way he describes it, help me out here Phil."

Corta, dressed in black slacks, a black turtleneck shirt and black Italian-cut jacket, the uniform of a late twentieth century architect, could barely be heard over the roar of the big earthmovers that were crawling like ants around the site. Cupping his hands over his mouth as he spoke, he said, "It is meant to create an oasis in the middle of the city where people will be able to work in a dramatic setting, enjoy the benefits of nature, and be at home in a relaxed atmosphere...truly a self-contained environment. I visualize it as the conjunction of an underground empire, invisible but ever-present, with a growing field of delicate structures, rising upward like flowering plants, shielded by a crystal canopy." While speaking, he raised his ballerina fingers and cut through the air, imparting form to his words.

"I wish I could understand what Phil just said," Alex exclaimed. "But he said it so beautifully and in that crisp accent..."

"Cheers," Corta yelled out, and then mumbled, "You spoiled bastard," as he thought about Alex's father, who would certainly never have been so crude.

Alex turned away from Philip. "Anyway, I can't wait to see the dream take shape. There are many others who have contributed to getting us to this groundbreaking but if I mentioned them all, we'd be here all day. For those of you who have forgotten who I am, I'm Alex Grant, and it's my development company that has brought us to this point. The actual construction will involve a substantial investment from outside financial institutions that have already made sizeable commitments. Chip, are you listening?"

As he stared directly at Alex, Chip Stewart, the banker, felt the whisper of a caress against his hand from another prominent attendee. He felt a warm rush of blood rising in his body, making him feel lightheaded but he dared not turn to acknowledge or rebuke the offender. *Later*, he thought, *later*. Fortunately, Alex dropped the subject of financial relationships.

"Now folks, this is the moment we've been waiting for, as I have the privilege of showing you the future. Here is Eden Center! Patrick, will you do the honors and unveil the model?"

When Patrick lifted the black-velvet shroud from the model, a murmur of awe spread throughout the small group, as they saw for the first time the incredible beauty and power of Eden Center. Towers twisted upward, surrounded by a graceful, undulating, curved lace roof that snaked around the towers, defining the nature complex. The composition was unique yet contextual and related beautifully to its environment. The face toward the city included a glazed galleria that invited in the public. On the riverside, a landscaped park with dining kiosks along a riverwalk and a boat basin were intended to bring life to a long-neglected part of the city. Although descriptions of the scope of the project had appeared in the press earlier, the full dramatic impact of the composition was only now revealed.

"Let me now introduce our distinguished guests from the political arena, without whose support and encouragement we would not be standing here today. Behind me are, from left to right, Senator Hamilton Johns, Mayor Roger Bartlett, and Governor Cynthia Davenport."

Alex introduced each of the guests with a compliment and a joke and each gave a brief speech lauding the project, promising their full support to achieve successful completion. Afterward, as the crowd began to disperse, some of the guests moved closer to admire the model. Alex engaged the politicians in discussions, smiling and shaking hands as photographers from media organizations framed them in front of the model. Within minutes, aides to the three politicians led them gingerly away from the thinning crowd and toward waiting vehicles. Philip stepped off the platform and onto the site, intent on viewing the progress of the work…his project!

"Wait up," shouted Alex as he ran to catch Philip. "How long have we been working for this day? It seems like an eternity." His face tightened and seemed ready to explode as he put his arm on Philip's shoulder and grasped it hard, feeling the thinly blanketed bones.

"Your parents would be proud." Philip thought back to that first meeting in New York twelve years ago and to a subsequent invitation for the Cortas to spend a weekend at the Grant country house in Truro. It was during the cocktail hour on the last day that the commission for an apartment building was offered and decided upon. He remembered Mr. Grant as a patrician-looking gentleman with gray hair parted above the center of his high brow and an erect posture belying his seventy plus years. He also remembered feeling embarrassed, as Mr. Grant took every opportunity to berate his son, saying, "I realize that I've spoiled Alex and that he certainly could learn a thing or two from your work ethic and accomplishments. I had never been able to convince him that rewards in life are the result of what you're willing to put into your work." Of course, now the elder Mr. Grant was no longer around to pressure the son, who greedily relished his newfound authority. "Actually, if it had not been for the success of the Landown Apartment building, the commission he gave me at your instigation, you might not have been in a position to trust me with this project. When Claire saw that building, she was able to convince you to hire me for Eden. I'll be in her debt forever for saving my career."

"Honestly," said Alex, "I did listen to her but was convinced from the day I first met you that you were the architect I wanted to work with. But let's not talk about dad today. I'm feeling too good. He's gone and mom might as well be, as she doesn't even recognize me when I visit her at the nursing home. Anyway, forget about all that! Don't you sense the energy? Look at this site. Activity everywhere with surveyors laying out grades and dozers digging into the ground for the basement, piles being driven to support the towers and, over in that corner, the first forms for the foundation. Christ!" His arms flew in all directions twisting his body as he spoke. "I can't wait to see the first concrete being placed, and then the steel. It's going to be fantastic!"

"I must admit that I never thought you would be able to pull it off. First, getting all the approvals—and I know that Claire was unbelievable in swinging politicians to support the project and, heavens, raising all that money."

"You've got enough to think about without concerning yourself with money issues. Stick to worrying about all the architectural details that are still to be completed." Alex turned and started walking back toward the dispersing crowd, raising a hand with two fingers pointed to the sky as a victory sign. "I'll take care of business; you take care of the design." His words faded as they blended into the background noise.

Philip thought again about the Grants; the father who never had a good word to say to his son and the mother who removed herself from conflict, unable to protect her son. He watched Alex, whom he now considered a friend, mingle with the thinning crowd, shaking hands, slapping backs, constantly in motion, moving closer to Claire until he stood before her. For a brief moment they spoke to each other. A truck roared between Philip and the platform, raising a cloud of dust. When it cleared, Alex and Claire were nowhere in sight, so with a shrug, Philip turned and continued his tour, reveling in the birth of his project before having to return to his office.

As HE LED CLAIRE TOWARD one of the trailers at the edge of the site, Alex saw Chip, the banker, talking intently with Congressman Jackson, who represented the West Village. He noticed that Chip kept turning his head nervously as if he were concerned that someone would see them when Jackson suddenly brushed a hand against Chip's cheek as they separated.

PATRICK CONNOLLY WAS ABOUT TO enter his office trailer parked against the southern fence of the site when Alex called out to him.

"Pat! Do me a favor." Standing in front of the closed door, he added, "Claire would like to know about the foundation construction that is now starting. Could you give her a primer? I'm sorry but I have to go back to my office for a meeting." Connolly did not directly acknowledge this request but turned to Claire and said, "Mrs. Fletcher, I'll be more than happy to tell you what I know if you'll tell me what interests you."

"Thank you," she said and turning to Alex asked, "Will I see you later?"

"I'll call you," Alex answered curtly as he turned to leave.

Claire flushed with embarrassment or anger; she did not know which, before facing Patrick. "What really interests me is the variety of foundation conditions you are dealing with on this site. I've been too involved in the politics of the project to appreciate the complexity of the site. And please, call me Claire."

"Why don't we go back to the platform you just left? I can point out what's happening from there."

When they reached the platform that had earlier hosted the opening ceremony, Patrick asked Claire to turn toward the river.

"Where we're now standing, the rock on which the towers will be founded is less than ten feet below your pretty feet. Now, as you look toward the river, that rock begins to dip, going under the Hudson River and then popping back up to form the cliffs on the Jersey side. See the bulldozers scraping the soil away and exposing the rock on the east side of the site? That's where we will pour our concrete footings.

"But why are they jack-hammering the top of the rock I can see near the platform?"

"Well, we're trying to make the rock under the footings relatively level."

"I see!"

"Now, the farther west on the site we build, the deeper we have to go to hit that rock. That's why you see those pile drivers banging away at those steel piles, some of them as long as a hundred feet."

"I suppose it takes a lot of your time to make certain that it's all done correctly."

"Actually, Mrs…uh, Claire, Sam takes care of that. He's the contractor's site manager and as you know I represent Grant Development."

"What's he like to work for? I mean, Alex?"

Connolly hesitated before answering, deciding in his mind how to phrase it, knowing that the two had a close relationship. "He can be difficult."

"So, I've heard," Claire answered. "Well, I don't want to take any more of your time. Thank you for the lesson. If you don't mind, I may come back when the structure starts moving up. Even though I've been involved in the development of the project, I've never actually followed a construction project in detail. It's been all paperwork and meetings, I'm afraid. I really appreciate being able to see the project come to life."

"It's my pleasure to talk to such a lovely lady. Please come back anytime."

As Claire left, Patrick followed her with his eyes. "Alex, you lucky devil," he whispered.

IN A LARGE WHITE TRAILER on the edge of the site, two men sat across from each other. Rising from his chair, the younger of the two, a coffee-skinned, powerfully built man gripped the edge of the desk pressing his fingers so tightly that his nails whitened. "I run this site and I don't want any trouble. If you think you can threaten me, you're sadly mistaken. We have agreements in place with all the unions and don't need any more protection from you or anyone else."

The other man, somewhat portly with a round face topped by a thin fringe of gray hair, hardly moved other than to raise his head and lift his eyebrows, causing the furrows on his brow to deepen. He spoke slowly, in a high, rather hoarse voice with a slight lisp. "Hell, there's no need to be defensive. We only offer you the opportunity of a problem-free site. You know we can deliver on such a promise but…"

Sam Ruth interrupted, "Just like you did for the apartment job? Let me tell you that for what you charged, I could have built another floor in that building. I've been in this business long enough to know what it costs to provide site security and you fall way above that." Sam recalled warning his boss, Mike Long, that allowing the Jersey Protective Association to provide site security would reduce the profit on that job to almost zero. However, Long seemed to have other considerations in mind when he agreed to their fees. Sam sat down and leaned back in his chair and in a more relaxed voice added, "So, you can see, Bruno, all you need to do, that is, if you want to work for us, is to cut your fees. Give me a reasonable proposal and I'll consider it."

Bruno Guardini was not used to being interrupted but forced a smile as he said, in a measured tone, "You know I can't do that. There are fixed costs and anyway, the level of protection we offer is much more complete than what you now have. But," he rose and turned to leave, "it's up to you."

As the door of the trailer closed, Sam Ruth pounded the table. "Damn it, damn it, damn it..." he repeated over and over again as he reached for the telephone with one hand and, with the other, massaged the closely cropped black hair on his head to dispel the tension that pressed against his brain.

AT THE OFFICE OF URBANLAND Construction Company, on the thirtieth floor of an office building in the center of the city, the telephone rang. Mike Long was leaning back in his chair, contemplating the view through the floor-to-ceiling glass façade that opened onto the cityscape on two sides. After all these years, he still often thought about how far this view was removed from what he now only vaguely remembered of his homeland in Cambodia. He recalled the sultry warmth of the air and visualized the expansive green carpet of vegetation covering the ground, an image that stood in sharp contrast to the gray masonry and concrete of the city he now faced.

He was only seven years old on that horrific day in the time of genocide, when he was forced to watch the Khmer Rouge execute his father. His mother tried to cover the boy's eyes, as a pistol was thrust under his father's chin, but a soldier ripped her hands apart with the muzzle of a gun and threatened to kill the boy as well as the father if she moved again. The boy watched transfixed as the pistol was fired and his father's skull exploded, spraying blood and tissue into the air as the pitiful sounds of his mother's wails enveloped him. He could not help releasing a muffled cry, filtered through his mother's fingers. Despite his fear and anger, it never occurred to the boy to question what was happening or why. After all, in his seven years, he had been taught never to question an adult. It was bad form and simply not done.

The phone continued its insistent ringing, dragging Mike out of his reverie. His face was slightly flushed and his hands moist with sweat as he pushed away the angry past and picked up the handset.

"Yes," he yelled into the mouthpiece.

Somewhat surprised, Sam responded, "I thought *I* was mad, but you..."

"Sorry! What's up?"

"Our 'friend'," letting the word float unnervingly across the airwave, "from Jersey came to see me. I thought all that was taken care of! I'll tell you, Mike, I'm not about to deal with these guys again. I had too many problems on the last project and it was simply too expensive."

Sam had worked for Mike on the first major project he undertook shortly before the elder Mr. Grant's death. The construction of a high-rise residential tower was a modest project when compared to the Eden Center but represented the coming of age for Mike as a contractor, driving him to work tirelessly to assure its success.

"I understand that you had to pay to avoid any problem that could slow or stop that project," Sam added. "But remember that it cost you a bundle. We're friends and I'm telling you if you give in this time they will suck you dry. You'll be in their debt for life."

Mike leaned back in his chair and remembered how, on that earlier project, he could barely constrain his anger and had wanted to kill Guardini, but Marion, his wife, said to him, "Honey, this is your first major project and you need to be a little flexible to ensure that it will be completed promptly without inviting a problem." At the time, he swore that he would never again allow himself to be made to feel so powerless.

"You're right. I'll make some calls to see if we can nip this problem in the bud. But just to be safe, place extra guards around the site after hours. It may also help avoid having material walk off the site." It was not uncommon for petty thievery to cause the loss of valuable material and small tools from a construction site, especially one as large as this one. "Let me know if you get any more nasty visits. By the way, how's the family?"

"OK. And say, what were you mad about when you answered the phone?"

"Nothing to do with you. I was looking out at the scene from my window and suddenly had an image of what happened to my father. This still haunts me after all these years."

"I get it! It's a crappy way to start your life. But you made it safely to the States, that's what really matters."

"I know, and I am eternally grateful for that, but the voyage out of Cambodia was what a shrink calls a traumatic experience that's hard to shake off."

"Look, let's get together one evening and you can tell Sam all about it. I'm not a shrink but I'm a good listener."

"Alright, I'll have the wife call yours."

"Fine! But see if you can convince her to keep their conversation to under an hour." They both laughed as their wives behaved like sisters who never had enough time to talk together. The two families would try to meet at least once a month for a dinner or a family outing. Marion often offered to babysit for the Ruths as she had no children of her own and thought of Jan's children as her nephews. Mike and Sam genuinely liked each other. Growing up in a middle-class society had buffered some of the worst prejudices, but as an Asian and an African-American, both experienced a subliminal sense of alienation in the majority-white society. Their common experience drew them together.

Sam added, "I hate to bring up another problem, but Grant made me fire one of the carpenters. You know I can't really do that under our union contract so I simply reassigned him but I can tell you, it was unpleasant. Perhaps you can suggest that Alex stay away from the workers. If he's got a problem let him deal with you. Actually, I'm meeting with Patrick after work and I'll remind him of that myself but it wouldn't hurt if he got the message from you as well. Our guys work for us, and not for him. He may be the developer but he's got no authority to fire them."

Before completing the conversation, Mike half-heartedly promised to talk to Alex. At the moment, he was unsure that either of the problems Sam brought up could be resolved, recognizing that the Jersey group was dangerous and Alex was so often irrational. Construction of the Eden Center was barely out of the ground and Mike was anxious to resolve potential problems before they became more serious.

WHEN THE WHISTLE BLEW, INDICATING the end of the workday at the site, Sam walked over to Patrick's trailer. "Why don't you and I amble over to that nice Irish saloon on 11th Avenue, you know the one I mean."

"Let's say that I have a passing acquaintanceship with that establishment," answered Patrick with a smile. "I'd be pleased to walk over there with you for our little chat."

They were an odd couple, the older man with a fierce shock of white hair above a round, pink face, and a slightly stooped stance and the younger man, somewhat shorter with close-cropped black curly hair and broad shoulders on a square body. When they entered the bar, the patrons looked away from the TV above the bar, blaring forth an analysis of the Yankees and—in this unusual sports year—the ascendant Mets. Patrick was warmly welcomed by several of the patrons who glanced suspiciously at his companion. "This is my friend, Sam," he proclaimed, causing the welcoming patrons to change their scowls to grins as they warmly shook Sam's hand.

"Two whiskeys, please," he bade the bartender. "We'll be in the booth by the back." This elicited comments from one of the other patrons, "Our

Mr. Connolly must have serious business to discuss," followed by knowing winks from his buddies.

"Ignore them," said Patrick as he led Sam to the booth far from the bar area. "We won't be disturbed here." After they slipped into the booth, he added, "So, what can I do for you?"

When the bartender brought over the drinks, Sam raised his glass, took a sip, and said, "We're going to be working on this project for a long time and I thought we should get better acquainted."

"Are you sure it's not because of what happened with my boss, Mister Grant, this morning?" Patrick stretched the *S* sound, Missssster Grant, like a hiss across the table.

"Well, maybe that was the spark but, dammit, you know that I had to reassign the carpenter because I couldn't just fire him."

"I'm sorry about that whole incident but I have real difficulty with Alex sometimes. I'll see it doesn't happen again."

"I appreciate that. But fill me in here. I can't help wondering what an old guy like you is doing working for him?"

At this remark, Patrick slapped the table causing his whiskey to slosh over the rim of his glass as he glowered at the younger man. "What do you mean, old? Next you'll be telling me I'm not competent to do my job."

"Whoa! I'm sorry. I didn't mean it that way. I just thought that a man with your long experience might be getting ready for a well-earned retirement by now."

Patrick waited a minute before answering. "It's not that I didn't think about it… but this project… I've never before seen anything like it. It was something I always wanted to be involved with and I needed it. But, even if I end up leaving in disgust, because of Alex,….and to tell the truth, I still have options, but…how about you? What I mean is that, as you said this morning, we have similar backgrounds and we both ended up at City College in engineering… of course twenty five years apart as you just so pointedly reminded me."

Sam hesitated before responding as he was not used to sharing his history with anyone other than Jan, but he felt comfortable talking to this blustery Irishman. "I don't know how it was for you back when you were a kid but I can tell you that there were so many temptations in my neighborhood, with drugs and petty crime, I bless my parents every day for the sacrifices they made to make sure that I stayed away from all that and got a good education."

He paused, raised his glass, took a sip, and, looking directly at Mike, continued slowly, "My father was a doorman for one of those fancy co-ops on the eastside and my mother was a domestic worker. Together, they saved and did without until they were able to buy a brownstone in Harlem when the market was depressed. You remember, the seventies was a time of renaissance when a new middle class was rising up in Harlem with all kinds of people, not just blacks but white and Latino families, buying vacant properties. My parents then spent all their free time converting a floor in the building to a rental, which made it possible for them to afford their mortgage. During all that time they made sure that I stayed off the street and pushed me to study."

"You're lucky. I never knew my father," interjected Connolly. "He died in the war."

"I'm sorry to hear that."

"It was a long time ago. You weren't even born then. Anyway, he had been a longshoreman before the war and volunteered for the merchant marine. His ship was torpedoed and he died a month before I was born."

"It must have been hard on your mother."

"It was. She was crazy about my father and spent the rest of her life living in his memory. Of course, she never married again and she tried hard to raise me but since she had to work all day, my grandmother was really the one responsible for me."

"How did you end up at City?"

"I have to give the credit to Father O'Shea. My grandmother was really close to him. I always suspected that in their early life they had a thing for each other. Anyway, he really pushed me to study and came to the house at least once a week to review what I had learned the previous week. During that time there were gangs in the neighborhood, and one in particular, the Westies, tried to recruit me. Father O'Shea heard about it and that was the last I heard from the Westies. He was relentless but because of him, I did well in school and was able to get into college." Patrick called the barman to bring another round.

"I'm not sure I should. Jan will wonder where I am."

"That's why I like my life," said Patrick, exuberantly. "No one to report to! Call her and say you'll be late."

"Easy for you to say. She can't wait dinner for the kids. By the way, how come a good-looking guy like you didn't ever marry?"

"There was a girl a long time ago. When it didn't work out I kind of fell into wanting my own space. I loved my neighborhood even though it was changing. You know, gentrification, which meant that houses on my block that had been rooming houses were bought and converted. I jumped at the chance. Just like your parents, I saw this as an opportunity and with my savings, bought the house I had lived in all my life, converted two floors to rental units and kept the apartment on the second floor, the one I was born in. It's still the only home I ever knew! I thought about wanting kids, but you know, I decided I didn't want to be tied down."

"Don't you miss the companionship?"

"Hell, I've got my buddies and there is the occasional lady, if you know what I mean. As I get older, I don't miss it so much any more."

"For me, I think I'd really miss Jan and the kids if I didn't have them. Look, I'd like to stick around and talk some more, so give me a minute while I call home."

Patrick nodded his head in acknowledgment as Sam walked to the pay phone near the front door of the tavern to place his call.

For all his outward bravado, Connolly was an intensely conflicted individual. What he told Sam that evening was true but he left out many salient facts about his life. He lived with his mother long after his graduation from college, a time when most of his friends had ventured out to establish their independence away from the parental nest. At first he justified this behavior because of his mother's needs; who was there to help with the shopping, who would take out the garbage, who would accompany her to Sunday Mass? But the truth was that his mother had many friends who were more than willing to help her and she had urged her son on many occasions to move on. "Soon, Ma, soon."

As months turned to years, Patrick became more attached to his routine: work on a job site during the day, a drink with the boys after work, time with his mother over dinner, but never a serious relationship with the opposite sex. "Why don't you find a nice Irish girl and get married so that I can have grandchildren to comfort me as I get older?" It was not to be, and years later, when his mother died, Patrick was left alone but he didn't feel alone. He had his routine.

When Sam returned to the table, he said, "I told her to go ahead and feed the kids and that I'll be late. And, it's OK with her."

"Well," said Patrick somewhat sarcastically, "I'm glad she gave you permission to stay. So anyway, I was about to ask you how you ended up in this business."

Sam took a sip. "In my teens, I helped my father when he was doing the renovation work on our house. I learned to move partitions, make plumbing and electrical changes, and I began to enjoy building things. So, when some of the other families on the block heard that I could do some construction work, they would hire me for small jobs. I bought myself some tools and was able to earn extra money doing freelance construction work even after I started at City."

"Sounds like you were a real hustler. I like that! In my day, I went to City when it was free so I had a pretty easy time of it financially and then, with Father O'Shea's help, I was able to get a job with a contractor right out of school."

Sam said, "You know, it wasn't that easy for a black man in construction. When I graduated, all I could get was a job supervising laborers. It made me damn mad that I spent four years learning to design steel and concrete structures and had to end up leading a bunch of trench diggers.... Don't get me wrong. I have nothing against laborers but I felt I was being underutilized.

"Frankly, most contractors didn't know how to deal with a black man supervising white workers so I was frustrated until I met Mike. As an Asian, he was in the process of qualifying as a minority firm. You remember that the city mandated such firms for public projects some years back. He was looking for a minority engineer to improve his chances. So, when I heard this, I sent in an application. When I received a letter asking me to come to the office of the Urbanland Construction Company, I told Jan...we had just gotten married... 'I think my life is about to change.' And you better believe that it did!"

"How about another round?" asked Patrick.

Feeling a little lightheaded, Sam answered, "Why not?"

Patrick and Sam continued exploring each other's lives for the next two hours. There was a lot to talk about beyond construction. Patrick's Yankees were battling with the Red Sox in the American League East, and Sam's Mets almost tied with Atlanta in the National League East, nothing much to argue about there unless it turned into a subway series. Neither man watched a lot of movies, but Patrick recommended American Psycho and Sam confided that with his family, 101 Dalmatians was a lot more likely. When they finally left the tavern, Sam was unsteady and had to be helped into a taxi. When he reached home, Jan led him to the bedroom where he fell on the bed and almost instantly was sound asleep. The next morning, he told Jan, "God, I don't know what happened to me last night."

"Well, I do," said Jan in her mellow alto voice. "You were drunk! It's something I haven't seen you do before. I got the children off to school already so they didn't see their daddy passed out."

"I'm sorry, honey. It got away from me somehow. Pat and I were having a great time."

"Well, I'll get you a cup of coffee while you wash the fuzz out of your brain. I'll be back in a minute and you can tell momma all about it."

The Ruths had married while Sam was finishing his last year at City. They had met at a students mixer a year earlier and for Sam, it was love at first sight. Jan was the most striking girl he had ever seen; warm brown skin, a well-curved but not-too-slender figure and magnetic dark eyes that he could not resist. Although Jan was not immediately drawn to Sam, his gentle insistence over the next few months won her over.

She returned with the coffee in a few minutes. "Here's your coffee. Now, suppose you tell me what happened last night. Honestly, I was getting worried when you were so late."

Sam sat on the edge of the bed and took a large swallow of the warm liquid to clear his head. "I'm sorry about that! You know, I don't often spend a lot of time hanging out with other guys. Remember, I told you that Dad used to keep me busy so I wouldn't get into trouble with the other kids in the neighborhood. I never had a chance to make friends until I got to college. Then, I was so busy studying that the friends I made were mostly interested in things connected to the school.

"But this evening with Patrick turned out to be special. A rare time for me, when I felt I could talk to a guy and feel that he understood me and that we could talk like equals. Can you believe it, he is also a City graduate. I know he's a lot older than us. In fact, he's almost as old as dad. But…I feel we could be really good friends. I could tell him everything …and I think I did! Not that I can remember everything we talked about later in the evening, but I definitely told him about you and how much I loved you and the kids. He has no one in his life and I thought we should invite him out here for a weekend. What do you think?"

"You're going pretty fast. You barely know the man. What did you tell him about us?"

"Don't worry. Nothing intimate….at least I think not."

"Listen Sammy, I've got to go to work so why don't we think about this and we'll talk again tonight."

After they married, Jan completed her nursing degree before starting a family, a career track that suited her outgoing personality. It utilized her healing skills and was a profession she could have her whole life. So, ministering to a hung-over husband was no problem. Although she had to postpone starting work while the boys were young and still at home, she had entered the profession once they started school.

"Yeah, I know. And I'm sorry again about last night. What time is it?"

"9:30"

"Oh my god. I've got to get going myself. I'm already way late. You go ahead. I'll see you tonight."

Jan kissed Sam goodbye while Sam dressed quickly to go to the site.

TWO
The Architect

A FTER COMPLETING HIS TOUR AROUND the site, Philip Corta strolled back to his office, a short 15-minute walk. His long face was reminiscent of a El Greco figure with arched eyebrows overhanging deep-set green eyes. Behind round, black-rimmed glasses, his eyes darted in all directions looking at architectural elements of the buildings along his path; an elegant brick archway; a crenellated overhanging cornice, the proportions of openings in a wall, the scale of buildings relative to each other. He drank it all in, adding the wealth of details he observed to his quiver of architectural knowledge. Architecture was his life and his mistress.

When Philip was still an infant just prior to the start of the Second World War, his uncle had taken him to London from his home in Spain. Philip was descended from Marranos, Sephardic Jews who, in the 16th century, were forced to convert during the Spanish Inquisition, a detail that became diluted through intermarriage after many generations so that he inherited from his parents and grandparents a conventional Catholic upbringing. Fiercely republican, his parents fought the rise of the nationalists and were imprisoned late in the Spanish Civil War. While being moved to another detention center, they died in what was officially called an accident but was suspected to have been a murder by Franco's thugs.

Growing up in England, Philip was introduced to the beauties of buildings and the science of construction by his uncle, who worked as a mason. Educated at the university to be an architect in a modernist

32

wave that had spread west from its Bauhaus origins in Germany, Philip searched for a warmer mode of expression that was closer to his Mediterranean origins and away from the sharp angles and cool materials that were the Miesian norm.

Unable to find an outlet for his dreams in London, he moved to America and traveled through the Southwest and Mexico to discover the soft curves of Adobe construction and the soaring curvilinear concrete structures of the Mexican architect, Candela. He adapted these ideas in developing his unique style, incorporating in his designs soft flowing lines and elegant curvilinear spaces that he compared to the organic structures of the human form and plants. He slowly built his reputation through his illustrated writings that described his design philosophy, and with the design of a few houses that blended seamlessly into the landscape and made the occupants feel a part of their environment.

A major turning point in his mid-life career was the commission he received from the senior Mr. Grant that provided him the first opportunity to expose his design ideas to a wider audience. But he never lost his sense of wonder at the many forms that architecture could create and, of course, he never gave up his sense of curiosity about the world around him.

Corta had recently chosen to move his office to the third-floor loft of an old industrial building on the west side of Manhattan because it afforded him a view of the project site… his project. He also needed the space for his expanded staff.

Prior to starting the design of the Eden Center, Corta's largest commission involved the design of a twelve-story apartment house for Mr. Grant that featured an undulating façade that was somewhat reminiscent, but a more modernist interpretation, of the work of the Spanish architect, Antoni Gaudi.

The scale of what he now had to create both challenged and frightened him at first. How was he to translate a program of such breadth into a unified concept? He needed to find the big idea, something beyond the usual platitudes that often accompanied architectural descriptions. He first asked his young staff, most of whom were his former students, to diagram the program in a series of bubbles signifying the size of each project element: the office space, the apartments, the public spaces, the entertainment complex, and the needed service elements. The staff then identified adjacencies—what elements needed to be near each other and how strongly they needed to be linked together.

Along with his staff, Philip studied the site and the building code restriction that defined how much could be built on the site and how high buildings could be in various parts of the site. From these exercises Corta's staff cut Styrofoam blocks to represent the building volumes that satisfied all the code constraints and defined what could possibly be built. This resulted in faceless blocks glued to a model of the site.

But none of this provided Philip with a grand vision for the project. To find it, he needed to think about the project in an environment free from the rigid geometry of the city, so he gathered all the diagrams and sketches and retreated to a rented cottage on Cape Cod. He knew that for a few days he would be alone, as his wife, Diane, was on an assignment photographing a construction project in California. She was an exceptional interpreter of the dynamics of a construction site—expressing, with candid photos of workers, the grit and strength of the process of erecting a building.

After settling into the cottage, Philip put himself in a relaxed mood by opening a bottle of nice vintage Barolo wine and pouring himself a glass. He tacked up the papers he had brought with him onto the wall of the living room—a plan of the site, the diagrams laying out the size of the various functions, the limitations dictated by zoning. He also placed the model of the site with the characterless white blocks on a table that served both as his desk and a dining table.

After staring at them a while without finding any inspiration, he went for a walk on the beach. He often felt that such solitary walks allowed him to synthesize a problem, helping to arrive at a solution. The gentle surf licked at his naked feet as he walked along the beach listening to the churning sound of the water and the sorrowful cries of the gulls flying overhead. He felt one with the elements and completely at peace.

As he leaned his slender body into the wind, his mind free, he began to visualize graceful curving arcs climbing toward the heavens, spiraling like a seashell, intersecting one another in an almost random manner. He raised his arms and twisted them upward as he imagined how a tower would look. Starting from a broad base with a firmly anchored foundation or taproot, as Frank Lloyd Wright had called the base of his proposed Mile High Tower, three towers would rise separately, spiraling around an invisible center. As the towers tapered upward, each would carry its own spire. A blaring, horn-shaped element would surround them at the base.

"Yes!" he cried out, heard only by the gulls and the silent sea and dunes as he scratched lines in the sand with a stick, a quick sketch that would vanish with the rising tide. Energized and excited, he turned back toward the cottage, walking and then running. Before this vision faded, he had to memorialize it on paper.

After that epiphany on the beach, Corta worked tirelessly to translate his vision into a skin-and-bones building. He would arrive at his office at dawn and rarely left before eight or nine in the evening. On those occasions when Diane was out of town, his staff would find him in the morning sound asleep, stretched out on his conference table surrounded by crumpled paper. Philip preferred to use a pencil and paper to illustrate his ideas, even though the rest of his young staff had long ago switched to computers. He needed that direct connection between the pencil in his hand and the image on paper and did not feel that same connection on a cold-blooded machine. "Maybe, some day…" he told his chief designer, when obliged to explain why he insisted on living in the past. In so many ways he was a modern technocrat but he was not ready to surrender his art to cyborgs.

THE GROUNDBREAKING CEREMONY HE HAD just attended was a success, but a great deal of work remained before construction could move forward. The detail plans needed to be completed and the coordination with manufacturers of materials and equipment had barely been started.

When he arrived at his office, Philip called together his staff and encouraged them to work as many hours as necessary to ensure that no detail, down to the last door handle, would be forgotten.

"The next few months are going to be hell. I expect you all to work harder than ever so we can all be proud of what we're going to achieve. We'll have the developer pressuring us on one side and the contractors on the other but I'll deal with those conflicts personally, so please let me know the minute there is a problem or if you receive a nasty call." There were a few moans but one after another agreed to work more diligently than they ever had in the past.

Philip sometimes thought of them, admiringly, as boys and girls with great facility in using computers, young and enthusiastic, unafraid of meeting challenges. They reminded him of his own apprenticeship and his eagerness to learn when working for a leading British architectural firm almost forty years earlier. Back then, he was constantly proposing design ideas that were, more often than not, squelched as being outlandish or too costly. He had fought to hold onto his ego until the time came when he could design buildings that met his sense of fantasy and order…a new style of seeing buildings not just as containers but as beautiful objects in the landscape of the city! He persevered and the day he opened his own practice, he promised himself that he would listen to, and carefully evaluate, proposals from his young staff to avoid destroying their spontaneity and fresh views as he realized that he could also learn from them.

This morning was perhaps too perfect, but Philip felt an undercurrent at the site that made him nervous. Perhaps it was the fact that Alex tried so hard to keep him in the dark about issues regarding project finances. After all, if he was to be responsible for maintaining the project within the budget, he had to know where it now stood.

He asked his chief estimator, a man in his late fifties, at least two decades older than most of his young architects, to show him the latest cost figures. Jack Mahoney was not an architect but spent many years working for a construction company, a fact that made him totally familiar with the costs and complexities. "Jack! What do you think?"

Standing next to Philip, Jack unrolled on the conference table a large sheet that was peppered with quantities and costs. Passing his fingers, gnarled and callused from years on construction sites, across the sheet, he said, "This is the latest printout where I've taken into account all the latest changes your kids came up with." He often disparaged Philip's young crew as being too inexperienced for such a huge project. "As you can see, the total cost estimate is now a bit over eight percent above our earlier budget. To be honest, Phil, unless you reign in these hot-shot young designers, we're in trouble." Philip looked down at the dizzying array of numbers and asked, "Can you see any possibilities for cost reductions?"

"I can always come up with a list of possible changes that will bring us back down to budget but I'll have to shrink the space in the buildings unless you're willing to give up some frills. There's simply too much granite and marble in areas that could as easily be painted drywall and the huge size of the nature complex is wasteful and very costly."

Philip looked despondent and started to walk away. "That's the essence, the core of the project and must be protected at any cost. Do what you can," he said, "to find savings in other areas and give me a list of proposed cuts." Why couldn't he, just once in his life, have a client with elastic financial pockets?

Two weeks later, Jack presented Philip with a four-page list of possible cost reductions. As he read through the list, Philip nervously ran his hands through his long graying hair and became more and more agitated, finally exclaiming, "You're cutting the heart and soul out of my project!" He turned, and, dropping the papers on the table, walked away saying, "There's no way I will agree to these cuts." Jack called after him, "You don't have to make any decisions now. Please," he implored, "think about it. You're going to have to do something or Grant is going to do it for you."

The thought that Alex, his patron and friend but a man totally lacking in aesthetic judgment, would dare touch his beautiful project infuriated Philip and caused him to feel weak as the blood drained from his head. He walked back and grabbed the papers Jack had prepared and turned toward the door, weaving and bumping into furniture, trying to gain control of his mounting rage.

He left the office and rushed home. Diane would know what to do, as she always had, from the day they first met twenty-five years earlier.

FOLLOWING GRADUATION FROM SMITH COLLEGE, Diane had taken a position as a magazine editor. After more than a dozen years she became disillusioned with the work and decided to obtain a graduate degree in art history. She was drawn to Columbia University because of the reputation of the art historian Meyer Schapiro, and enrolled there the year after Philip was engaged to teach Architecture.

On many afternoons, Philip would sit in Avery Library, reading architectural books that he could not afford to buy. It was on one such afternoon that Diane, who would use Avery's extensive collection to study the use of art in architecture, spotted a man in round-framed glasses and with a slightly disheveled appearance intently studying the image of a recent house by Marcel Breuer. Looking over his shoulder as she passed by his table, she commented, "Nice house."

"Nice," Philip observed in a raised voice, obviously annoyed. Looking up at this lady with auburn hair pulled back into a ponytail, he then exclaimed, "It's not nice, it is brilliant." Not waiting for an answer, he continued, "Look at the beautiful proportions of the rooms and their orientation bringing in light and air and..." It suddenly struck him that he did not know this woman. "I'm sorry, I thought you were one of my students."

"I'm Diane Sherwood and I'm in Art History, but don't stop, professor, I would like to learn why you think this is such a great design."

Somewhat taken aback by this young lady's directness, Philip stood up and, extending his hand, said "Philip Corta, and please sit down. I'll be happy to discuss the design with you." A lively discussion ensued that became somewhat noisy, so the librarian suggested they leave. Since it was a beautiful spring day, Philip proposed that they continue the discussion on the lawn near Low Library. Philip soon realized that he was dealing with a woman of intelligence and taste complementing her quiet beauty, and considered asking her to dinner.

Philip believed he had finally found a woman who understood him and was able to guide him when he lost his direction. For her part, Diane was attracted to the fact that here was a man who listened to her and respected her opinions—he was shy, but in a loving way. Both were attracted to each other, but Philip was nervous about seeing her again because she was a student, so he did not call her. A year later, they met again at a lecture Philip gave. That meeting eventually led to their marriage.

As a photographer, Diane had the patience of a saint, waiting for the perfect moment to click the lens, capturing an image that revealed the strength or weakness of her subject or the range of an action. This patience served as a mediating influence in her marriage, as Philip would often become frustrated when the order of their lives was disturbed. This ability to calm a tense personal situation would have made her a wonderful mother. To their infinite regret, the Cortas were unable to have children and, after years of trying, Diane shifted her energy toward photography, expanding what she had started as a hobby into a profession.

At first, she accompanied Philip to construction sites to take pictures of workers as they performed their everyday tasks: framing a wooden house, guiding steel members into place, hammering, bolting, pouring concrete and operating machinery, all expressing the ruggedness of the place. Her presence on the construction site was resented at first by many of the workers, but, after seeing some of her early pictures, these same workers had begun waving at this petite woman with an oversized construction hard hat covering her hair and shielding her face, calling after her, "Hey, take my picture; am I holding the wrench the way you like it?" After her early photographs were published, she was engaged to photograph other projects that often took her to various parts of the country.

The Cortas lived in the Greenwich Village area of Manhattan, less than a mile from the Eden site. They occupied the second floor of a wide brownstone that provided them with two bedrooms, one of which Philip had transformed into a study lined with art and architecture books along one wall. The room was utilitarian and devoid of any decoration. The only elements that seemed out of place against a stark white wall were two faded sepia photographs in simple black frames. One, of a fierce-looking older man with a sunbaked face looking directly at the camera, holding a carpenter's level in one hand and a trowel in the other, against a background of a partly completed brick wall, was his uncle. The other was of a young couple holding hands, the woman in a longish faded print dress and a sweet smile, the man looking more robust with a brush mustache and wrinkled cheeks, looking down at the woman; in the background, a Moorish church…. his parents! Against a window looking out on a communal garden was a table Philip used for creating drawings and pen-and-ink sketches of buildings he designed, most of which, until the commission for the Landown Apartments, remained images on paper and illustrations for his articles.

WHEN HE ARRIVED HOME ON this day, Philip knocked on the door of a closet that Diane had converted into a cramped darkroom and called out, "Diane, are you in there?"

"Obviously, I'm in here" she said impatiently in a voice muffled by the heavy wooden door, "You see the red light above the door. What are you doing home so early?"

"I have to talk to you. Please come out," he said in a pleading voice.

"Give me a minute. Is something wrong? You sound so strange."

"I need your advice." While he waited, he let his long body drop into a black leather lounge chair in the middle of the sparsely furnished living room and stretched his feet out before him, leaving his head dangling behind the back of the chair.

The room reflected Philip's admiration for organic design with fabrics in muted earth tones salted with burgundy pillows providing a bright accent. The only furniture in the room, other than the Eames lounge chair Philip now sat on, was a sofa with geometric lines covered in a light bronze fabric, and a small dining table, designed by the woodworker George Nakashima, that emphasized warmth and strength in the use of naturally shaped, polished wood. The four chairs that surrounded the table had only three legs each, to emphasize the minimum required for stability yet sufficient to satisfy the need for balance. Windows on the north side of the room faced the street to provide natural light while two large impressionist-style paintings dominated the east and west walls, which were painted light tan.

When she saw him, Diane exclaimed, "What's wrong with you? You look like a skeleton. Have you been losing weight?" She constantly worried that Philip was too thin and would crumple like a scarecrow from lack of adequate nutrition.

"No! No! It's nothing like that. It's the project. It's in trouble and I need to find a way to keep Alex from emasculating it because of money."

"Well, that sounds dramatic," she said, putting a hand softly on his cheek and kissing his brow. "Can you be a bit more specific?"

Diane sat on the sofa facing him as Philip sat forward in his chair and proceeded to tell her about the problem with the cost of the project and his fear that Alex would step in and make arbitrary cuts, denuding the project of all its visual drama and strength. All the while, his hands kept flying up as in a supplicant pose, emphasizing each perceived disaster.

"You know that when I design, I see more than just a picture in front of me. The shape of the building comes to me as a song in which every note is a cell in a three-dimensional puzzle. Every one of those cells is special and calls for a particular object to fill it. Now, if any of those cells are emptied, the whole balance of the design is lost. That's what Alex wants to do just to meet his budget. It's a disaster!"

Diane answered in a soothing alto voice, "Darling, I know you see your designs in a unique way and you have worked so hard and put your heart and soul into this project. There surely is a way of dealing with this problem. Had you thought of calling Alex to see if, perhaps, there is any more money available? You have told me how devious Alex could be, but you know that developers often have a slush fund that they use to cover contingencies and you might find out that he is willing to consider a budget increase if he understands the need."

She sounds so calm and reasonable, thought Philip. *Perhaps I should call Alex?* "No, it wouldn't work. Alex told me early on that the budget was it and there would be no more money available."

Calmly, Diane answered, "It can't hurt to try. Don't forget that after the groundbreaking, Alex has to deliver a project that many people, important people, have now seen. There are expectations that have to be met."

"Well...."

"Come on, darling," she said in her sweetest yet most insistent voice. "Just pick up the phone and call him."

Philip hugged his wife, still feeling nervous but somewhat rejuvenated. He stared at her as she turned to go back to the darkroom. Her smile warmed him; her blue eyes penetrated his soul; she radiated confidence that overcame his fears. What was it, he wondered, that could change his mood and wash away his doubts and give him the conviction to act? *What would I do without her? I would be lost*, he thought. *I can't think about that now.*

Not ready to give up, Philip went to his study in the back of the apartment and closed the door. Spreading the cost estimates across the table, he began making a list of those cost items representing cells in his three-dimensional puzzle that could be modified without damaging the overall vision he had for the project. He then listed those items that would create a void in the puzzle that would lead to its conceptual collapse, essentially denuding his vision of the Center. For days he continued refining these lists until he reached a final tally that represented how far he was willing to compromise. He then picked up the phone.

ENTRACTE

Construction projects always start with the development of a site: surveying to locate the buildings shown on the construction plans; staking out the corners of each building to guide the excavators; and finally, excavating the ground. Installing foundations continues even in winter, as earth can be moved to level areas for buildings, as pile drivers can continue their staccato hammering of steel piles, as rock can be blasted out to the required depth, and as concrete poured for foundations can be protected from freezing by a covering blanket of hay. An expensive portion of the construction budget, foundations represent a hidden strength that is necessary for the support of a building but that frustrates owners since it is no longer seen or appreciated once construction is complete.

On an overcast day weeks after the groundbreaking ceremony, footings were being poured directly on rock that had been blasted to create a smooth base. On the western side, closer to the river, piles were being driven to reach the deep supporting rock. Throughout the site, workers were bundled in multiple layers, hooded to keep out the misty rain and chilling morning wind and some could always be seen pressed against a construction trailer seeking shelter while sipping their morning coffee from paper cups. In the fall and winter, weather slowed the pace of construction, yet when viewed week after week more and more portions of the site show signs of organized growth as footings are completed, delineating the outline of the buildings that were soon to rise.

THREE
The Consultant
October 2000

WHILE A STUDENT AT WELLESLEY, Claire Fletcher attended courses at Harvard in city planning and architecture, exposing her to the role that politics plays in moving projects forward. Developers generally faced a labyrinth of regulations and had to satisfy design commissions and government bureaucrats, all contributing to a slow approval process. The more she learned of the difficulties in shepherding a project through this paper obstacle course, the more she realized that her inherited character traits were perfectly suited to undertake a career as a consultant to developers. From her mother she had learned the value of gentle manipulation that complemented an aggressive, persuasive personality she inherited from her father.

However, the opportunity to enter this career would have to wait for the end of her failed marriage. Her former husband, Douglas Fletcher Jr., was the son of a family who traced their roots to the founding of the thirteen colonies and whose generations amassed a fortune, profiting from the new country's many wars. Claire was, at first, seduced by the strong conservative values that she shared with her husband in the historical traditions of New England's elite. She enthusiastically entered into the social and political arena that Douglas inhabited and, with her charm and obvious good looks, she was welcomed in. She proved to be an invaluable asset in her husband's first election campaign for a seat in Congress.

However, three years into her marriage, she discovered that Douglas was having an affair, an event that left her feeling violated. This led, after a period of confused disillusionment, to a cathartic change in her views; she dissolved her marriage but, recognizing the need to establish herself as an independent person, maintained friendly relations with the many business and political contacts that she had made and would later be useful in her new career.

During this period, her political leanings shifted as she gravitated toward liberal activist causes and, feeling free, she cut herself off from the narrow social milieu that surrounded the Fletcher family. Claire became sought-after as she proved to be exceptionally successful in obtaining approval for one development project after another.

In order to be closer to her clients and to establish her independence after her divorce, she moved to an apartment on the east side of Manhattan. She felt free to express her newfound modernist taste in designing her apartment, and followed the precepts of her favorite architect, Frank Lloyd Wright, with rooms that flowed into each other without the interruptive severity of walls and doors. The living room, dining area and kitchen were one room, though the three areas were angled from each other in such a way as to hide the kitchen when sitting on the living room couch. Never one to blindly follow a master, Claire did not share Wright's penchant for severe, angular and uncomfortable furniture, preferring softer and more ergonomic forms, more suitable to the gentle curves of her body, yet with modern, cool clean lines and occasional sparks of color; the bright orange pillow she brought back from her trip to Peru, the abstract painting on the wall with brilliant blue brush strokes slashed diagonally across the canvas.

The floors, which were of a light tan bamboo, extended from the entry hall to the wall of glass overlooking the cityscape. She never tired of looking at the ever-changing patterns formed by the buildings spread out before her and absorbed the sparkling energy radiating from the myriad lights emanating at night from the thousands of openings punctuating building walls. It was a magical view that every day reinforced her decision to move to this city and escape the stifling atmosphere of her ex-husband's too-perfect faux-Victorian suburban house.

With her coat buttoned up to ward off the chill of this cool October morning, Claire was walking toward the entrance of her apartment building on East 74th Street just as Alex's car approached. The car stopped and Alex was about to step out as a brass fanfare announced an incoming call on his fancy new flip phone. He was about to answer it when he spotted Claire passing below the awning in front of her apartment building. "Wait up!" he called out to her as he replaced the phone in his pocket. "I was coming to see you."

Without stopping to answer, Claire moved past the doorman, who held open the door as he saluted her, touching the visor of his hat with the tip of his white-gloved hand. "Good afternoon Mrs. Fletcher," and he added a moment later, "and Mr. Grant," as Alex sped past the door trying to catch Claire. The doorman was used to seeing Alex visiting Claire and, although he disapproved of their relationship, he did not betray his feelings other than to allow his eyes to sternly follow them as they passed into the elevator.

When they entered her apartment, Claire moved toward the kitchen and asked, "Would you like a drink?"

"It's not a drink I need," Alex said as he approached her. He often came to Claire's apartment without first calling her. Claire's initial reaction to these visits was to scold him. "You can't just barge in here like this without letting me know first. It so happens I have to go to an important meeting in an hour." But she actually looked forward to these visits. It felt good to know she was desirable, as contrasted to how she had felt during her frigid, emotionless marriage to Greg.

When the door to her apartment closed behind her, Claire said coquettishly, "If you want me," placing her hand on the top button of her blouse. Alex grasped her roughly and pulled her toward him as their lips met. He hungrily devoured her, moving from her lips to her neck and the top of her breasts as his awkward fingers unbuttoned her blouse. She eagerly responded to his urgency and backed toward the sliding doors of the bedroom as her blouse dropped to the floor.

Leaving a trail of discarded clothing, they fell on the bed. Alex raised himself to look down at Claire as if for the first time. There were thin lines radiating from her tightly closed eyes, whose color he could not remember. Her somewhat full lips were partly open, revealing a small gap between her top front teeth. Why had he not noticed these before? His eyes dropped toward her breasts, two sensuous globes with small volcanic protrusions that stiffened as he took each in his mouth.

As he began his rhythmic movements, Claire surrendered to her feelings of warmth under the protective weight of the body above her. He kissed her and she felt the chafing of his stubble as he brushed against her cheek. "Careful," she said, forgetting the passion of the moment and wishing that he had shaved a little closer. She moved her hand to her face to ease the burning on her cheek and totally lost the desire she had felt only moments earlier as he finished and rolled off her body to lie beside her. Breathing out heavily, he gazed at the ceiling and quietly exclaimed, "There are stars up there. When did you do that?"

"How many times have you been here? It's typical of you not to have noticed before."

"Sorry! But…stars? That's for kids!"

"It just so happens that I always wanted them when I was a child. You might say that I was deprived and I'm making up for it."

This was totally outside the image Alex had of Claire and he did not know how to respond. Fortunately for him, his cell phone began its musical interlude and he rose to retrieve it from the living room as Claire called out in a tight voice, "You're not going to answer that now, are you?"

He picked up the phone and turned to Claire. "Someone keeps ringing me, so I assume it must be important." Not waiting for her reaction, he answered the phone. Hearing Philip's excited voice on the other end, he said, "Calm down and tell me what's all this about money?" He sat down naked on the living room couch as Claire walked about picking up her clothes and throwing his at Alex. He cupped the phone to his ear and slipped on his shorts as Philip explained that the construction estimates were coming out high but that he expected to have the project built as it had been designed and that it was Alex's responsibility to find the necessary funds.

Balancing the phone on his shoulder as he tried to pull on his socks, Alex said, "There is no more money! I'm stretched to the limit and unless I can get the bankers to go along, you're just going to have to cut whatever is necessary to stay on budget. Look, it's a fantastic project and I'd like to have it built with all the trimmings, but that's simply not possible." He placed the phone on the coffee table while he grappled with his shirt and trousers.

When he had slipped on his pants, Alex picked up the phone again and heard a sigh on the other end of the line. This was followed by a minute of silence and then Philip's pleading voice. "Please, Alex, do me the favor of going back to the bankers just once more. I know you can be very persuasive. I just spent an agonizing week trimming the costs but I'm still over by twelve million. I realize that as a developer, you have to control the cost of the project so that it will meet financial objectives. But look at it from my viewpoint. There are aesthetic objectives as well. The design is based on my concept of how the people who will occupy it—and those who will see it—will react. Will they be dazzled when they see it? Will they be comforted by its practicality? Will they feel that it is a home in which they can work productively and live in pleasant surroundings?"

He also added in an authoritative voice, "Consider the comments you received at the groundbreaking. After seeing the model and your description of the project, you've created expectations that you have to meet. People will demand it! And, remember that you said yourself, I have to take care of the design and you'll take care of the financing."

Alex was getting impatient to conclude this conversation and did not want to argue with his friend since he felt certain that his bankers could be swayed to consider an increase in the construction loan. "OK,

OK! Just for you, old buddy. Send me the papers and in the meantime, I'll make the call to test the waters. But don't hold your breath!" Philip thanked him profusely before hanging up. By this time, Claire was fully dressed and was walking toward the door. "Make yourself at home and lock the door when you leave. By the way," she added, hiding a frown from Alex, "I wonder who is the child here?"

Unfazed by that remark, Alex turned to see her already halfway out the door and waved, "Bye," as he picked up his phone to dial another number.

FOUR
The Banker

CHIP STEWART WAS SITTING AT an antique oak desk in his office, which adjoined the office of the president of the Losey & Sons Trust Co. when the phone rang. It had taken Chip almost twenty years since his graduation from Dartmouth to achieve the position of senior vice president and he was confident that within a few years he would be asked to move next door and take over the leadership of this century-old bank. After all, he was a cautious and successful banker, belonged to the right clubs and had a picture-perfect home with wife and children cut from the same social milieu as the current president. He catered to the members of the board and could be counted upon to fill in when a fourth was needed at tennis, or when a round of golf needed a loser to boost the ego of a client. "Charles Stewart, here! May I help you?" he said in the studied rounded tones of his Connecticut set.

"Chip, old boy, how are you," Alex said. "We haven't spoken since the groundbreaking ceremony. What did you think of it?"

Chip instinctively tightened his grip on the phone as he responded. "It was quite a show and I imagine that you must have felt a great deal of satisfaction in having carried out the project so far."

"It has been a long road and it's far from over. Actually, that's one thing I wanted to talk to you about." He proceeded to describe the development of the project and the effort that Philip and his crew had put into making Eden Center such an exceptional design. "So you see, buddy, we have a little problem at this time. I've been talking to Phil about the budget and we seem to be a few percent over. I need you to extend your commitment to meet these obligations." Alex proceeded to detail the increase in funding he was seeking.

After a moment of silence, Chip responded, "I should have guessed when you started to call me 'old boy' and 'buddy' that you wanted something from me. The truth is that the bank cannot commit any more funds at this time. The pro forma does not indicate sufficient income to justify a cost increase. The only way the bank would do it is if you would put up your other properties as collateral." Adding in a conspiratorial tone, "Of course, that would mean that if the Eden Center project failed, you would be flat broke."

Chip did not see Alex becoming red in the face as he heard these words and how he tightened his lips as he tried to control his anger. "There's no way I'm putting up any more fucking collateral. You better find another way if you want to keep enjoying that house in New Canaan with the perfect wife and kids," adding in a measured tone, "I saw the way you and that fag Jackson were pawing each other at the groundbreaking. What do you think would happen if your boss and the board found out about your little 'encounters?' That cushy VP's desk with all the perks; the country club membership and the city club would all vanish in an instant. All I have to do is make one phone call! Think it over but don't wait too long. I don't have any fucking patience with guys like you."

As Alex slammed down the phone, Chip, his face drained of color, continued to hold his handset in a tight grip and let it drag against his cheek as he whispered, "Christ!"

LATER THAT DAY, A MAN in a perfectly fitted dark gray overcoat walked hesitatingly down the commuter rail platform at Grand Central, gazing furtively into each car, avoiding making eye contact with the commuters already on the train. He had faded sandy hair with a touch of gray at the temples and his clean-shaven oval face was marred by a twitch that exaggerated the hatch wrinkles between his nose and his full lips. As he approached the last car, Chip recognized one of the commuters and quickly turned away, retracing his steps and finally settling into a seat in a middle car. As he reviewed the events of the day, his face sank into his upturned collar and he shook noticeably.

Earlier, after his late-morning conversation, Chip at first felt like a cornered animal and sat frozen in his chair for what felt like hours but were barely minutes. No, he decided, no boorish oaf like Alex was going to destroy the life it had taken him all these years to cultivate. Perhaps his family no longer held the social standing they once did, but the name Stewart was still respected in New York society.

Leaning back in his high-back plush leather chair, he had reviewed his available options. He could refuse to give in to Alex and face the possibility of losing his position at the bank. What about Alice and the children? They would be devastated. He loved them and was not ready to lose them. Of course he could confess his weakness, but he did not really believe that it was a weakness. It was, rather, a greater openness to a variety of physical and emotional experiences.

In his mind, a number of scenarios played themselves out, flashing like movie shorts one after the other. He saw Alice standing with him as he bravely announced to a gray audience of his friends that he was a little gay. What's a little? A little hungry, a little warm or cold, a little tired; somehow, a little gay was not the same. He imagined a scene in which he walked bravely into his club with questioning eyes following him around the room as he settled into his favorite chair by the high Gothic window. And a scene with his son, too young to understand, being confronted with that dreaded word in school: fag! How could he explain? This was a new millennium. Attitudes had changed starting with the sexual revolution of the sixties yet in his milieu, the new order had yet to overcome stilted, age-old prejudices.

As he turned all these thoughts and images over in his mind, it became clear what he must do. He brushed aside all negative thoughts and pulled out the Eden file from the wooden cabinet behind his desk, opened to the page outlining the income projections and resultant mortgage limits, and began to pencil in modified numbers showing increases in both.

He then drafted a memorandum justifying the increases based on forward-looking interest in the project and early results from advanced condominium sales and office rentals. It was a rosy picture full of optimism spawned from enthusiastic reviews of the project but with just enough skepticism in the form of footnotes qualifying the statements to make it seem balanced. Chip was conscious of the occasional error he made in assembling a table of numbers and joked with Jill, his assistant, as he asked her to check his math and read over the revised pro-forma for obvious errors.

After Jill left the room, Chip sank back in his chair, relieved and yet still unsure he was doing the right thing in doctoring up a document that could cause the bank, and more importantly, him, personally, to face charges of questionable banking practices. But the die is cast, he told himself.

Jill, now in her early forties, had been his assistant for a dozen years. Befitting the institution she served, she was always properly dressed in a dark jacket and skirt, with a high-neck white blouse showing the subtlest line of color along the buttoned front. Her dark brown hair was pulled back into a chignon, which, combined with a narrow chin, made her face appear as sharp as the head of an axe. Of course, what made her valuable to the bank was her keen eye for numerical errors. She entered Chip's office waving papers and walking around the desk to stand over him, placed the papers down and with a pencil pointed to the balance sheet.

"Do you realize that with these income projections, we could increase the bank's loan limit even higher than you suggested here... in fact about four percent higher?" Chip thanked her and agreed that he would review the figures and if necessary change them. Having deliberately placed a lower limit on the loan increase, he now felt justified to increase it, allowing a margin of error, to the figure Alex had given him. All that was needed now was for Chip to present the revised calculations to the bank president and obtain approval from the loan committee. Within two weeks the changes would undoubtedly be approved and his nightmare would be over.

On the train home, Chip mused, this was a job well done. In a few days, his life could actually be back in order and "Alex be damned!"

When he arrived home, he was warmly greeted by Alice who, like a suburban wife from the sixties, hugged him and kissed his cheek asking in her characteristic bell-clear tones, "How was your day, dear?" As Chip turned away from her and took off his coat to hang it in the closet he answered jokingly, "Just another day in the financial world," adding, as his voice dropped almost to a whisper, "Nothing for you to be concerned about!" He walked toward the bar in the living room. A martini would quiet the fear in his racing heart as he sat in his favorite leather wing-top chair watching the evening news on the television

As she turned away, Alice stifled the tears that were stinging her eyes and walked quickly to the kitchen where she felt safe. All the while, she wondered why Chip could not share more of his life with her. What could possibly be so terrible? He surely could not be concerned about money, knowing full well that she had a substantial inheritance that could carry them both for the rest of their lives. Besides, they were so much alike, both having come from old-line New England Presbyterian families. They belonged together and had seemingly been happy these past fifteen years. It was only in the past year that there had been an almost imperceptible change in Chip's attitude toward her. He seemed so absorbed in his banking business that he had less time for her and used what time he had at home to spend with their children. *But...* thought Alice, *that's understandable. After all, they had been together a long time and nothing is forever, yet he still seemed to love her.* She remembered their last anniversary when he took her out to a romantic dinner and dancing. Of course, nothing happened afterward...but....

THE FOLLOWING AFTERNOON, CHIP CALLED Alex, who immediately called Philip at home, exuding with the confident voice of a general who had just won a major battle. "I've bought you some leeway, but from here on out you'd better rein in the costs because there won't be any more ways to dip into the well." Before Philip had a chance to answer, Alex added, "But tell those kid designers of yours to stop fiddling with the project because I liked the design you originally presented and I don't want to see any more changes."

"Believe me," Philip answered, "I don't want changes any more than you do but you have to understand, there will naturally be some adjustments that are needed. Above all, as the design is fleshed out and we find that some details don't work, we may need to modify them. But, trust me when I say that I absolutely want to see this project built. At my age, I can't afford another paper project." After a moment, he added, "By the way, thank you for getting us this added financing. If you hadn't, I don't know what I would have done. I'm actually flabbergasted that you were able to get a signed commitment so quickly."

"Phil," added Alex after a pause, "don't worry about the contractual details. I'll take care of them. Listen, why don't we get away from this project one evening and just socialize with the wives."

"That sounds great! It's been a long time … actually the last time we four got together was last summer at your house in Truro."

"Has it been that long? That's terrible. OK, I'm going to tell Lila to fix a feast for us next Saturday."

"Please don't have her go to any trouble. After all we're practically family."

"No arguments, it's done!" said Alex before hanging up feeling somewhat concerned that he may have been too optimistic. After all, he did not have a signed commitment letter in his possession, only Chip's word that it will be forthcoming.

AFTER HE HUNG UP THE phone, Philip was jubilant and ran to the kitchen to embrace his wife. "That was Alex. He was able to increase the budget just as you thought he could."

"That's wonderful," she answered. "Now perhaps you can relax a bit. You always worry too much, and it's not good for you. Come, let's sit and have a relaxed evening starting right now. Perhaps a celebratory drink is in order."

"You're right, as always. I feel so lucky to have found you. It's just that I have demons that keep chasing me. Last night, for instance, I…"

"Before you start, bring out that great bottle of Bordeaux you've been saving."

Philip opened the cupboard and obediently took out the bottle and two glasses and placed them on the coffee table. He opened the bottle and poured the deep plum-colored liquid, lifting his glass to taste it before offering Diane hers. "It's still good. Now, let me tell you about my dream."

All right," said Diane. "Come, sit by my side on the couch."

Anxious to get on with his story, Philip started. "You know that even the most successful architects design more buildings than are actually built. Frank Lloyd Wright, for instance, conceived of a mile-high tower for Chicago, a visionary project that never went beyond the drawing stage. That was only one of dozens of projects that were conceived by him and never built. But, he was lucky, since he left a school of his disciples to carry on after he passed away. Because of that, some of his paper projects were eventually built, but his was an exceptional case. Well, I had this nightmare last evening that the Eden Center was never completed and sat on the site like some ancient ruin and that I would never again have a project built. I'm almost 62 years old and I don't have enough time to start over if this project doesn't succeed. In this profession, time is my enemy as it takes so long for a new building to go from concept to completion."

Diane put her arms around Philip and pulled him close to her, tightening the grip on his shoulders. "This is just what I was saying to you a few minutes ago. Eden Center is real and taking shape. It's not just a paper project. You can't let your demons take over your life. Look, you survived the time when war devastated half the world, and you overcame the cynicism of some of your colleagues to get this far. Today, Alex was able to solve the financing problem but you have to expect that there will be more hurdles before this project is completed. It's time for you to stop always seeing the negative consequences of a situation and become more positive."

Philip turned to face Diane and shaking his head said, "How come you are always so rational when I lose my way? I wish I had your brain."

"It's not the brain you should look at. Not letting your emotions control your reasoning would help."

Suddenly standing, Philip took Diane's hands in his and kissed her gently on the lips. "I swear I'll change!"

"We'll see," she answered, pained by the certain knowledge that this was a promise he could not keep.

IN THE SITE OFFICE AT the edge of the project, Patrick Connolly was at his desk, which was a flat-panel door supported by two wooden horses, when the phone rang. The office was in a trailer, which was raised on concrete blocks to immobilize its wheels above the rough ground. The exterior white walls of the trailer were decorated with undecipherable graffiti of swooping black lines like a modern-day version of Chinese calligraphy, the work of nighttime intruders with cans of spray paint.

As he picked up the phone, Patrick raised his head to look out at the site teeming with activity and heard the jumble of sounds that were only slightly damped by the thin walls of the trailer. "Connolly!" he boomed out into the phone. After a minute of garbled, undecipherable sounds, he repeated, "This is Patrick; you're going to have to speak up. It's a bit noisy here."

Alex raised his voice and explained the situation with the budget. "It's good news but you're going to have to be tougher with both the contractors and with Phil and his guys. There simply will not be room for any more change orders. You've got to stick to the letter of the contracts."

"OK, boss!" Patrick answered tersely and added apologetically, "You realize that it's too early in the construction process to guarantee anything and to make such unqualified statements...." but the phone went dead before he could complete the sentence. Instead, Patrick walked over to Sam's trailer to pass on the message.

When Sam Ruth heard the news, he felt only slightly relieved, knowing full well that such a unique project presents a wide range of uncertainties. "You understand," he said, "we're barely out of the ground, and the foundations are far from complete, so we could still face unknown problems with financial consequences."

"Of course I understand," Patrick answered, clearly annoyed. "I tried to tell that to Alex but he hung up on me, the son of a...."

"That figures! Oh, there is another thing. There have been a number of nighttime petty thefts at the site in the last few days, and I'm not talking about a bunch of nails or a hammer but some of our expensive power tools. You know that since the opening-day ceremony, I haven't heard a peep from Guardini so I suspect that this might be a not-so-subtle hint from the JPA that it was time to make a deal."

"You may be right but remember that you're in charge of the site. You might consider supplementing the nighttime guards and have them report the presence of any strangers."

"Mike already had me add guards at night but you're right, a few more wouldn't hurt." It was all he could do for the present, yet Sam still had an uncomfortable feeling that something terrible might happen.

Sam immediately called Mike to inform him of the increased project budget. This was welcome news since it meant that Mike could negotiate an increase in the contract cost to cover expenses that he had not anticipated.

"What does it look like?" asked Mike.

"They're talking about adding twelve million to the project."

"Great!" answered Mike. "I'll get with Alex to negotiate a contract adjustment. Anyway, it's good news since I was working with a really tight budget." To assure himself that he would win the original bid, Mike had made a number of risky concessions that reduced his margin and did not allow for unforeseen problems. The threat from the JPA was one such issue, which he now felt more confident to fight.

THE FOLLOWING SATURDAY, THE CORTAS arrived at the townhouse that Alex had purchased with his profits from the first office building he developed on his own after his father had passed away. Similar to the other midblock four-story townhouses on a fashionable eastside street, Alex's had a limestone façade but an interior that had been completely modernized. Before moving in, Alex had Philip develop plans to remodel the old structure and add an elevator, "just in case I need it one day."

Philip, to his dismay, had no control over the interior design as Lila introduced furniture and carpets that were eclectic at best and in poor taste at worst. For this reason, the Cortas rarely visited and preferred to meet the Grants for dinner at a restaurant or to spend a weekend in the Truro house that Philip admired and that had remained just as he remembered it from the time the senior Mr. Grant had asked him there to offer him the commission for the Landown Apartment project.

Philip told Diane that they had no choice this time. Alex met them at the door and, after taking their coats, led them to the second-floor living room. A kitchen separated the room from a dining area overlooking the back garden. On the way, they passed Alex's office on the ground floor and could see a family room in the back that opened onto the garden. The bedrooms were on the third floor.

Before they reached the living room, Lila stepped out from behind the kitchen counter and embraced Diane as both blurted out almost simultaneously that it had been too long since their last get-together and why didn't the husbands arrange more frequent dinners. Before the Grant children were sent downstairs to the family room, Diane expressed wonder at how they'd grown, and listened as Lila gushed about their latest school accomplishments.

Meanwhile, Alex showed Philip a bottle of 18-year-old single-malt scotch he had just bought and, pouring two glasses, said, "Taste and tell me that this isn't the best you've ever had."

"Don't forget Diane," Lila yelled across the room while taking a sip of her usual vodka that sat on the counter in a large water glass.

"Thank you, but I'm afraid I've never developed the taste for scotch. If you don't mind I'll wait for the wine at dinner."

"Would you try just a sip?" asked Philip. "It has a delightful nutty, smoky flavor that I remember from my school days."

"I guess you weren't just studying hard at old Cambridge U," said Diane.

Smiling nervously, Philip interjected, "Maybe we should move on to another topic."

They all laughed and began two conversations divided by gender. Alex and Philip retreated to two leather easy chairs in the living room and, sipping the precious scotch, were unable to stay away from talking about Eden, although they had promised each other that this was supposed to be a social evening. Diane and Lila stood in the kitchen talking first about the progress the children were making in school, all the while watching a *coq aux vin* simmer on the stove, exuding a sweet intoxicating smell. As they talked, Lila would periodically take another sip of vodka.

"Is everything all right?" Diane asked.

"I guess so," she responded in a whispered voice and after a moment added, "I don't know. It's Alex. He seems to be pulling away from me and I don't know what to do about it. It gets me so depressed that maybe I drink a little too much and then he gets cold and distant." She wiped away a tear.

"I'm so sorry," said Diane as she put her arm around her friend. "Maybe it's just the pressure of the project that is having a negative effect on both Alex and Philip. Honestly, there are days when Phil is so wrapped up in himself that I can't reach him."

"I know what you mean. But I feel I don't have a husband anymore and it's painful. I worry it's affecting the children as well."

Before Diane could answer, Alex called across the room, "How's the stew coming along? Philip and I are getting hungry."

"Hold your horses," answered Lila, "and it's a *coq au vin*, not a stew."

"A stew by any other name..."

Diane interjected cynically; "Don't be in such a stew, boys, Lila and

I are going to have a little chat on the terrace while the chicken finishes cooking."

Pushing Lila by the waist, Diane led her to the little terrace overlooking the garden and closed the door to the dining room.

"OK, before we both freeze to death out here, tell momma. There is something else going on here, isn't there?"

"Ever since Erin was born, I've been trying to get back to my art work but I can't seem to concentrate on it. I've begun to suspect that Alex is having an affair. That started me drinking and then things just got worse. I don't know what to do. It's like it was before we got married and I had to give up acting because I became pregnant with Marc. Believe me, I love my children and I don't mind having to give up acting or art for them, but I want Alex to respect me and love me."

"Actually, I think you do mind," said Diane, "but I don't blame you. You should be able to follow your dreams while in your marriage. When I found out that I couldn't have children, I was devastated but Philip pointed out that there were other options. That's how I discovered photography and I've enjoyed every minute of it even when there were problems. Of course, Philip encouraged me, and that was important. You need to talk to Alex and tell him of your doubts about his fidelity and of your need to pursue your art. If you don't, it will eat away at you."

"I know you're right but I'm afraid! What if he wants to leave me?"

"You're going to have to be strong. If Alex truly loves you, he'll support your decision."

"But, what if he doesn't?"

"You'll only find out if you talk together."

Ten minutes later, the four friends sat around the dining table chatting as Alex poured an appropriate Cabernet. Philip raised a glass to give a toast, complimenting the chef as Lila looked embarrassed and Alex scowled impatiently.

"You're so lucky to have a wife who is such a good cook," said Diane.

"I don't often have a chance to taste her fare." Alex shot back.

Lila glared at Alex and blurted out, "Well, maybe if you were home more often, you would have a better chance to enjoy my cooking."

Alex dropped his utensils in his plate and stared menacingly at Lila. Sensing the tension, Philip interjected, "The project claims so much of Alex's time as it has mine, but I know he must miss the chance to eat at home."

"Thanks, Phil! But you don't have to defend me. Lila knows perfectly well why I don't spend more time here."

"Listen, you two," Diane exclaimed, "If you have problems I'm sure they can be worked out. I remember when you just adored each other and now you've got two wonderful children. Maybe the pressure of this project is weighing you both down. Please, we're your friends. Perhaps we can help you work through this difficult time."

Lila had tears in her eyes while Alex stood up and took a deep breath before looking in the direction of the Cortas and saying, "We don't want to burden you with our problems but maybe you're right when you say we've all been under a lot of pressure lately." Turning to face Lila, he added, "Truce! I'm sorry. Let's try again."

Wiping her tears Lila took a deep breath and said, "OK. I'm sorry too." Then turning to Diane, added, "You're really good friends. I was so happy to cook this meal for you, so let's try to enjoy this evening." Pushing away her glass of vodka, she added, "Alex, can you pour me a glass of that lovely wine, please?"

All four smiled and spontaneously bust into laughter as Diane hugged Lila. Philip raised his glass and exclaimed, "To friendship!"

"Here, here," the others responded as they clinked their glasses together.

Alex stared at Lila as he wondered whether he should make more of an effort to cement his marriage. Diane was right when she pointed out that his family was really quite perfect. He loved his children and he still loved Lila. *So, why,* he thought, *did he still cling to Claire? Maybe he should break off that relationship?*

ENTRACTE

An air of excitement pervaded the site with activities taking place everywhere. Machines were digging and drilling into the earth and rock toward the very core of the planet. Concrete trucks were disgorging their soupy gray mix into prepared wooden forms, and trussed steel columns on flatbed trailers were waiting their turn to be unloaded near the entrance to the site. In contrast to this high-energy environment, the flowing river to the west and the city traffic to the east appeared gentle and benign.

The ground, consisting of soil stabilized with gravel, easily supported the trucks carrying the story-high trussed steel sections of what would become a tower crane that would be needed to lift material and equipment to each floor that would rise from the foundations. A mobile crane on a truck, with four outriggers making it appear like a giant Jurassic spider, lifted the first section and positioned it on a prepared foundation where workers in gloved hands bolted it firmly to the concrete.

The sun shone brightly on this crisp early winter morning as the work of building continued slowly, at a measured tempo, in keeping with the cool air temperature. The ironworkers were careful not to touch naked steel or bolts without gloves, knowing that their fingers could be instantly bonded to the surface, which was cooled below freezing by an overnight frost. On this day, four sections of a tower crane were to be erected to await the horizontal boom that would house the counterweighted hook of the crane.

In another part of the site, another mobile crane unloaded the first sections of the steel columns that piece-by-piece would eventually rise to the top of the towers. The first of these were now being jockeyed into position so that holes in their base plates lined up with steel anchor bolts projecting from concrete footings. As more columns were to be erected during the day, they would stand as sentinels announcing the beginning of the visible embodiment of the buildings that were to occupy the site.

FIVE
The Protector
December 2000

S AM RUTH PUT ON HIS parka and hardhat as he prepared to take his
morning tour of the site when a two-tone bell announced an incoming communication on his computer. Impatient to visit the site, he ignored the message and stepped outside his trailer. After all, most emails
were either advertisements or requests for action that he felt were not
urgent. Furthermore, for the first time in weeks, the site had been free
of petty thefts and work was proceeding smoothly. Why tempt fate by
opening a message that might announce bad news!

Walking onto the site, Sam pulled up the collar of his parka as he felt
the chill of this mid-December morning licking his skin. He spent some
time watching a steel column section being jockeyed into position onto
its concrete foundation and noticed that the concrete spalled easily as the
base plate scraped against it. He called out to the crane operator to be
more careful and avoid any more damage to the concrete.

Driven by suspicion aroused by years of experience, Sam removed his
gloves and picked up chips of the spalled concrete, ground them between
his fingers and was surprised at how easily they disintegrated. He called
over the concrete superintendent and asked, "Where did this concrete
come from?"

The super, a sturdy man with unruly, thinning hair and rumpled
clothes that gave him the appearance of an unmade bed answered, "Our
regular supplier. Why?"

"Look at this stuff. It falls apart. This isn't structural concrete; it's crap! Where are the test reports?

"They were e-mailed last night. You should have received them this morning," the super responded.

Without waiting for further discussions, Sam hurried back to his office and opened his e-mail. The reports were all there and indicated that the concrete strength was a little low but not terribly so. Turning away, Sam reached into his cabinet and pulled out a Swiss hammer, a tool used to obtain instantaneous strength readings of concrete, and hurried back out onto the site and went from footing to footing testing the strength of the concrete. He became more and more agitated as he realized the concrete strength was not just a little low but, in many locations, more than forty percent below the required values. He turned to the concrete super who was trailing him and screamed, "What the hell is going on here? Where were you when this material was delivered?"

Without waiting for an answer, Sam returned to his trailer to make a call, ordering further tests by a second independent laboratory. If his suspicion was right, that the concrete was seriously under strength, it would endanger the ability of the foundation to support the future towers. It was obvious to him at this point that the reports he received from the concrete contractor were deceptive or, at worst, fraudulent. Sam called Mike to advise him of this problem. "How bad is it?" asked Mike.

"I stopped the contractor from erecting any more columns and I think about half the footings may have to be jack hammered out and replaced. The most serious problem we have is that the main tower foundation may have to be replaced and that's a huge job that could delay us over a month."

Mike raised his voice to exclaim, "Shit! How could this happen? Isn't the concrete checked at the plant before it is placed into the trucks that are supposed to be driven directly to the site?"

"Well, you know, sometimes the drivers stop for coffee and donuts even though they're not supposed to." After a moment, Sam added, "Somehow I think Bruno's guys may have salted the concrete." It was well known that ordinary salt added to liquid concrete could seriously diminish its strength.

"That bastard could easily be so vindictive. Before I call Alex, I need more details of what's going on. Question some of the concrete truck drivers and call the lab to find out what they did with the concrete test samples."

Sam spent the next few hours questioning drivers, knowing that they could not easily be cowed with fear of physical violence, so he threatened to have them fired, which, in the current economic environment, was more persuasive. What he learned was that at least some of the drivers had indeed stopped on the way to the site and were away from their trucks for at least half an hour, long enough for someone to introduce a substance into the hoppers, such as salt. Checking on the testing laboratory that had prepared the reports he received earlier in the day, he also discovered that one of its owners was a corporation with the same address as the JPA. Sam concluded that Bruno could easily have influenced the preparation of inaccurate lab reports.

Sam called Mike with the information, asking, "What do we do now?"

Mike held the phone away from his face as he tried to contain his anger. "There'll be hell to pay but you'll have to pull that concrete out. Talk to Patrick and I'll let Alex know what's going on but…" and after pausing for a moment added, "I want you to get hold of Bruno and arrange a meeting away from the site, somewhere we won't be disturbed. Just the two of us! I don't want anyone else at the meeting."

"What are you planning?"

"I don't know yet. Just make the arrangements."

"Stay cool." Sam remembered his conversation with Mike in the fall after Bruno Guardini had first proposed a protection deal and was worried that Mike might act on his earlier threat to kill the man from Jersey. Nevertheless, he made the call and arranged a meeting for the following afternoon at a roadside diner near the Jersey Meadowlands.

Later that afternoon, as Alex was preparing to go home, he received a call from Patrick Connolly. The words flowed threateningly in the ether between the two men: defective concrete, delays, sabotage… At first, Alex thought only about the effect this could have on the project finances but as Patrick explained the situation, Alex became increasingly angry and finally screamed into the handset, "Incompetents, fucking incompetents!"

The following day, after a quick sandwich lunch in the construction trailer, Mike left for his meeting with Guardini. Driving through the Lincoln Tunnel and onto Route 3, he went over in his mind how he would handle this meeting. Before leaving, Sam had reminded him again to be careful to maintain control and not fall into the trap of uncontrolled anger.

The diner, an unimpressive building sheathed in dark wood vertical slats, was partially hidden from the road by a deteriorating picket fence meant to hide the parking area. A small sign on one side of the turnoff from the highway identified it as Emil's Diner. It had been chosen for the meeting not for its cuisine, which consisted of a greasy mix of burgers and omelets, but rather for its relative isolation and for Emil's discretion and respect for the privacy of his customers.

Mike parked near the entrance and pushed open a light aluminum-framed glass door, entering the fluorescent-lit diner. Walking past the counter, he settled into a booth far from the entrance, ordered coffee, and waited. Every few minutes he looked at his watch and toward the door, all the while becoming more agitated as he reminded himself of Sam's parting words, "Keep cool." But it was not that simple! There was a great deal at stake; the future of the project, the cost of replacing the weak concrete, and the question of the money.

Mike understood that often, money changed hands to smooth over a situation; when, for instance, a building inspector was willing to turn a blind eye to a minor infraction of ridiculous rules or a contractor offered to speed up a process in exchange for an under-the-table payment. However this situation with Guardini was different because Mike saw no clear value in making any payment for which he would receive no real benefit. "It's a fucking bribe!" he hissed.

Having never met Bruno, when a man wearing a dark wool coat punched through the door of the diner and walked directly in his direction extending his right hand, Mike decided it had to be him. Mike had become so agitated that rather than taking the offered hand, he could only nod his head in greeting.

Bruno took off his coat and carefully draped it over the bench opposite Mike. He unbuttoned his pin-stripe suit jacket revealing a white shirt and purple tie. The top button of the shirt was open to accommodate a thickening neck. His face featured flashing eyes and broadly spread nostrils on a smooth face with a perpetual tan below a hill of dark brown hair tinged with streaks of gray. He smiled, exposing nicotine-stained teeth and said, "Mike, my friend, it's good to see you. I hope Emil has taken good care of you...Emil," he screamed, "a cup of coffee for me and top off my friend."

As he slid into the bench to face Mike, he said in a raspy voice, "So, what do you want talk about?" When there was no answer, he continued, "I told your boy, what's his name...Ruth... sounds like a girl's name... that we're here to help you. Construction's a tough business. Something's always happening at the site you didn't expect. We can make it easy for you. You know, smooth things over, " he said, smiling as he raised his head and tilted it back so that he appeared to look down at Mike.

Emil placed a fresh mug in front of Guardini and poured more coffee into Mike's mug.

"Maybe you don't know much about us but the JPA's been my baby for almost twenty years. We provide protection services for contractors and manufacturers." Waving his arm as if to brush away a fly, he added, "Hell, I don't hafta tell you, we helped you out in the past. You had no problems, remember! That's our motto. In all the time we been in business, no complaints about our service. Hell, in fact our clients come back to us for their next job. On top of that, since we provide employment for guys who would otherwise have their hand out, you can say we provide a social service."

Bruno presented himself as a successful businessman, dressed as he was in an expensively tailored suit. He leaned forward and stroked the edge of his coffee cup, revealing a gold chain bracelet below the cuff of his left arm.

"You and I, we're businessmen and should understand each other." After a pause, he added, "I offer you a service to help you with gettin' a job done at the lowest cost and with no problems, as I said. With us, you don't hafta worry about security at the site and…"

Mike interrupted brusquely, "Maybe you don't understand the reason for this meeting."

Deaf to that remark, Bruno continued, "Sure, I understand, you got laborers who don't know what they're doing and you put them at the front gate of the site. Our guys are trained just for this job: it's all they do. Your people are amateurs and we are professionals."

Mike placed his hands on the table and started to get up. "Not interested! I asked for this meeting for only one reason and you know perfectly well what I'm talking about. What happened to our concrete is unacceptable and I'm pretty sure you had something to do with it. I want you to listen very carefully and understand that the next time anyone even stubs his toe accidentally on the site," leaning forward, Mike added in a voice barely above a whisper, "I'm coming after you. I don't want to hear about any more incidents at the site. None! Is that clear?"

Lowering his voice and crossing his forearms on the table, Bruno was seething inside but answered, "Are you threatening me?"

"If that's the way you choose to hear it."

Bruno stood up slowly as if to leave and looking down at Mike said, "This meeting's over. You're making a fuckin' big mistake. I offer you a legitimate business deal and you choose to turn it into something ugly. I don't like being disrespected. That's not the way I work and if you can't have a civil conversation with me, there's no point talking." Without waiting for a reply, Bruno turned and left the diner.

"You forgot to pay," Mike yelled out, taking a five-dollar bill out of his pocket and laying it on the table. He smiled in a self-satisfied way, convinced that he had made his point but was concerned that this was not the last time he would hear from Bruno. He hoped that the added security he had ordered for the site would resolve any further problem.

Upon his return to the site Mike met with Sam and Patrick to report on his meeting with Bruno. "I'm pretty sure we won't have any more trouble from the Guardini bunch," he said, "but, just in case, let's keep the guards on their toes. The concrete problem we just had is going to cost me a bundle and I can't afford any more sabotage on the site."

"I don't know," said Patrick, "I've dealt with people like this in the past and believe me when I say that they generally don't respond well when they've been challenged. A cornered dog can be dangerous."

"Mike," interrupted Sam, "remember the problem you avoided when you paid off the JPA on your last job."

"You agreed with me," said Mike, "that we weren't going to talk about that again, so let's drop it."

"Hold on," said Patrick. "What's that about?"

"It's got nothing to do with you."

"It's got everything to do with me," Patrick replied angrily. "When you talk to me, you're talking to Alex and as he keeps reminding me, in his not-so-subtle way, everything that happens on this site is my responsibility. So let's cut out this bullshit."

Mike yelled back, "You weren't even involved with Bruno on that job. I was! So don't get in the middle of this."

"Well, I'm involved now, so…"

Sam broke in, "Guys, it's time to ratchet down a bit…. Listen Mike, let me tell Patrick what happened on that other job."

Mike stepped back and sat on the edge of the desk. "OK."

"First, let me tell you Pat, I'm with you. I wouldn't trust Bruno for a minute. Anyway, it was a few years ago when we first became involved with the JPA. Mike was the contractor for an apartment building that Alex was developing. Guardini offered to provide protective services and since this was Mike's first major job, he didn't want any trouble so he made a deal. It turned out to be a costly mistake because the fees we had to pay the JPA wiped out any profit on the job. Now, here we are today, barely out of the ground and we've already had an expensive problem with those guys. I don't know what else we can expect but to tell you the truth, I'm worried."

"Damn it Mike, you should have told me about this earlier," said Patrick. I'll have to tell Alex. It's possible he can help us. He's got good relations with the mayor and the police commissioner. Perhaps they could apply a little pressure to make Bruno back off."

Mike started pacing around the limited space between the desk and the wall of the trailer. "I don't like it. Getting the mayor and the cops involved makes everything more complicated. When it was just between us and Bruno, I could see containing the situation but I'm afraid involving more parties will complicate what's already difficult enough to deal with."

"I'm not sure I understand you. I thought you would be happy to have someone else take the heat off you."

Sam interjected, "I don't know why you would object to letting the cops take care of Bruno."

"I just don't want the cops involved in my affairs, that's all," replied Mike.

"Now you're making me nervous," said Sam, and added with a smile. "What affairs are you talking about? You've been cheating on your wife or something?"

"Christ, It's nothing like that. It's just that my business is private and I don't want anyone digging into it. Look, let's drop this. I'll find a way of dealing with Bruno without involving Alex. If there's a problem, I'll get back to you." Turning away abruptly, he added, "Sorry, I have to leave now."

Mike then walked out without saying another word.

Sam turned to Patrick, "I don't know what's eating Mike. There must be something wrong. I'll try to see him in the morning to see if I can pull it out of him."

"I'll give you a couple of days, but then I've got to tell Alex," replied Patrick.

TEN DAYS LATER, THE RUTHS drove to visit the Longs for Christmas Eve dinner. They lived in adjacent townships in North Jersey. Sam soon arrived at a quiet residential street and stopped in front of an old Victorian house ablaze with lights of all colors outlining each window and door. The small front lawn also sported a pair of wire-mesh reindeer, speckled with myriad miniature lights, pulling a red and green sleigh. The Ruths' sons in the back seat exclaimed, "Wow!" They were delighted to see such a grand display, since their house had no such decorations.

"Mike seems to be competing with his neighbors to see who can burn more power," said Sam.

Jan turned to face him, a frown cutting lines on her milk-chocolate brow. "Remember, Sam, this is supposed to be a joyous occasion so no negative comments and try not to bring up any problems tonight."

"But...."

"No buts," and turning her head to the back, "and boys, I expect you to be on your Sunday behavior."

Sam stepped out of the car and said, "Well, boys, I guess we've been given our orders. Let's just march up to the front door with a smile on our faces."

"It's not a joke," replied Jan. "I expect all my boys to behave."

Marion greeted the family at the door and immediately sent the two boys to the basement that had been converted into a playroom with a ping-pong table and a television corner.

"Now, be careful not to break anything," Jan called out as the boys ran down the stairs, practically tripping over each other.

"Don't worry," Marion said as she hugged Jan. "The boys have been here before and the room is pretty well childproof. Come in and let's sit down." She was led into the kitchen while Mike and Sam went to the living room.

With the sound of ping-pong balls echoing from the basement,

Marion whispered, "I've been trying different recipes to remind Mike of Cambodia but I'm afraid many of them involve fish and I wasn't sure the boys would eat them so I made a Khmer beef salad. And…just in case, I've got some burgers in the fridge."

"You don't have to cater to my boys," answered Jan. "They eat what I give them with no arguments. It's bad enough that I have to deal with Mr. Fussy who was spoiled by his mother," turning her eyes toward Sam. "I swore I wouldn't let that happen to my kids. Anyway, thanks for the invite. I don't think we've ever been together for Christmas Eve."

"I thought it would be nice for us since I haven't seen you or the boys for a while. I guess you haven't had a chance to go out much lately with the job ramping up. I know that Mike seems to spend every evening at the office or out in the field. He doesn't tell me everything that's going on but I gather there have been some serious problems."

"Serious is an understatement! Sam tells me there's been sabotage at the site. He's been trying to get Mike to agree to call the cops but for some reason, Mike is delaying…"

"He has been nervous lately so maybe this is weighing on his mind. But, let's forget issues of work tonight and just enjoy each other."

"OK! Let' s bust up the guys and have a drink."

They brought out some appetizers that Marion had prepared, and bottles of beer for all. Mike and Sam had no opportunity of conversing beyond "hello" and "what's up." Sam had wanted to press Mike for a decision about involving the police because Patrick, who was anxious to start an investigation into the sabotage of the concrete, was pushing him for an answer, but that discussion had to wait.

At the end of the evening, as they walked toward the car, Sam put his arm around Mike's shoulder and said, "Thanks for this evening. The kids really enjoyed being here. And, listen, I'm sorry we never got a chance to talk but I wanted to find out when you plan to answer Patrick about calling Alex."

Mike pulled away, clearly annoyed, and grumbled, "Stop pressuring me. I'll get to it soon."

"Don't get defensive on me. I'm only trying to prevent a nasty confrontation because Pat told me that he planned to call Alex right after Christmas."

Mike expressed surprise, as he had not yet reconciled his concerns about having police involvement with his affairs with the need to further deal with Guardini. "I'll leave a message to have Pat call me before he contacts Alex… If that's OK with you, that is."

"Sorry to pressure you but …"

"Don't worry, I'll take care of it."

The evening ended as the Ruths all climbed into their car and drove off.

"Are you coming in?" asked Marion, as Mike stood staring at the departing car.

"In a minute," replied Mike as he went over in his mind what he could possibly say to Patrick to give him more time to deal with Guardini rather than have Alex involve the police.

THERE WAS LITTLE WORK GOING on at the site during the week between Christmas and New Year's day, and Mike had decided that this was the right time to meet with Patrick. When Mike arrived at the site office, Patrick was waiting for him impatiently and blurted out, "Well, you certainly took your sweet time getting back to me. You were going to get back to me in a couple of days and now it's almost two weeks. You're lucky that I didn't just call the cops myself. If it weren't for Sam, that's exactly what I would have done, so now what?"

Mike was taken aback by this barrage and paused before answering. "What can I tell you? I'm sorry, but I had to be certain that involving the cops wouldn't hurt my firm or the project. Now, before you jump in, let me explain. This project is a big deal for me. If anything goes wrong, I could lose all credibility. If I can handle the kind of problem we now have with Guardini, I will have built up a positive reputation in the industry and owners will trust me in the future with their projects. I realize that the way I dealt with Guardini two weeks ago was a mistake. I ended up aggravating him instead of negotiating with him. Now, I think he may come after us again. I plan to call him and get together again to see if I can smooth things over. In the meantime, involving the cops would be a mistake."

"I don't know," answered Patrick. "It may already be too late to correct the situation. When do you propose to get together with him?"

"I'll wait till after the New Year. It won't hurt to let him stew a little while."

"OK, but don't wait too long. Guys like Guardini are unpredictable and you never know what will set them off." Patrick added before leaving, "And let's hope we all have a Happy New Year."

ENTRACTE

Little hillocks of fresh snow covered the steel erection towers that lay on the ground like wounded abstract animals. The air was filled with the deafening whine of compressors whose tentacles of plastic hose led to workers manning their jackhammers, gouging out concrete from the defective footings and throwing up clouds of gray dust that enveloped the site in an impenetrable, choking fog.

Dump trucks moved into the site in straight columns like a well-disciplined army. Front-end loaders clawed into the chunks of concrete torn from the defective foundations and picked them up before dropping them into the waiting mouths of the trucks. Leaving the site in marching order, the trucks headed to a waiting dump site on the New Jersey side of the river. Apart from the concrete removal, little other work was being performed and several groups of workers were huddled around steel drums in which fires, fed by scraps of lumber, burned, radiating much-needed warmth. The site was in turmoil!

SIX
The Persuader
January 2001

IN THE SITE OFFICE, WITH garlands of green and red lights interspersed with sagging branches of pine and spruce left over from a Christmas party ten days earlier, Patrick Connolly faced the project's architects and engineers around the conference table and said, "I know this is a lousy way to start the New Year."

As he explained the reasons for the removal of the defective concrete, a gray silence hung in the air. Sam was slumped back in his chair, his legs outstretched, his deep-set brown eyes almost closed, his full lips pulled back leaving only a thin pink line dividing his face, his hands folded on the table in supplication restraining an inner rage.

For a moment, after Patrick stopped talking, people around the table looked at each other until Philip raised himself in his chair and, speaking in a barely audible voice, started, "Where were the controls that are supposed to assure us of a quality project? Today, it is concrete. What's it going to be next, steel welds, missing bolts, even the quality of the steel itself, and what about the quality of the rock under the footings? How do we know it's any good?"

The more he spoke, the higher the pitch of his voice became. "We're building a major building in a major city and I would think that this kind of problem could be avoided. I've talked to Alex and he assures me that this was an unfortunate incident but I have certain responsibilities toward the City Building Department in reporting what is going on and

77

I need more than vague assurances that this will not recur. My structural engineer tells me that if it had not been discovered, this concrete problem could have resulted in a catastrophe with the possibility of a major collapse later, leading to I don't know what consequences."

Slamming a fist on the table, he stared at the three construction men. "I need to know that controls have been instituted that will absolutely guarantee—I say again, *guarantee*—that we won't have another such problem." He faced Patrick and nervously combed his hair with his fingers and rubbed the back of his neck, concluding, "I've been sick with concern about what could have happened. Now please tell me how you will prevent a similar problem in the future."

Patrick was used to dealing with emotional architects and stood to face Philip and spoke sternly, "If you don't think we're taking this seriously, you're sadly mistaken. Since we discovered the problem, Sam, Mike and I spent the Christmas holidays looking into this thoroughly and we're certain we know what happened and why and are taking steps to make sure that it won't happen in the future. This isn't the first job that has had problems during construction and it won't be the last! Trust me; we know how to deal with them."

The engineer sitting next to Philip whispered in his ear.

"This isn't just any old construction problem," said Philip. "This is clearly a case of sabotage and maybe the police should be involved."

Patrick was visibly upset and waved his hand, cutting the air. "No police! As I said, we'll handle it in our own way." He turned and left the room followed by the other two construction men, leaving the architect and engineer shaken by the sudden outburst.

Philip was unsure how to react but after a short conversation with his engineer, the two decided there was nothing they could do but let the construction men deal with the issue. Once outside, Sam pulled Mike aside and asked, "Have you called Bruno yet?"

"For Christ's sake, don't pressure me," Mike answered brusquely. "I said I'll do it and I'll do it in my own time."

"Sorry," said Sam. "I only brought it up because you had seemed anxious to get back to him to make sure we have no more trouble at the site."

"I'll call him first thing in the morning, so relax."

THAT SAME DAY, IN A residential neighborhood of Jersey City, beyond the rocky cliffs across the river from the Eden site, a broad-shouldered young man paused in front of a house on Baird Street that differed from its neighbors only by the muted earth tones of its clapboard siding. Number 178 was the color of faded sand. Justin Cameron climbed the sixteen steps of the stoop leading to the entrance door and furtively looked left and right toward the street corners on either end; seeing no one, he pressed the entrance buzzer above a small tarnished brass plate engraved with the letters JPA.

As the door clicked open and before entering, he glanced down at the shiny black roof of the Lincoln town car parked in front of the two-car garage adjacent to the stoop. As he stepped inside and before his eyes adjusted to the relative darkness of the hallway, a heavy voice called out, "Come in the office."

The Jersey Protective Association had, long ago, converted the townhouse for its own use, although the signs of its residential origins remained. A front office usually occupied by a receptionist had been transformed from a living room on the parlor floor that faced the street. Two heavily curtained windows severely rationed the light entering the room. An open doorway led to Guardini's office at the rear of the building. From behind a desk on the sidewall of his office, Guardini called out through the open doorway, "Come in and sit. Thanks for coming on Sunday when my guys are not here."

As Justin sprawled into a chair on the side of the desk he faced a wall of photographs, all including Bruno and either a political figure or some famous personality. Several also showed him with buddies on a fishing boat exhibiting their catch of the day. "You see that," Bruno said when he saw Justin staring at one particular photo in the corner, "that's the day we caught two dozen stripers off Montauk. Beautiful! Best day I ever had." He spoke in dark, authoritative tones of someone who had clarified an early accented speech. "So," he continued, "I hear good things about you. You work hard and you know how to keep your mouth shut and don't blab about what you're doing. So…you know what we do here?"

"I think so."

"Let me finish. We provide protection services to keep the bad guys away. And, we do it by hiring guys like you who need work and also know how to stand up to trouble. What I've got now is a situation that needs to be helped along with your kind of talent. We've got a reluctant client who doesn't want to sign with us even though we've offered him a good deal. Anyway this outfit needs a little more persuasion and that's where you come in."

"If you think I can be of help." Justin spoke in a high gargled voice.

"You understand, I'm not looking for any rough stuff. That's not what we do…that's old fashioned. But some guys just need a friendly push so they understand that we're offering a service that they can't do without."

"If you want friendly persuasion, I'm your man." With his legs outstretched and his arms hung loosely draped on the sides of the chair, Justin gave the appearance of a totally relaxed individual were it not for his fitted tee shirt that defined a physically tight upper body. He appeared capable of exerting pressure without resorting to violence.

"OK, here's what I want you to do." Bruno then explained the lack of response from the contractor at the Eden construction site and what he wanted done to encourage a positive response. He ended with, "And, the sooner the better!"

"Mr. Guardini, consider it done!"

The night following this meeting, Justin, accompanied by an accomplice, parked his car a block from the project site and waited for the construction workers to leave. A light snow covered the ground. Lights were still on in the project office and in trailers belonging to mechanical, concrete, and foundation subcontractors. One by one, these were extinguished and its occupants left the site until only one lighted trailer remained.

"I can't wait any longer," Justin said to Tom, the brutish looking man next to him. "Let's go, and bring that bag." Dressed in parkas and watch caps pulled down over their heads to ward off the freezing temperatures, the two walked toward the wooden gate that was loosely chained shut, and Justin took a bolt cutter from the bag. Snipping open the lock, the men then slipped onto the site and headed toward an equipment trailer.

"Hand me that can and keep it quiet." Justin spread the contents of the can around the base of the trailer when suddenly, the door on the adjacent trailer opened and Steve Crocker, a large man framed by the light radiating from his trailer, yelled out, "What the hell are you guys doing here?" Justin was about to light a match when Crocker ran toward him and pushed him roughly to the ground.

Crocker was a superintendent for the concrete contractor and used to having to use muscle to keep his men in line. "Get the hell out of here before I call the cops and..." Before he could finish the sentence, Tom locked his muscular arms around Crocker's chest and Justin stood up and punched him in the abdomen. Wild with fury, Crocker twisted around, loosened the man's grip, and turned to smash his fist into Tom's chin, propelling him backward toward the side of the trailer. Justin lunged forward with fists flying but Crocker was ready for him and parried his blows, hitting him back violently, causing Justin to stumble. Crocker stood over the fallen man shaking his fist and yelling, "I told y..."

Unable to complete his sentence, he felt a stabbing pain as a knife thrust upward through the flesh below his left shoulder blade. As the knife penetrated his heart, Crocker stared transfixed and slowly crumpled to the ground. Blood drained from his body, staining the white snow. Turning to Tom, Justin snarled, under his breath, "Shit! I told you no rough stuff. Now see what you gone and done. How are we going to clean up this mess? Grab his legs and pull him next to the trailer."

Not waiting for a sign of acknowledgment, Justin picked up the matches he had dropped in the snow earlier and, lighting a dry one, dropped it on the ground together with the remainder of the pack that immediately flared up. As the flames spread, igniting the kerosene-soaked clothes on the body on the ground and the tires of the trailer, one of the guards at the other end of the site could be heard yelling and running toward the trailer. Justin and Tom hurriedly left the site and drove away as they heard the sound of sirens approaching, followed by an explosion as the propane tank attached to the trailer blew up. In the rear-view mirror Justin saw flames and smoke enveloping the trailer.

MIKE LONG WAS SOUND ASLEEP when the telephone startled him in the midst of a dream in which giant bees, the size of bats, were buzzing all around him, swooping down to attack him as he flailed his arms to prevent them from biting. Marion pushed him away; "Stop hitting me and answer the damn phone," she insisted. Brushing his face to wipe away the haze of semi-consciousness, he reached for the phone. "Yea!"

"Mike, it's Sam. I'm sorry to wake you so early but there's been an accident at the site. There was a fire in one of the trailers and Crocker's dead. The police called me and want us down there this morning."

Fully awake now, Mike sat on the edge of the bed with one hand holding his brow as he tried to gather his thoughts. "Do they know what happened?"

"All I heard was that they suspect arson. As far as Crocker, they are not sure because the body was badly burned and we'll have to wait for an autopsy. I've called Patrick and he'll meet me at the site in an hour." Mike promised to join them and turned to see Marion frowning. "That was Sam. There's been a problem at the site. I'm going to have to go."

"It's five in the morning," she said.

"I'm afraid it's serious. One of our men is dead," he replied as he dressed and prepared to leave. "Do you mind opening the office and handling things until I can get there?"

"Of course, but let me know when you find out what happened."

When Mike had first opened his office, he had asked Marion to join him as executive assistant to handle the management of the office and the bookkeeping that he did not feel comfortable trusting to someone he did not know. Since then, Marion has been his wife and his business partner, as Mike became totally dependent on her judgment.

When the sun began to rise behind the city's highest buildings, long shadows fell across the ghostly site of the Eden project. Bright lights illuminated one corner of the site where the twisted, charred remains of the burned trailer stood. A bitter stench pervaded the atmosphere as Sam and Mike silently looked at the scene. The area, cleared of snow by the heat of the fire, was a muddy bog. Sam, his teeth clenched tightly in anger and his bass voice shaking, said, "This is no damn accident. Somehow, and I'll lay odds on it, Bruno's involved. Did you ever call him? This goes way beyond anything we experienced on the last job. There, it was only threats and money. This time it's murder."

"We had better join Patrick and wait to hear what the cops say before we jump to conclusions," Mike replied, as he turned to go to the trailer where two detectives were talking to Patrick. "I don't like it," said Sam as he followed. He wondered whether Mike had called Bruno. Why was he always so secretive? We're supposed to be friends!

Before entering the trailer, Mike turned to Sam and warned, "Just listen and let me do the talking. And don't bring up the Jersey guys. We'll take care of that ourselves." Before Sam could respond, he added, "And don't argue." At this last remark, even though he was angry, Sam could not help smiling.

The police detectives, along with an investigator from the fire department, wanted to know if Mike and Sam knew of any reason anyone had for starting a fire at the site and if Crocker had any enemies who would want to harm him. Mike explained, "Look, this is a construction site and sometimes things happen. At least we haven't had anyone buried in the concrete foundation... at least as far as I know." It was common knowledge that on at least one major construction project in New York, where a serious conflict erupted between the union and some non-union workers, one of the latter ended up missing, under suspicious circumstances. Without specific evidence, the authorities were not about to jack-hammer the foundation to try to find the missing worker, so it just became part of the lore of a dangerous trade.

The investigator from the fire department pointed out that the fire was of suspicious origin and was definitely ignited with the use of a petroleum product, of which they found traces around the site. He also noted that the chain on the front gate had been cut and that a guard had seen two men running away from the site just before the explosion. As for Crocker, no definite conclusions concerning the cause of death were available since the body was badly burned and the medical examiner had not completed his autopsy. A preliminary report would be available later that afternoon.

The police detective pressed Mike to name specific individuals who might have been responsible for this arson but Mike was evasive, insisting that he could not identify any single individual as there were always some conflicts between the various trades and between workers and contractors, although most were of no consequence and harmless.

"This was obviously not harmless," the detective insisted and asked both Mike and Sam to prepare a list of individuals whom they knew to have had conflicts with Crocker. Mike hesitated, but, realizing that the detective would not give up, finally agreed and promised such a list by the next day.

When the detectives had left, Patrick asked Mike and Sam to accompany him on a tour of the site. "It's kind of cold outside. Couldn't we talk in here?" Sam asked.

As he firmly led the other two toward the door of the trailer, Patrick responded, "This place has ears and is like Grand Central Station. What I have to say is best said in private."

They walked side-by-side, hands in their pockets and the collars of their jackets pulled up to cover their ears. Mike was a little taller and slimmer than Sam, but Sam was broader and more firmly rooted to the ground as he took short steps, leaning left and right with each, to keep up with Mike's long strides. Patrick, walking behind the two construction men, called out, "OK, guys, I told you before Christmas that Guardini was dangerous but you assured me that you would deal with it. Now it's too late because we have a serious problem on our hands and the cops are involved, even though you didn't want that."

Sam broke in, "To be honest, I never thought it would go this far."

"I don't care what you thought" interrupted Patrick. "This killing, and I'm pretty sure it is murder, will cause us all a great deal of trouble. Remember Mike, that you may be the contractor and what happens on this site is your responsibility. But I represent Alex. It's his development and he owns this site, which gives him plenty of responsibilities as well, and needs to answer to others including the city and the bankers."

"You're right," said Mike.

"When Alex hears about this murder," said Patrick, "he's going to go ballistic and I'm going to get a call to ask how such a thing could happen on his site. A fair question, since I didn't tell him about Bruno and the Jersey guys... and that was only because you told me you needed a little more time before meeting with Bruno again. Now, I need to figure out how to explain this...actually, we need to figure it out. It was one of your supers who was killed."

"Listen," answered Mike, "I'll help all I can, but I'll tell you honestly, I don't like the cops digging into my relationship with my subs. I had to push hard to get this contract and some of my subs resent the fact that I squeezed them to reduce their price and would like nothing better than to cause me trouble."

Angrily, Patrick screamed, "It's too fucking late to avoid the involvement of the cops. They are involved. By the way, you're not talking about anything illegal, are you?"

"No, no!" said Mike. "But you know that sometimes there's a thin line between a little arm-twisting and what someone thinks is illegal. Anyway, I'm sure that Bruno is responsible for this killing. I just don't know how to point the finger at him without getting personally involved with the cops."

As they walked, making fresh tracks in the thin snow, Patrick considered the issue and then spoke almost in a whisper that made it difficult to hear over the rising din of the early morning activity on the construction site, causing Mike and Sam to move closer. "As I think about it, I need to get Alex involved now. I don't want him to hear about this first on the morning news. He has contacts in the police department that could be helpful. Coming from him, the suggestion to have them look into Guardini's operation would be perfectly natural and would not have to involve the two of you."

They continued walking to the edge of the central tower of the complex before returning to the trailer where Patrick made a call to Alex. After revealing what had happened at the site, Patrick was immediately interrupted. "What the fuck!" Alex yelled, "I don't believe this. You guys are trying to ruin me."

"Before you blow your top, we should meet and discuss this."

After a heated exchange, a meeting was agreed upon, to be held the following morning for breakfast at El Capitan, Alex's favorite restaurant near the site.

Later, before he left the site, Mike received a call from Sgt. Murphy, the policeman who had interviewed him, saying that the autopsy on Crocker's corpse showed that he had died from a knife wound to the upper torso so that the death was clearly a murder case. Mike didn't know whether to be relieved or shocked by this news although he certainly had already suspected that Crocker's death was meant to send a message, but why did he have to die?

This was the first time in all his years in construction that a killing had occurred on one of his projects. There had certainly been any number of accidental deaths, most of which were due to a worker falling from a high elevation. Construction, after all, was a dangerous business with the third highest death rate nationwide from job-related injuries at work sites. But murder!

The more he thought about it, the more Mike became convinced that Crocker had not been deliberately targeted. He must have been an accidental witness to the fire and then killed to prevent him from identifying the arsonists.

THE MORNING *POST* FEATURED THE story with a gruesome headline; *Murder in the Garden of Eden.* With this one act, the project had become associated more with hell than heaven, tainting the dreams of both the architect and the developer. Seated in at a corner table of El Capitan, Alex waited for Connolly to arrive.

When he read through the article in the *Post*, his fingers crumpled the edge of the newspaper. The tendons in his neck stiffened as he became increasingly angry. Why, he wondered, why on my site and at this time when the final commitment letter had not yet arrived from the bank? He worried that the bank would use this event as a reason to delay issuing the commitment letter. Putting off releasing the money he needed to pay the contractor would seriously jeopardize the continued progress of the project, as suppliers would be hesitant to keep on extending credit.

Alex had already spent several million dollars of his own capital to advance the project to this stage, and he was loath to use any more of his own funds without the assurance of financial support from the bank. What he now needed was a guarantee from Patrick that there would be no more such incidents, and that this one would quickly be resolved. To Alex, the death of a worker was an "incident," no more than a minor annoyance, and he expected that it could fade away, like a bad dream.

"Let me have another cup of coffee and this time," he admonished the waitress sharply; "use a fresh pot." At that moment, Patrick came through the door of the restaurant and was directed by the headwaiter to Alex's table. He nodded his head in greeting and sat down.

"You're late," said Alex sharply.

"I had another call from the police before I left and had to answer them."

"Suppose you tell me what the fuck's going on. You're responsible to keep a secure site. Where were the guards that I'm paying for?"

"I'm still looking into that but you realize this is a big site and guards can't be everywhere at once. As far as what happened to Crocker, that may be a response to Urbanland not hiring a protective service, the JPA... which is really a group of thugs who've been hounding us. Mike had trouble with them on a previous job and decided not to give in to their demands this time."

"Why wasn't I told about this at the time?" Alex said, squeezing out the words to keep from screaming. "I want to know everything that happens on this project. If you think you're trying to protect me, you're not. If you've got some mob guy trying to weasel his way onto the project, I want to know about it, and especially if there's a connection to the murder. There could be serious consequences for the project, some that you can't even imagine."

"Honestly, Mike and Sam never thought the JPA would go this far. Sure, a little muscle perhaps, but murder? It's not their thing."

"No excuses! I've told you that a thousand times over, no excuses!" Alex screamed as he tightened the grip on his coffee cup. A family at an adjoining table stared at the source of this outburst as Alex hid his face behind a menu. After a minute, he took a sip from the cup and deliberately placed it back on the table. In a quiet measured voice, he said, "Now, suppose you now tell me everything you know about this JPA group."

Connolly explained what he had heard from Mike and Sam and then added, "Anyway, we thought you could help by talking to one of your friends in the police. You could say that you've heard that the Jersey Protective Association has been nosing around the project and ask the cops if they were aware of that as part of their murder investigation. That way, we might find out if the cops suspect that the JPA may have an involvement in this murder."

"Why don't you tell them yourself?" said Alex. "You're in touch with the detective on the case and you're the one who was contacted."

"There are reasons it would be best coming from you."

"What reasons?"

"Well, for one thing, you're the developer and have a big stake in this project and beside, you have political connections and a special relationship with the police. They trust you!"

'What are you not telling me?"

"No big mystery! You're a big man in this town and it'll just be better coming from you."

Alex hesitated for a moment and looked suspiciously at Patrick. "I still think you're not telling me the whole story. But, this is not good for the project and the quicker it's resolved, the better I'll feel. So, OK, I'll talk to them."

Patrick left the meeting with a mixture of satisfaction and concern. He had achieved his goal of shifting the investigation away from Mike and Sam. However, he was worried that if Mike's actions in pressing his sub-contractors surfaced, Alex might draw the wrong conclusion that this whole mess is somehow Mike's fault.

Patrick understood that he owed loyalty to Alex, who was his boss, who had showed confidence in hiring him for such an important project. But Alex was too unpredictable and selfish, often outright mean, and could never be his friend. *I'm not even sure about Mike*, he thought, *but Sam I like and respect. I trust him and think of him as a friend. I would never let Alex try to implicate him in the murder investigation. But, I'm not sure I feel quite the same way about Mike.*

CLAIRE UNFOLDED THE MORNING NEWSPAPER that was left outside her front door and was surprised to see the front-page item about the murder at the Eden site. She sat at her dining table with a cup of coffee in one hand and the paper in the other, while viewing the dramatic panorama of the Manhattan skyline spread out beyond her window. She wore a short yellow nightgown that was loosely tied at the waist and seductively open from her navel to her neck.

Having woken late after a long planning board meeting the night before, her golden blond hair was still plastered to the back of her head. The smooth features of her face belied her age but as she read the news, worry creases appeared on her brow. She had not seen Alex for well over a month and had taken the time to re-invigorate her career by meeting with city officials and other developers, restoring her independence after almost a year dealing with the needs of the Eden project prior to the groundbreaking. Although in a way she still remained attracted to Alex, he was not wholly in her life and could never be as long as he was married to Lila. As she thought about this situation, she began to resent being on call to satisfy a man who was unable to make a long-term commitment.

Her emotions wavered. As she read the article about Eden, she felt a tightening in her chest that she interpreted as sympathy for the pain that Alex must feel when reading about such a terrible event occurring on his project, a project that he so often had expressed was the culmination of a dream. She reached for the phone to call him to let him know how sorry she was that this had happened but, as she looked out over the city, she realized that her feelings for Alex had changed. She looked away and walked into her bedroom to dress for a meeting with the mayor.

WHILE THESE EVENTS WERE TAKING place in New York, a meeting took place at the JPA townhouse in New Jersey. Bruno Guardini was furiously interrogating Justin. "When I asked you to do a job for me, I made it clear that there was to be no rough stuff. What the hell happened?"

"It was an accident, Mr. G. When we got to the site, we didn't see no one and then this guy comes charging out of a trailer. And I tell ya, he was big, real big and tough like a bull. Then Tom, he's my partner; he had no choice but to stick him."

Bruno growled, "There's always a choice! The two of you have made quite a mess of it. You sure that no one saw you?"

"We got out of there fast and didn't see no one following us."

"I hope you're right. Anyway, after what's happened, I want you gone. You're going to have to disappear—for good as far as I'm concerned. I want you out of the state or even better, out of the country." Guardini reached into his desk drawer and took out an envelope, leaning across the desk to slap it into Justin's hand while warning him again, "I don't want to see you or hear from you again. I want you to vanish, not tomorrow but now!"

ENTRACTE

Fresh snow covered the site, obliterating the evidence of the burned-out trailer like a coat of whitewash on a soot-black wall. Nevertheless, the workers who knew and loved him did not easily forget Crocker's murder and moved about cautiously, trying to ignore the suspicion that maybe one of their own comrades could possibly have been the culprit. Of more immediate concern were the rumors that the project was in financial trouble, a problem that could directly affect their continuing employment. In the wake of the bursting of the dot-com bubble after the millennium, the construction market had collapsed with a resulting drop in opportunities for construction workers. The fear of layoffs, as well as the freezing temperatures, resulted in a significant slowing in the pace of the work.

Yet, construction was nevertheless moving forward. Most of the bad concrete had been removed and fresh concrete was being poured, with Sam watching the arrival of every truck and questioning each driver to assure himself that no stops were made in the drive from the concrete plant to the site. Sam also took the foot-high cylindrical samples of each truckload of concrete and placed them in a locked cabinet in his trailer.

In four weeks, the samples would be tested to verify the concrete's strength. Finally, Sam ordered thick insulating blankets to be placed on the fresh concrete to prevent any chance of freezing. Construction in the winter is never easy. but with the added pressure of trying to catch up with the delay caused by the bad concrete, it was that much more difficult and stressful. On those parts of the site that had not been damaged by the concrete problem, steel construction moved forward with the framing for the lower portions of the towers rising like a child's jungle gym. In the center of each of the future towers, a trussed column stood with a counterbalanced trussed beam, delicately balanced on its peak. These tower cranes would be used to lift each of the thousands of steel beams and columns needed for the framework of the towers and raise them to their defined position in the structure.

SEVEN
Spouses And Lovers
February 2001

I N HIS OFFICE, CORTA SAT despondently staring at the drawings on his desk. When he first heard about the murder, his first reaction was to sympathize with the family of the victim, but then he quickly became mostly concerned with the effect on the project, his project. How would Grant react? Would the financing be in jeopardy? Was there some kind of conspiracy that would doom the project?

Regardless of how many precautions are taken, death was not a stranger on a construction site. This usually involved a worker plunging from a high floor or scaffold, being struck by a falling piece of construction material, being trapped and squeezed to death when a trench suddenly collapsed, or being accidentally electrocuted either by touching a high-voltage line or by operating a piece of equipment that touched an overhead power line.

Corta remembered the shock he felt when a worker died on his first project. It was such a stupid accident, one that should never have happened. The worker had slipped on a carelessly placed board near the edge of the third floor of a small office building Corta had designed. As he fell, the man struck his head on a portable pump that was sitting on the floor, and he then rolled off the edge of the floor head first, breaking his neck as he struck the ground. There was no scream, no apparent pain, no agony except for that felt by Philip as he suffered through sleepless nights, blaming himself for the accident.

With later accidents, Philip began to accept them as tragic but normal events—the inevitable result of practicing a dangerous profession—so he learned to focus his concerns on the effects that an accident had on the project. Diane recognized that Philip was trying to steel himself against the sadness of an accident but it bothered her deeply. "Please, Philip," she would say. "Think about the loss to the family. It wouldn't hurt you to express some sympathy."

"I'm sorry, I just can't do it," he would respond. "It's too painful for me to even think about the fact that someone died on a project that I designed. I can't help thinking that I should have been able to prevent such accidents by somehow modifying my design. Maybe I shouldn't even be designing buildings."

"That's crazy, Philip. There's nothing you could have done to prevent it so you just have to face the fact that it happened." Diane was never able to convince him of the inevitability of the event and that it was not his fault. The discussion usually ended when Philip walked away mumbling an excuse about having to get back to work.

Corta realized that the current situation was different. This worker did not die due to an accident; he was killed. It was murder, and that had never before happened on one of his projects. He did not know how to react to this. Also, only weeks earlier there had been the problem with the bad concrete. Two extraordinary events on this one project. It did not make sense.

That evening, Philip stared past Diane at the dinner table, oblivious to the fact that he was using his spoon to stir an empty soup bowl.

"Darling," Diane said sharply, "what's wrong with you tonight? You seem far away, and for heaven's sake put down that spoon."

After an eternal moment of silence, Philip responded with a pained expression, "It's Crocker, the dead super at the site; I remember meeting him…he was so full of life… I can't get him out of my mind. And, after the problem with the foundation concrete, I'm beginning to feel that this project is cursed. If anything more happens, the project could stop and even die. If that happens, I'll die because you know it's my last chance at real recognition. I'm too old to start again."

Before he even had a chance to finish talking, Diane walked over and leaned over the back of his chair to hug him saying, "Don't be so morose. You're blowing the situation totally out of all proportion. Tell me, has Alex said anything to you to make you think that the project is in trouble?"

"No, but…"

"No buts! If there were a real problem, Alex would tell you. After all, he's our friend as well as your client."

Philip responded rather sheepishly, "I don't know! He hasn't been totally open with me about the financing so he could be holding back."

"Sweetheart, you're the architect for the most prestigious project designed in this city in decades, a project that's already garnered all kinds of acclaim in the press. As you've said so often, this is not some paper project but one that's actually being built."

"Ever since I had to beg Alex to increase the budget last fall, I felt constrained; as if I could no longer control the direction of the project. Ideas keep coming to me all the time to improve the design but I hesitate to propose them for fear that Alex will cut me off. It's as if now the project is more his than mine."

"You're right, in a way! It is now more his project. You finished your design and it's perfectly fair for Alex to ask you to stop making any changes that could result in cost increases. You've done the best job you could and you saw the reaction after the groundbreaking ceremony where everyone there couldn't stop praising the design."

"You don't understand, I'll never be satisfied and always feel that I could improve the design." Philip stood and looked down at Diane and added, "But of course, you're right, I must stop obsessing about it."

Nevertheless, Philip had never been able to switch off his active imagination like a light bulb. Driven by a constant desire for perfection and a fervent belief in his aesthetic judgment, there was always a better way.

After the completion of the Landown apartment building, whenever he passed the site he saw only missed opportunities, even though the occupants delighted in its unique design and told him so whenever they saw him. He left the dinner table and retreated to his office, unable to resolve his conundrum.

EARLY THE NEXT MORNING, ALEX was at his desk in his study on the ground floor of his townhouse, looking through the day's mail hoping to find a letter with the bank's increased commitment, and wondering if he perhaps misplayed his confrontation with Chip.

How will he be able to honor his promise to Phil without that letter? Perhaps the murder at the site had spooked the bank. He became increasingly frustrated until Lila brusquely opened the door to enter. She was dressed in a flowered dressing gown that was tied at her waist and extended down to her knees. Her rounded frame was topped by unruly hair falling over bloodshot eyes on a face with a sallow complexion. Alex nevertheless noticed how the dressing gown flattered the curves of her body. Leaning against the door-frame, Lila exclaimed,

"Nice of you to drop by. When did you come home last night? If you had warned me, I would have stayed up."

Alex responded impatiently, "Not now! I've got real problems. Can't you see that I'm busy?"

"Oh sure, you've got time for your floozy but not for your family."

"First of all, I was working last night and didn't want to disturb you when I came home late and secondly, I thought that after our dinner with the Cortas you were going to straighten yourself out. What happened?"

"You bastard! I didn't see any change in your attitude. I thought you were going to make more of an effort."

Alex pushed away from his desk and walked toward her. "For God's sake, pull yourself together before the kids get up."

Lila turned and ran toward the bathroom and locked herself in.

"Go ahead," he yelled after her. "Hide!" Shaking with rage and feeling helpless, Alex went to the kitchen and poured himself a cup of coffee. The warmth of the liquid soothed his throat but the caffeine only intensified his raw nerves as he opened and tightened his fist mumbling, "Damn, damn, damn."

This is one more problem that I don't need, thought Alex. *First there was the financing shortfall and then the problems at the site with the bad concrete and to top it off, a murder. And now Lila giving me her injured-wife bit… it's just too much. It's a hell of a project and a hell of a life.* He wished he were back in his office where he could reach into his desk drawer for the envelope with the white powder. Instead, feeling frustrated, Alex reached for the phone and punched in a number. After three rings, Claire answered. "I need you," was all Alex said before hanging up.

CLAIRE SAT BACK ON THE bed while Alex lay with his head in her lap. She gently stroked his hair, letting the strands filter through her fingers. When she received the call, she had hesitated before agreeing to have Alex come to her apartment. After having read about the murder at the site, she had resolved to wait for Alex to call her. Yet, she felt guilty for not acknowledging his pain and realized that her feelings toward him had not totally vanished. So she received him warmly and embraced him when he arrived.

Their lovemaking had been less hurried than usual, with the urgency replaced by warmth that extended the pleasure they both felt. Alex let all his anxieties drain away, leaving only the insecurity of his conflicted situation. "What am I going to do?" he asked, but did not wait for an answer. "I put so much energy into this project."

Claire looked down at him and frowned. "Which one? The building or your marriage?"

As if he had not heard Claire, Alex closed his eyes and said, "I remember when it all began. It was shortly after dad's death and I took Lila out to the desert near Las Vegas. I was trying to decide what to do with my life now that I was no longer shackled to the old man. God, how I hated him when he put me down all the time.

"It was in the middle of the day and you know how when you look out at the horizon in the desert, it seems as if there are waves coming toward you like those rolling in the ocean before they reached the beach. But, in the desert, the waves always remain in the distance and never come closer. I decided that I'm going to chase one of those waves and catch it and build a project that my father could never have even dreamed of."

"But as you just pointed out, no matter how hard you try to reach out for them, those desert waves always remains distant, more like the end of a rainbow that you can never reach. Listen Alex, it's an illusion and you can't build your life on that."

"You don't understand. This project is my life. If it fails, I'm finished in every way. It's not just the money. I've put my reputation on the line… to the mayor and his damned development commissioner, to Philip and the contractors and even to you. I just can't fail… and I won't. I don't care what I have to do."

Saying this, Alex climbed out of the bed, slipped on his pants and walked toward the living room. When he pulled open the sliding door a vertical sliver of light rapidly expanded until it framed his body as a black silhouette, appearing like a medieval warrior preparing for battle. The image faded rapidly as Alex moved through the door.

Claire called after him, "Don't leave yet. We need to talk this out." Alex ignored her as he often did. It was, after all, his problem and he needed to solve it alone. No matter how sympathetic Claire seemed at this moment, he could not resign himself to the idea that a woman could possibly help him. After all, his mother, a bright and capable woman, had never been able to help him when his father belittled him. It was only when he established himself after his father's death that Alex gained the confidence to deal with people, and for the first time was able to gain, however grudgingly, the respect of his associates. Turning back toward Claire who was walking toward him, he said, "I'm sorry but I have to go back to the office. There is something I have to do and it can't wait."

Turning back toward the bedroom, Claire responded, "You're making a mistake. I could have helped you." As she thought back to her marriage to Greg Fletcher, she added, "I thought you were different." Different how? Who was she kidding? After all, both Greg and Alex were unfaithful to their wives; both had been spoiled by their parents although in Alex's case he had, in the process, been beaten down by an imperious father. Both were controlled by expansive egos and both showed little respect for women. This led Claire to question again why she should remain in a relationship where she was "the other woman" and where her opinions were not respected.

"This is the last time I'm going to be here for you. If you leave now, don't bother to call again."

It had been three years since she first met Alex when he approached her to help him gain approval for zoning changes he needed to make the Eden project viable. Under the restrictive zoning regulations then in force, it was impossible to build any structure over twenty stories tall on the site even though another rule, using the allowable floor area, would have permitted a sixty-story tower. Through her contacts within the city administration, contacts she had carefully nurtured from the years of her marriage to Greg, she focused on two city councilors who she felt could be swayed toward sponsoring the needed changes. It took her many months of friendly persuasion and constant meetings and late-night meals with Alex. By the time a resolution was passed by the council, Alex had become her lover.

Now, although she still had feelings for Alex, she resolved to end her relationship with him before she became further entangled.

"For Christ sake," said Alex, "I've got enough on my mind without having you suddenly threaten me. I just can't deal with this now!" He slammed the door as he left Claire's apartment. *I've got to concentrate*, he thought.

Pushing aside thoughts of Claire, he focused on finding a way to fix the problem that seemed to stand in the way of the success of the project. Until he solved the issue of the increased commitment letter, nothing else mattered. It was the key to the success of the project and only then could he allow himself to turn his attention to sorting out his relationships with Claire and Lila.

Claire was shocked and a little frightened by this outburst and stood frozen in place for a moment. Alex had often been insensitive, to say the least, but had never spoken to her with such an angry voice before. "No more," she promised herself. "No more." She felt a shudder enveloping her body but no tears. Perhaps it was best this way. As she recovered her composure she vowed to move on with her life, a life that would not include Alex.

BY THE TIME HE REACHED the sidewalk, a light snow was falling and a cold wind blew against his cheeks. Alex suddenly realized he had just made a terrible mistake. Within the last twelve hours he had turned the two women in his life against him. The project, the commitment letter; nothing had any meaning any more if he could not repair this problem. He could turn around and go back up to Claire's apartment; or maybe he should go home to Lila? "What's happening to me? I'm losing control."

Not since that day in the winter of his junior year in high school, a day much like this one, when he had been criticized by his father once too often and had viciously lashed back to avoid crying, stalking out of his house, had he felt so lacking in control. As usual, his mother had left the room the moment his father started spewing a litany of failures on Alex's part.

What's wrong with these women? he thought. *When I need them, they abandon me.* He pulled up the collar of his parka and leaned his head down to deflect the wind and started walking west on 74th Street.

But his thoughts remained on that long-ago day when he had left his house in anger and frustration. On that day, he had also walked the streets for hours and did not return home until nightfall. He tried to be as quiet as possible when he returned and was about to walk up the stairs to his room when his mother called out to him. "Please come and sit with us a moment." Us? Yes, "us" meant both his parents. When they were seated, the parents on the couch and Alex in a wing-top chair facing them, Mr. Grant started, "Son, your mother and I have been talking. We were concerned about you. You gave us quite a fright staying out all day, but, ..." taking his wife's hand in his, "maybe I've been too hard on you."

There ensued a discussion that Alex never could have imagined at that time, with promises of greater understanding and professions of love. "You're my only son and I've always had such great hope that one day you would take over my company. Your mother has convinced me that is not going to happen if I push you away so I hope you'll understand if, occasionally, it seems as if I demand too much of you."

After that day, his relationship with his parents improved dramatically for a time. Even his mother began to express her love for him with the occasional hug and "I love you, Alex." But, as the years passed and Alex graduated from high school and chose Columbia for college, his father questioned that choice. "You know, I went to Princeton. Did you consider that? To succeed in business, you'll need a better grounding in mathematics. You'll need to choose the right fraternity because those contacts will serve you the rest of your life."

By the time Alex enrolled in Philip's architectural design course, his relationship with his parents had again descended into the old patterns. His father would criticize his academic standing. His mother would retreat into her cocoon and spend much of her time outside the home with friends or participating in club activities.

Now, as he reached Central Park, snow had begun to fall at a steady rate and the ground was covered in a white blanket. He approached a park bench and, after looking around, realized that this was the exact one he had sat on that day when he left his parents' house. On that day, he walked for hours, and finally sat down exhausted, shaking from cold. Or was it from a sense of loss.

So much had changed in the intervening years. His father had died and Alex took over the firm and developed the Eden Center, a project greater than anything his father had ever developed. His mother had only recently died without ever rekindling the warmth and intimacy of those months of temporary family reconciliation. He had wooed and married Lila and had two wonderful children. And then there was Claire! He had been flattered by her attention and the ease with which she entered into an intimate relationship with him, but after today he realized that his family was more important.

He did not sit on the bench this time. It was simply too cold and he was no longer a brooding teenager and there were no parents he wanted to punish, but he was punishing Lila for being a good wife. With quickened steps, he headed downtown.

When he reached his house, no one was home so he took a hot shower to drain the chill from his bones. Steam was seeping into the bedroom when Lila walked in.

"What are you doing home in the middle of the day?" she asked coolly.

He blurted out, "I love you."

Taken aback, she responded, "After you left this morning, I wasn't so sure. What changed?"

Alex heard a bitter edge in her voice. "I can't blame you for being upset with me. I've been walking in the snow all day, trying to figure out what's wrong. I thought about my parents and their distant relationship and I don't want to end up like them. I want us to be better than that. I want us to be closer." He didn't tell her about Claire, he couldn't. "After our dinner with the Cortas, I tried to make things better but with the problems I've had with the project, it hasn't been easy and then, when you accused me this morning, of something I hadn't done, I guess I just snapped."

"Maybe," Lila said cautiously, "maybe I was too quick to judge. But, you must understand that after your... I don't know what else to call it. After your affair with that woman, what did you expect me to think?"

"OK, we've both been a bit on edge but I'm here now and I meant it when I said I love you. I need for us to succeed."

Lila walked up to Alex and embraced him saying, "you smell clean."

ENTRACTE

The structure of a building is articulated by the joining together of columns and beams into a skeleton that will support the load of the building's floors and walls, as well as its occupants. These are the building's bones and muscles while its façade is the skin, and its ducts, wires and pipes are its circulatory and the nervous systems that give it life. Like a ballet in slow motion, when following construction day by day it appears as if little or no progress is being made. Especially, during the first few months on a site as large as Eden's, an added batch of concrete or another steel beam could not be immediately discernible from those already placed or the many still needed. Viewed from a broader time scale of months, progress was clearly visible but on the days since the death of Crocker, progress seemed even slower than usual as knots of workers extended their coffee breaks while discussing their shared concerns about safety at the site.

Moreover, Mike Long had ordered security at the site tightened, with added guards monitoring the movement of workers and of trucks entering and leaving, further slowing progress. In order to bolster activity, and aware of the need to keep the project on track, Sam toured the site at least hourly, urging superintendents to keep their crews active but he found it difficult to change the gloomy mood of apprehension, tension and suspicion. Rumors that the project financing was in trouble and that the project might be stopped persisted among the workers. To make matters worse, the weather was uncooperative with frigid gray skies hanging threateningly overhead, contributing to the gloom at the site.

EIGHT
The Ruse
March 2001

THE ARRIVAL, ON THIS EARLY March morning, of the white limousine at the main gate telegraphed as a bad omen to workers across the site. Here comes Mr. Bigmouth, the name the workers on the site had attached to Alex Grant. At least that was the name used in relatively polite company. More often, he was called the Big Asshole or even more uncomplimentary terms. But what was he doing here now? Was there more bad news?

Alex barged into the developer's trailer and walked directly to where Sam and Patrick were meeting in a room at the far end, separated by a flimsy plywood partition. "Connolly, what the fuck is going on here? The place looks more like a funeral parlor than a construction site. If you guys can't do better to control this situation, I'm going to get myself people who can."

Patrick, shaking off his irritation at the intrusion, answered first. "Look here Alex, we're doing our best... but it doesn't help having you come down here and screaming your accusations so everyone can hear you."

Grant planted his hands on the table and bent his trunk so that his face stopped inches from Connolly's. "Don't tell me what to do. This is my project and my site and I'll talk any damn way I want to."

Trying to defuse the situation, Sam interjected, "Look, Mr. Grant, It's not every day that we have a murder at the site and my guys are

103

understandably nervous. Until we find out who's responsible, there will be tensions at the site."

"Sit down," Alex ordered confidently. "And listen. I've been talking to my contacts at the police department and they assure me that they are making progress on the case. In fact, they now have a suspect…a small-time crook, who was seen in the neighborhood. They're now looking for him and when they have him in custody, we'll know more. And Sam, for some reason, the police are looking into your boss's business." He turned to leave. "But in the meantime, get this site moving or I swear I'll…" He brusquely turned away from Connolly and left the trailer as the rest of his words melted into the general din of the construction site.

Patrick and Sam were not satisfied with the progress of the investigation Alex had just revealed, especially since the police did not link the responsibility for the murder to the Jersey Protective Association. Perhaps the individual who was seen near the site was working alone, but that was not likely since there had to be a motive for the attack. It was also unlikely that the suspect was a disgruntled former employee, because Sam had reviewed the status of dismissed employees and found none who had not found other jobs or who conceivably held a grudge against the contractor. Somehow, if this individual was responsible for the murder, there had to be a tie to the JPA, so why weren't the police questioning Bruno?

As hopeful as was the news of the possible identity of the murderer, the rest of Alex's revelations were very disturbing. The police were examining the circumstances surrounding the award of the contract for the project, while seeking a possible motive for the attack at the site.

"I don't like it," said Patrick. "It's been over a month and the cops are no closer to finding the killer. A person of interest is not what I'd like to hear. If they know the bastard, why isn't he in jail? Something's not right. And, what the hell's all this about the cops looking into your company."

"I have no idea why they should be checking on Mike but I'll find out."

When Sam returned to his own trailer, he called his boss. Mike Long assured him that there was nothing to be alarmed about. "I certainly did nothing that could involve me with the murder, so don't worry," said Mike, cheerfully but without much conviction in his voice. After all, there is a difference between lack of involvement in a murder and lack of damaging information that could emerge from a police investigation.

The icy barrier of the Hudson River separates the island of Manhattan from New Jersey. Floating shards of late-winter ice floated lazily down the river, bumping together and mounting one another near the shore like animals in heat. As he looked out across the river, Sam wondered if that made the island an impenetrable prison, or something more like a gated community, imperfectly defended from intrusion. Sam measured this dichotomy as he thought about the murder and the ongoing investigation that threatened the progress of the work at the site and, more importantly, seemed to upset his boss and friend, Mike Long. He picked up the phone to call him again.

"This is Mike."

"Yeh! And this is Sam again."

"As if I couldn't tell from that gravelly bass voice. What's up?"

"Listen. Because of all the problems at the site we haven't really had time to talk openly and I was going to suggest that we get together for a cookout next weekend. It will be warmer, courtesy of climate change, and no showers are in the forecast. We can do it at my place, and on the off chance that it rains, I can set up the grill in the garage and the ladies can stay warm in the kitchen. It'll give us a chance to talk."

After a moment during which he thought about it, Mike said, "Maybe that's a good idea. There is one thing I did want to talk to you about. It's nothing about the project."

"Sounds mysterious. Anyway, I'll ask Jan to call Marion and set it up."

After he hung up the phone, Sam wondered what Mike had on his mind. If it's not about the project, then what?

Sam remembered the time of their first meeting. He had answered an ad for a project manager for a new public school project. On the day of the interview, he arrived in a suit and tie and was greeted by Mike, wearing an open blue shirt and jeans, who remarked, "I hope you don't plan to dress like this on the site." Feeling somewhat embarrassed but immediately relaxed, Sam loosened his tie and opened the top button of his shirt, giving his carotid artery the freedom to let the blood flow back to his brain. That day transformed both of their lives as a strong professional and personal friendship was formed.

Of course, there remained a barrier between them, more than just the usual separation between a boss and his employee. It was more like a wall of silence, or maybe a fear that Sam could not penetrate. Perhaps their proposed meeting would help to release whatever Mike has been holding onto these past few years and help to further cement their friendship.

WHEN HE REACHED THE LIMOUSINE, after leaving his meeting with Patrick and Sam, Alex slumped into the back seat and wiped his brow on the back of his sleeve, drying the moisture that had formed even in this cold weather.

"Damn!" He hated confrontations because they fed his innate insecurity, but he felt they were needed to establish his authority. In truth they gained him nothing as his words, no matter how loudly spoken, could not change the facts.

"Where to, Mr. Grant?" the driver asked.

"Just drive." The project was in trouble and no amount of yelling could change that. He eyed the drawer with the magic powder. No, not today! What he needed were solutions and resolutions, not a drug-related boost. Think, think! The voice in his head offered some reassurance. The murder will pass and soon be forgotten if I can get that commitment from Chip at the bank. Then everyone will calm down and the work will get back on schedule.

"Go to Park and 47th."

One more confrontation and maybe we can get back on track, he thought.

The offices of Losey & Sons occupied the 18th to the 21st floors of the gray-granite clad building facing Park Avenue. Grant took the elevator to the 21st floor, which housed the executive offices, and calmly walked past the receptionist, then opened the door marked "Charles Stewart, Executive Vice President."

Startled, Chip looked up from behind his mahogany desk to confront the intruder. He loved that desk, a vestige from a nineteenth century banking magnate that he had found at an auction. Closing the door behind him, Alex walked directly toward the desk and was about to speak when the door behind him opened and the receptionist looked in saying, "I'm sorry Mr. Stewart but I couldn't stop him."

Holding up his right hand, Chip replied, "It's alright, Nancy. I'll deal with the gentleman." Turning to Alex, he said, "You've got some nerve barging in like this and scaring my receptionist. What is so urgent?"

Standing and leaning forward so that his knees pressed hard against the desk, Alex said, "Fuck your receptionist. I've waited patiently for you to send me the papers about the increase in the loan. I don't appreciate your stalling tactics. I would think that your bank would do what's necessary to keep the project moving forward, especially since you already have such a large stake in it."

"Who do you think you are?" answered Chip, leaning forward in his chair to stare directly at Alex. "You can't intimidate me. Let me remind you that we own you and without us you are nothing." Leaning back, he added, "The reality is that the management committee became concerned when reading about the murder at the site. Until that issue is clarified, the bank will move cautiously. Sorry!"

Feeling deflated, Alex sat down. "Listen, the police are dealing with that and I've been told they're focusing on a suspect who has nothing to do with the project. It may simply have been an unfortunate incident when one of the contractor's men interrupted a thief. You know, we often have petty thievery at a construction site." He added, in a sarcastic voice, "Give me a break."

Chip now recognized that he was the master of this confrontation and responded confidently, "We will get back to you in a few days. I'm certain that I can discuss this with the committee and convince them that this murder will not interfere with the progress of the project, that is, if you can assure me that this is the last time you will come to us with a request for an increase in the loan commitment."

Chastened, Alex answered, "You have my word."

Chip smiled as he said, "Thanks for dropping by. I'll get back to you." The exchange left him feeling empowered, more so than he had felt before in his 43 years. It no longer mattered what Alex suspected. He could deal with his desires openly and no one would ever again make him hide behind the veil of conventionality.

ALEX LEFT THIS MEETING WITH a sense of failure. *The damned commitment letter! I'm no closer to having it in my hand than when I walked into Chip's office*, he thought. *Damn you!* It was too dangerous to continue along this path without having a contingency plan, so he called Philip. "Good! You're there. Listen, I'll be in your office in fifteen minutes. We have something to discuss." He hung up leaving Philip nervously awaiting his arrival. When he walked into the architect's office, Alex closed the door between the drafting room and Philip's office.

Philip then said enthusiastically, "I haven't seen you here in a long time....In fact I don't think you've ever been to my office. What's the occasion?" The two men faced each other as Alex said, "Phil, you'd better sit down. You're going to have to help me out."

Philip tried to control himself but in a shaking voice barely above a whisper asked, "I can't imagine what you could possibly ask of me now. The plans are essentially complete and the building is under construction. But..."

Suddenly concerned, he stretched out his hand, "If it's not the project, is it something between you and Lila?"

"No, no, actually we're fine since you guys knocked our heads together, better than fine, actually. No, it's about the project. Listen, I know you're aware that the bank hasn't sent me the new commitment letter yet. Well, since the recent problems at the site, the murder and all, they have been slow to process it and well, you know, that without that money, I can't finish the job."

While Alex remained standing, Philip now sat down. "You gave me your word that you would build what I had designed. Anything else would be a failure to complete my vision of the project."

"Believe me I want to, and I plan to build what you designed, but what I need now is a backup plan that I can use to hold over the bank if they don't come through. I need you to come up with changes that would bring the project within the original budget. Please listen and don't fail me now. I gave you this project because you were the best and that means that you are part of my team. It also means doing something that you may not like but that is important for the team to succeed. You understand that?"

Philip turned away from Alex and looked out the window where he focused his eyes on the top of the tower crane that projected in the distance above the low buildings that separated him from the Eden site. "Alex," he began, "please try to understand what I'm about to tell you. When you gave me this project I was extremely grateful. I saw it as the fulfillment of my professional career. But, I also saw it as a way of creating a vision of what the future of urban architecture should be. Not just as a group of buildings, but more, much more. This project can change the urban landscape away from the monotonous sameness of cookie-cutter boxes plunked down with no seeming relation to their environment. Look out this window. What do you see? One building after another, each ignoring its neighbor and what is worse, turning away from the street and the people who walk by it; that's no way to create a warm and inviting future for the city.

"What I think I've been able to demonstrate—with your help, of course—is that there is a better way. Our project marries the public amenities to the street, inviting people to come in and enjoy beautiful gardens and a waterfall. Yet, the private areas, the hotel, the apartments, the offices are all secured away from the public without creating a fortress-like environment. I..."

After listening impatiently, Alex broke in. "Yes, yes. I understand all that but what are you driving at?"

"I can't imagine compromising the project as it is designed and I can't see my way clear to doing what you want."

"You ungrateful…." Alex raged, "Have you forgotten that you work for me? This is not just some academic exercise we're talking about. This is the real world and in the real world you sometimes have to make compromises to achieve a desired result. Now, I'm not going to ask you, I'm telling you. Either you do what I ask or I'll fire you and find someone else who understands the realities of this business."

Philip stood frozen in place as Alex left the office slamming the door behind him. Ricardo, Philip's chief designer, came into the room sheepishly and asked, "Philip, are you all right? We heard shouting and became concerned that you were being attacked."

Ricardo Vegas was one of Philip's former students and, in his late thirties, was somewhat older than the other architects on the team. After graduation, he had worked at one of New York's larger architectural firms but when he heard that Philip was going to design the Eden Center, he immediately contacted him. When Philip offered him the position of chief designer, he accepted without yet having given notice to his current employer. He was completely devoted to Philip's vision of architecture and knew that this was an opportunity of a lifetime. In carrying out Philip's vision he could also put his own stamp on the project. When they started working together, Philip had only crude pencil sketches of the buildings he had imagined, more of an outline than a completely formed idea. This allowed Ricardo to interject suggestions reflecting his own aesthetic when translating soft gray lines into the hard black lines of the finished drawings. The more detail he added to the design, the more protective he became of what was a collaborative effort, albeit one clearly dominated by Philip's vision.

"I don't know what's going to happen," Philip said, all the while still staring out the window. "I've been asked to make changes to the project and I refused. It's quite possible that Alex and I have reached a breaking point as he threatened to fire me."

"No!" Ricardo interjected, "I can't believe he would do that. He needs you to finish the project and beside, he has too much respect for you to do something so crazy. What happened?"

Turning to face Ricardo, Philip sat down dejectedly. "He wants me to make changes to the project to reduce the cost down to the original budget. I just can't do that. We spent too many hours trimming the project as it is, and there just isn't any more we can cut."

"Why does he suddenly want to make these cuts?" asked Ricardo.

"He claims it's to force the bank to act on the commitment letter but I know that once we make changes they will be permanent."

"What if Alex is right," said Ricardo, "and all he wants these changes for is to use as a lever against the bank?"

"I'm just not convinced."

"Maybe," answered Ricardo, "the team and I could prepare a mock set of drawings that would satisfy Alex and allow him to use it as a ruse against the bank without really being a buildable set of drawings."

Philip was not keen to undertake such a subterfuge but answered, "Let me think about it."

WHEN ALEX LEFT PHILIP'S OFFICE he could not contain his anger and frustration and did not return to his office but headed home instead.

"Lila," he shouted out when he slammed the front door behind him. "Where the hell are you?" He took the stairs to the second floor two at a time but did not see anyone in the living room. "Are you in the bedroom?" When he did not receive an answer, he poured himself a drink at the bar and looked at his watch. Damn, she must be picking up the kids at school, he realized, and retreated downstairs to his study, bottle and glass in hand. Thirty minutes and two drinks later, he heard the key turning in the front door. As they entered, the children ran to embrace their father, who said without waiting, "Hi, kids, daddy loves you but could you go up to your rooms? I've got to talk to your mother."

Puzzled, Lila asked, "Give them a chance to take off their coats please."

"Sorry! I'll see you later kids." Then, turning to Lila, "Please come in the study. It's important." Closing the door, he said, "I'm sorry I was so snappy with the kids, but something's happened I need to talk to you about. I met with Phil and kind of lost my temper when he got up on his high horse about his principles. I only asked him to do me a favor and he started in on his vision of the project. I just couldn't take it and maybe said things I shouldn't have."

"Maybe you had better start from the beginning," said Lila, "I'm a little confused."

Alex explained how concerned he was about not yet having the commitment letter from the bank, how his meeting with Chip had ended in a standoff, and what he had asked of Philip and how he thought it had been a reasonable request, and how angry he became at Philip's response.

"Look," she answered, "you lost your temper. I've become used to that lately. I…"

Alex interrupted sharply, "What do you mean! Haven't things been better between us?"

"Of course they have, but you're not the most patient person in the world. The children have noticed it and maybe that's why they were so anxious to embrace you when they saw you today. And then, you were so brusque with them. Perhaps you should go up and talk to them. Perhaps even apologize to them?"

"What? They're kids. I told them I love them. What more do they need?"

"Perhaps they didn't feel it from you when what you told them was to go up to their rooms. And, as far as Philip is concerned, you owe him a phone call to reassure him that you're not about to fire him."

"The hell I do! I've got a problem and he's got to understand that he's part of the solution."

"Are you sure he understood that you were only proposing a paper exercise and not a change in the project?"

Alex considered this for a moment. "Maybe you're right. But, he didn't have to react in such a high and mighty manner. Do you know what you're doing? First you want me to apologize to the kids and now to Philip?"

"Well, that's not a bad idea, is it?"

Suddenly, relaxed, Alex took Lila in his arms. "I can't stand it when you're right."

THERE WAS A STARTLING SYMMETRY to what just occurred in the Grant house and what happened in the Corta apartment later that day. Diane was in the kitchen preparing dinner when Philip walked in with a long face and went directly into his study. "What's this? No hellos?" Diane put down the spoon with which she was stirring a tomato soup and stepped into the study to see Philip staring dejectedly at a drawing on his desk. "Now, what's the matter?"

Philip looked up at her and then sat down and continued staring at the drawing, a pen-and-ink rendering of the Eden Center he had drawn years ago, and said, "Alex threatened to fire me."

Diane was dumbfounded. Her eyes wide, she practically screamed, "He can't do that. He wouldn't do that." Then, more calmly, "Tell me what's really going on."

Very slowly, Philip recounted what took place when Alex arrived at his office. He went on to repeat what Ricardo suggested concerning the preparation of a mock set of documents to satisfy Alex's demands.

"I think that's a very sensible idea. I don't know why you wouldn't accept it," said Dianne when she heard about Ricardo's suggestion. "You should tell Alex you will do it and explain that you consider this to be a means to an end of obtaining the commitment letter."

"What if he decided to build the cheaper version?"

"What if… what if… there are too many possible "what ifs." What if I were to die tomorrow?"

"Don't even say that," interjected Philip. "I would be lost if that were to happen."

Diane placed her hand on Philip's cheek, gently stroking it. "Of course I'm not about to die. But if I did, you would be fine. You're a strong person."

Philip took Diane's hands in his and said reluctantly, "I don't know, but let's not have any more such talk. As far as Ricardo's suggestion, I suppose you are right. I should choose my battles carefully and not stand firm on one I could potentially lose. I'll get in touch with Alex and try to straighten out this problem."

After Diane went back to the kitchen, Philip looked again at the rendering of the Eden Center and wondered if he would see it finished as he had conceived it; three linked towers rising majestically, overlooking the drab environs surrounding them. He needed to reassure himself that nothing would stand in the way of his grand concept; not even the vagaries of an uncommitted financier and developer. Diane was right and Ricardo, dear Ricardo, whose loyalty was unflappable…he owed them both.

Yes! Alex had to understand that although he would prepare a set of modifications to the project there should be no illusion that these were actually to be carried out. Just paper, to serve the purpose of completing the financing of the project. Ricardo understood this but he needed to have Alex to commit to the ruse. As he considered this, the phone rang and he answered it with unaccustomed vigor. "Hello!"

"Philip, this is Alex. I wanted to…"

Philip interrupted, "I was about to call you. I believe I can solve your problem."

ENTRACTE

With punched orange plastic sheets circling the edge of each built floor of the towers, casual observers would conclude that little progress was taking place. However, hiding behind the shrink-wrapped curtains, workers were installing ducts for air conditioning systems, pipes for cold and hot water, and myriad conduits for electrical and communication networks to service the telephone and internet needs of the future tenants. In fact, there were now more workers than ever at the site.

Overhearing their conversations, it was clear that these recent arrivals were unaware of the death of a job superintendent that had taken place on the site only three months earlier. Above this closed-in section of the structure were steelworkers adding beams and columns to push the towers ever higher so that every ten days a new floor sprouted, a clean geometric framework that was soon clothed in a wrinkled orange skirt.

Looking up at the towers, Sam marveled at the steelworkers who delicately walked across beams trailing a harness with belts around their waists linked to a cable that was clipped to a line that was firmly anchored to a previously erected column. Should a worker slip and fall, this harness would leave them dangling, although not necessarily protected from being hurt or even dying. In the early days of skyscraper construction, Mohawk Indians were hired as the first sky-walkers, as they possessed a strong sense of balance and would casually walk along a beam hundreds of feet above the ground as if they were taking a stroll in the park, and, of course, without today's mandated safety harnesses.

With so much activity at the site, Sam now relied on assistants to help him keep track of the progress of the project and ensure that no more quality issues arose. By the time Friday night arrived, he was exhausted from having dealt with myriad minor problems and a few major ones, so he looked forward to a relaxing weekend. He questioned why he had arranged a cookout with the Longs, as he would have preferred to sit in an easy chair and watch a Saturday-afternoon basketball game.

NINE
The Secret
April 2000

I T WAS SOMEWHAT COOL ON this first Saturday in April, as broken gray
clouds floated overhead. Sam, wearing a hooded sweatshirt and flow-
ery shorts, pulled the charcoal grill from the corner of his garage where it
had been stored for the winter.

"You had better clean that thing if you're planning to use it for cooking," Jan called out from the kitchen. *She must have X-Ray eyes*, thought
Sam. He also wondered if it had been such a good idea to invite Mike
and Marion this early in the season. Passing gray clouds threatened rain;
the grill needed cleaning and the boys were in a bad mood since they
were kept home from their usual Saturday soccer game and, worst of all,
were told to be helpful and to be on their best behavior when the guests
arrived. *This may be the last year I can keep them in line*, he thought, as the
oldest boy was entering junior high school and the youngster, only two
years behind, was already exhibiting a rebellious personality.

While scrubbing the accumulated dirt and grease from the grill, Sam
tried to imagine what Mike wanted to talk to him about and wondered
if perhaps he and Marion were having some marital difficulties. On the
surface they seemed to be a loving couple but he had noticed over the
years that they rarely touched or even held hands. And, he could not
remember the last time he had seen them kiss. Pushing these thoughts
from his mind, he called out to his children to please dress now, as the
guests were soon to arrive.

Jan was also aware that there had been some tension in the Long household. After all, she and Marion talked frequently and were quite open with each other in expressing their feelings and revealing their anxieties. Marion recounted how there were times when Mike seemed distant and lost, as if he were in another world. At those times, it became impossible to communicate with him and also made any measure of intimacy out of the question.

Mike had told her of his experience leading to his departure from Cambodia, of course, but had never volunteered details when pressed to complete the story that led to his arrival in Seattle. Marion was convinced that he was withholding a crucial part of the story surrounding his settling in the United States. No amount of prodding and cajoling would pry any further information from him.

MARION AND MIKE HAD MET in the mid nineteen eighties at the University of Illinois in Urbana. He was in a combined engineering and management program and she was a liberal arts major. Mike was not a brilliant student but he was outgoing and popular with the other students and had a natural ability to lead, which resulted in his successful campaign for the student council.

Marion was interested in student affairs and attended a meeting where Mike spoke of the challenges facing minority students. Who was this boy with the bushy black hair, the sad almond eyes and a light tan complexion, and where did he come from? He certainly seemed passionate in making the case for greater integration of foreign-born students into the general population of the University. He described how when he first arrived at the University, he felt alienated and would socialize only with other Asians like himself. A chance friendship with another engineering student introduced him to other engineers who were more interested in technical discussions than obsessing about a person's skin color or national origin. By his junior year, Mike had developed many friendships throughout the University, which gave him the confidence to seek election to the student council.

Marion went up to him after his speech to say how much she admired his position.

"Thank you," he said. "I hope that you did not take personally my comments about the 'Insular Midwesterners'."

"You were a little severe in your criticism of 'my' people, but I might have done the same if I were in your shoes. By the way, you don't have an accent so you've obviously been in the country a long time, but you never said where you came from."

A damn good-looking girl and with such a bright, open, midwestern face and a ready smile, he thought. "My family is from Cambodia. If you're interested, we could talk about it over a cup of coffee."

"Are you asking me for a date?"

"If a cup of coffee is a date, then yes!"

They spent the next few hours in a campus coffee shop discovering each other. It was clear that they had little in common, coming from totally different backgrounds. Marion came from a small town in rural Illinois, which she described as a homogeneous environment in which she felt smothered and could not wait to leave. Mike didn't talk about his parents, but explained that he lived with relatives near Seattle who pushed him to excel in school, and from whom he felt disapproval as he struggled to blend into an alien culture and fall away from his birth family's Theravada Buddhist beliefs.

When he heard from Marion about her family, he realized that his feeling of alienation was not too different from Marion's desire for separation from a constricted environment. The more they talked to each other, the more they felt a close bond developing. They would meet often during their last two years at the University as both experienced a growing affection for each other, held sufficiently guarded so as to prevent the blooming of love.

Finally, toward the end of that time, Marion asked, "Do you care for me or maybe even love me?"

By now, Mike was used to her directness, but was nevertheless taken aback and responded sheepishly, "I don't know. I think so. What about you, how do you feel about me?"

"I'd like to love you but I feel something is holding me back."

"What are we going to do?" asked Mike, knowing that he could not answer the question and neither could she. And so it went until the end of the year when Mike was to move to New York to take a job and Marion was going to Chicago to look for one.

"Why don't you come with me to New York?" asked Mike. "We could live together. I've got a good job offer and I'd really like to share my life with you."

"I can't do that," said Marion. "My family would be devastated if I moved in with someone without getting married."

"Well then, let's get married."

It was that simple. Not overly romantic but a solution to a conundrum that they both felt would suit them. In the years that followed, Marion became fully engaged in the construction company that Mike started.

JAN AND MARION WERE IN the kitchen preparing a potato salad as Marion finished her tale.

"So, when did you actually get married?" asked Jan.

"As you can imagine, it wasn't quite that simple. I had asked Mike about his parents and he told me that they were no longer living so that we were free to do what we wanted. Of course, my parents had a bird when I told them I was getting married, especially when they heard that he was Asian. So Mike and I decided to skip a ceremony and go to City Hall.

"All in all, it was the best thing we could have done."

"What about your parents?"

"Over time, they grudgingly accepted Mike but I can't say we have a close relationship with them."

Jan asked her boys to please help their father and go outside. She turned to Marion when the children had left and, cradling both her hands, asked, "Is something bothering you now? I had the feeling that all was not well between the two of you."

Marion tried to turn away but Jan held her hands tightly. "I don't know. Mike's been more distant lately as if something is weighing him down. He won't talk about it. He's always been somewhat removed, but this is different. I just can't get through to him. I don't know what to do. Maybe we need a little time away from each other. Being together all the time, both at home and the office…maybe I've lost perspective of our relationship. I feel he's hiding something."

"We have time before the guys will be ready for cooking so why don't we sit and talk."

Marion nodded her acceptance and followed Jan to the living room.

The threatened showers had melted away and were replaced with patches of cottony clouds against a blue/gray sky. Mike and Sam stood by the freshly cleaned grill that had just been loaded with charcoal. A little lighter fluid and a lit match started a fire that would now take half an hour before leaving embers hot enough to begin grilling the hamburgers that Jan had prepared.

"So," said Sam, "what's up?"

"What do you mean?"

"You know perfectly well what I mean. Let's not dance around the issue you hinted at last week."

"There's noth—"

"Listen," Sam interrupted brashly. "We've known each other for over ten years. Marion's been babysitting my kids since they were almost babies. You and I have gone hunting together since God knows when. Sure, we haven't exactly talked up any personal issues but I've been watching you ever since the murder at the site and man, something's not right. Please, I'm your friend. The least you can do is tell me what's bothering you." Sam put his arm on Mike's shoulder. With a shrug, Mike then pulled away softly as he turned to look at the swing hanging from a tree at the far end of the yard.

"The kids are going to get hurt if they swing that hard"

Sam grabbed Mike roughly and with anger in his voice said, "Fuck the kids. They can take care of themselves. You're just trying to be evasive and I'm not going to go along with that anymore. For God's sake, you can talk to me, whatever it is. There shouldn't be any secrets between us."

Mike put his head down and practically whispered, "OK, OK! But let's go a little further from the house."

They walked to a corner of the garden where Jan had planted a grape arbor that afforded them some privacy.

Mike said, "This has got to stay between us and you can't even tell Jan. I don't want her to know what I'm about to tell you. You must promise."

"OK, OK."

Mike took a moment to collect his thoughts. He was not at all certain how much he should reveal without putting his friend in an awkward position. "I've told you before that after my father was killed, the Khmer Rouge destroyed our home, and my mother and I took a barge down the Mekong River toward the delta. I don't remember how long it took but the only food we had were fish that my mother was able to catch. We were not alone and soon were joined by other skiffs with fleeing survivors seeking the safety of the open ocean and the hope of a larger boat that would take them away from the horror. I've never forgotten the violence that precipitated my departure from Cambodia."

"That must have been a horrendous experience for a kid. But, how did you finally get to the States?"

"You can imagine that when we left in that miniature version of Noah's Ark we had no papers, nothing! When we finally reached the ocean, we drifted into a shipping lane and a passing freighter picked us up. My mother was so happy, as she thought we had been saved. But the sailors who pulled us aboard were a rough bunch and dragged us up to the captain's cabin where we came face-to-face with a small man with a pregnant stomach, evil eyes, and a pointed goatee. He pushed my mother to the ground and started yelling at her in a language I did not understand. My mother was on her knees in supplication, and kept repeating, *aw-koon, aw-koon,* which means "thank you." All the while, the captain kept screaming in a high-pitched voice and finally pointed to one of the sailors who brusquely pulled me by the hand and pushed my mother forward, holding her by the scruff of her neck. We were led down to the bowels of the ship and locked into a empty cabin lit by a dim overhead bulb illuminating a narrow upper and lower bunk.

"I'll never forget the smell of the place, the sour odor of rotting vegetables that made me gag with every breath. We were not allowed to leave the cabin for many days and the only food we were given was a bowl of rice with an occasional chunk of boiled fish. Day and night blended together except for the few minutes each day when we were allowed on deck. All I saw in all directions were waves with the occasional bloom of white water.

"When I asked my mother what was happening, she explained that we were going to a new land where we would be free. After a few days at sea, I would hear our cabin door open on some evenings. I was in the upper bunk and had barely fallen asleep. My mother asked the visitor what he wanted, and in answer, he threw her into her bunk. I tried to sleep but kept hearing my mother moaning and felt the bunk shaking. Then, I heard thump, thump, thump, and my mother whimpering. I tried to close my ears but could not push away the sounds…my mother, the bunk…until finally there was silence as the visitor left the cabin.

"On other days, my mother was taken out of our cabin and I was left alone and frightened. When she returned, I noticed her reddened cheeks and disheveled dress and asked her what happened. She told me that she had visited the captain to arrange for our arrival in this new land. After what seemed like an eternity at sea, I one day heard the engines stop. It was night but we were allowed on deck where I saw twinkling lights in the distance and the vague outline of a shoreline illuminated by the iridescent breaking of waves. My mother told me that this was to be our new home, but that she was not yet allowed to go ashore. She told me that she loved me and asked me to be brave because I had to go to this new land alone and that she would join me later. I saw tears in her eyes as she put a life jacket on me, led me to the rail and, seeing that we were alone, had me climb over the rail and gently held my hands. She told me that once I was in the water I should paddle toward those distant lights. And, saying again that she loved me, she slowly released her grip and let me drop to the sea. That was the last time I saw my mother."

"That's a terrible story. You could have drowned. How could your mother do that to you?"

"You don't understand. I didn't know it at the time but I realized much later that this was my mother's greatest act of bravery. She sacrificed herself to give me a chance at life, knowing that she would never get off that boat."

"I still have a hard time with that, but how did you get ashore?"

"I paddled. That's all I could do because I didn't know how to swim. And I kept looking at the lights as they slowly grew, their halos merging with each other until all I saw was a band of light. I don't know how long it took. At the time, it seemed to me like an eternity and I was getting more and more tired as the sun began to light the shore.

"Suddenly, when I had almost given up, my feet hit something solid and I was on a rocky beach. Now this is where the miracle happened, or maybe it was providence or just plain luck. There were two men on the shore, fishing in the early morning light. When they saw me, they rushed over and pulled me out of the water and asked me, in a language I understood, where I came from. It turned out that they were Cambodians—from a colony who had settled near Seattle after having fled the country when the Khmer Rouge started a killing spree to eliminate religion from the country."

"I remember reading about that. You were lucky to get out when you did. I hear that over a million people were killed at that time."

Anyway, after I came ashore, I was so tired and weak that all I could tell them was that my name was Meaker and that I came from a boat. They talked among themselves and then one of them carried me to his car and took me to his home. The man, whose name was Haing Loung, lived in a small house with his wife and daughter. They took me in and treated me like their son. Somehow—and I never found out how—I became Mike, and part of their family, and was able to get a birth certificate and then a Social Security card. I suspect that the priest at the local church helped them."

"But I thought Cambodians were Buddhists."

"The Luong family had converted to Catholicism, as had some of their friends in Cambodia. Also, they Anglicized their name to Long."

"That's some story. But, what's the problem, since they adopted you?"

"Don't you see, they did not legally adopt me! When I was baptized at the church, the priest created a history of my birth and life as if I had always lived there. It was all done under the table and I've always been careful to stay away from any trouble with the law. Now, I'm concerned that if the cops dig too deeply, they'll find out."

'Hell, it all happened so long ago that I can't believe they'd dig it up now."

"I just don't know and that makes me nervous."

"Did you tell Marion?"

"NO! And I don't want you to say anything to Jan because you know how the two of them talk."

"You're going to have to tell her one day. It's not a secret you can keep from her. After all, you've been together for almost twenty years and she would be devastated if she were to find out about this from someone else. I'm not saying that she'll hear it from Jan or me but, to be honest, something could slip out. So, please, share this with her. She'll understand."

Mike grabbed Sam's shoulder and shook it. "Damn it. I know you're right but give me a little more time. I'll tell her soon. I promise."

Walking back to the open garage, they continued talking as Sam placed some hamburgers on the grill. When their wives joined them. Jan immediately asked, "What did the two of you talk about? You look so serious. The sun's peeking through the clouds and the burgers haven't burned yet, so lighten up."

Sam evaded his wife's eyes. With her lighthearted banter, Jan usually found it easy to redirect a potentially tense situation. However, the complexity of what he had just learned caused Sam to be careful to avoid exposing Mike's secret. He knew it would be difficult to keep such a secret from her, as she always knew when he was holding back. Luckily, Mike broke the silence to announce that the burgers were ready.

The talk then turned to the weather, food and the children. The afternoon passed without a single mention of the project.

THREE WEEKS LATER, PHILIP WALKED into Alex's office with a roll of drawings clamped under his arm. "I don't know why I ever agreed to this, but here are the changes we talked about." Before Alex had a chance to respond, he added firmly, "I expect you to keep your word and treat these as bargaining chips only. As I told you, this is not the project I want to see built."

"When we talked a few weeks ago, I made it clear that was my intention. Don't you trust me?"

Philip ignored this last remark and said, "I had Jack Mahoney look these over and prepare an estimate of proposed cost savings and he came up close to the dollar amount you were expecting, so you should be satisfied."

"Leave these with me and I'll follow through with the bank. And," he added, "I really appreciate your doing this for me. I know how painful it must have been for you to cheapen the project even if it's only to play this game of financial brinkmanship. Believe me, I have no intention of building from these drawings. I promise that I'll stick to the originals."

Philip turned to leave. "I'm counting on it," he said, while he thought, *More promises, always promises. I want assurances.*

ENTRACTE

Light brown tinted windows began to band the towers, alternating with horizontal bronze panels delineating the floor levels. Surrounding the towers, the outline of a wide ramp, the future nature walk that was to terminate at the top of the waterfall, was beginning to take shape. Concrete was being poured for the shallow pool below the waterfall and the surrounding gardens were beginning to take shape.

With the warmer weather, activity at the site exploded with hundreds of workers involved in the many varied aspects of the project; steel erection, pouring concrete for floors, installation of ducts and electrical conduits and glazing, Controlling all these tasks was an organizational nightmare that required Sam to hold frequent meetings with subcontractors to make certain that progress of the project was not impeded and the schedule was kept.

Patrick no longer had time to think about the JPA or the progress of the investigation into the death of Crocker. He was equally busy making certain that the construction conformed to the plans, meeting often with Corta, and keeping Alex aware of any changes.

TEN
The Investigation
May 2001

A THUNDERSTORM WORRIED AND GROWLED overhead but, like the dry heaves, brought forth no rain. In the offices of Urbanland Construction Co., Mike Long ignored the noise outside as he handled the myriad paperwork required to move the project forward, responding to invoices from subcontractors, preparing monthly billings to Grant Development Co., and responding to Sam's requests for more superintendents at the site. Marion, who had served as Mike's executive assistant since they started the company, was away visiting her sick mother. She was to return later that day. A temporary secretary had been assigned to handle Mike's routine tasks, leaving more serious matters to await Marion's return. Mike was surprised this morning when the temp announced the arrival of two gentlemen from the FBI.

"Just push away some of those papers on the chairs and have a seat," said Mike.

The two FBI men in dark suits, white shirts, and plain dark blue ties stood in sharp contrast to Mike in an open blue collared shirt and jeans. They presented their credentials and introduced themselves. Stephenson, the taller of the two by no more than an inch, explained that the case of the Crocker murder had become a federal issue because the suspected perpetrator had fled across state lines. In the process of their investigation, they had come across a number of questions that they believed Long could help them clarify.

"I'm always happy to help the feds. What do you want to know?"

Makovsky, the second FBI man asked, "We've talked to some of your subcontractors who complained that you pressured them into cutting the fees they had negotiated with you before you signed a contract with the Grant organization, a contract they claim you would not have gotten without them. You also threatened to go to another sub unless they cut their fees, in effect increasing your profit at their loss. This may have been a violation of existing statutes."

Mike replied confidently, "Gentlemen, this is a rough business and it's difficult to make a buck without squeezing the last penny out of every contract. It's a common practice in the construction business to negotiate a best and final offer before actually signing a contract and frankly, I don't think negotiation is against the law."

"We're not making any accusations at this time," replied Makovsky. "We're merely trying to understand what could have led to the death of one of your supers."

"If that's all, ask away!"

Stephenson paused for a moment and then asked, "It's not just the contract issue; there is another matter we would like you to clarify. It concerns your origins."

Mike fidgeted nervously in his chair and said, "What about it? All I know is that I was born in Seattle of Cambodian parents and that formalities were handled by the priest at our church."

"That's the problem. It seems that your birth is noted in the church records but a birth certificate for you was never registered at City Hall."

"Well I know nothing about that. It would have been handled by my parents or our priest."

"As you know, your parents died some years ago, as did the priest of the local church, so we will not be able to verify the authenticity of the birth certificate."

Mike stood and replied angrily, "That's really not my problem."

Stephenson walked around the desk to stand beside Mike. "I'm afraid it is your problem. You see, there's a question whether you are actually a US Citizen. Until we sort this out, you'll have to come downtown with us to make a full statement."

Stunned, Mike was led out of his office by the two FBI men. On the way out, he asked his secretary to call Alex Grant and apprise him of the situation.

Alex was in his car on the way to the Eden site when he received a frantic call on his cell phone from Mike's secretary. She hurriedly described what had happened with the FBI men as Alex kept interrupting. "Slow down! Now tell me again, where did they take Mike?" Alex then called his lawyer's office and told the receptionist to have Mr. Hammersmith meet him at the FBI office in Federal Plaza.

When he arrived there, Alex asked to be taken to whoever was in charge of the Long investigation. He was led to an interior room with faded lime-green walls and a long oak table that bore the scratches of age. Mike sat at the end of the table as Stephenson introduced himself and Makovsky to Alex. A young man with dark blond hair neatly parted in the middle of his head and dressed in a buttoned double-breasted dark blue suit stepped forward and extended his hand.

"Jim Hammersmith. I'll be representing Mr. Long on your behalf."

Taken aback, Alex replied, "No you're not. Jim Hammersmith is a much older man and I don't know who you are."

"I'm sorry. I'm James junior. My father was unavailable and asked me to stand in for him."

"Would you excuse us for a moment gentlemen," asked Alex sarcastically, "while junior and I have a little chat in the hallway?"

When the door closed behind them, Alex turned to the young Hammersmith and in a loud whisper close to his ear said, "I'm not used to being treated like this. When I ask for my lawyer, I expect to get my lawyer and not a junior version."

Unfazed, Jim stood close to Alex and in a clear voice said, "I understand, but in this instance, my father was out of town on another case and by the way, I don't value being put down in public, especially by the man I'm supposed to represent. For your information, I've been with the firm for over five years and handled many situations more complicated than this seems to be, so if you want proper representation I would appreciate your backing off."

Alex stepped back and smiled, "Well… the cub has fangs! All right, let's see what you can do."

When they returned to the conference room, Hammersmith took over the discussion with the FBI men and after a brief exchange, pointed out that there was no real evidence of a wrongdoing, only a technical oversight in not filing the birth certificate with the municipality, and that Mr. Long should be released immediately. Stephenson said that he would keep the case open as he still suspected that there was a question concerning Mr. Long's citizenship. Jim insisted that until such time as they have definite proof of an illegal act, Mike was not to be harassed.

Stephenson reluctantly agreed and Mike, Alex and Jim left. When they reached the street level, Alex turned to Jim and said, "You did well. Maybe I was a little hasty in my earlier judgment," then added, as he led Mike to his car, "and give your father my best regards."

At Alex's direction, the car headed toward the West Side of Manhattan and the site of the Eden Center. Alex closed the window to the driver's compartment and faced Mike angrily.

"What the fuck's going on here? Are you or are you not a citizen? At every turn, you guys are trying to sabotage my project. First it was the fact that you kept me in the dark about the JPA and their possible involvement with the murder, and now this. We're going to meet with Patrick now and I promise you, there will be changes made. I won't be kept in the dark any more by any of you guys. So I repeat, are you or are you not a citizen?"

"It's complicated."

"Complicated—Hell! I want a simple answer."

"The simple answer is, yes."

"You could have said so in the first place. And, I don't want to know about any complications." The rest of the ride proceeded in silence.

When they reached the Eden site, they joined Patrick in his trailer. Brusquely pushing a roll of drawings off a table to the floor, Alex sat in Patrick's chair and ordered, "Sit!"

The two men pulled folding chairs from the back of the trailer and sat down facing Alex.

"I told Mike," started Alex and looking directly at Patrick, "and I'll tell you as well. From now on, no secrets, no hidden agendas, nothing held back. In other words, I want to know every fucking thing that goes on here, and that means everything," emphasizing the last word.

"To start with, I need to know more about this fellow Guardini. When I talked to my contacts at the police, they told me to lay off the JPA. Something about the fact that they are a legitimate security firm and that they often work with the police. Frankly, it sounded like a too-cozy relationship...as if the cops were being paid off to turn a blind eye. Are you guys certain that Guardini's involved?"

Patrick answered first. "There's no question in my mind that he is, in some way, involved. Actually, Mike met with Bruno in January to confront him about the salted concrete. Perhaps he pissed him off when he asked him to lay off our project. But, none of us thought he would resort to murder to get us to use his services."

Mike added, "I never told you but on the apartment building we built for you two years ago, I did pay the JPA for protection. It was my first major project with you and I didn't want any hang-ups but I swore that I would never do that again and beside, it would have been too expensive this time."

Raising his voice in anger, Alex replied, "That's exactly what I'm talking about. I've told you before that on my projects I want to know everything that's going on!"

"I used my own money to pay them so..."

"I don't give a fuck whose money was used. Maybe I haven't made it clear. When you work for me, I will not have any dealings going on behind my back. Is that clear?"

Mike's face turned red and his lips tightened to a pencil line in obvious anger, so Patrick, seeing this, immediately interjected, "We get it. You're the boss and as I told you before, we're going to keep you in the loop from now on."

"I hope that's clear."

"Perfectly," said Patrick.

As Alex stood to leave he said, "There is one other matter. I have a set of drawings in the car that I want you to price out. These are changes that I may need to institute to bring the project back on budget. It's important that you keep this confidential. I don't want anyone else to know about this."

Mike said, "I'll have to have my estimator work on this and Sam…"

Alex interrupted, "No! Sam is not to be involved. I understand you need your estimator, but that's all. I want no one else to get wind of this. Make that clear to your estimator."

The three walked out to Alex's car as he retrieved the drawings and handed them to Mike.

As he entered the car, Alex said, "I'll be in my office if you need me."

The moment the door closed, Mike turned to Patrick and said, "That self-righteous bastard. From what I hear it's the bank that owns this project and not mister Bigmouth. It really pisses me off the way he treats us. I don't know how you take it."

"I'm just trying to get this damn project finished and then I won't have to deal with Alex any more." Patrick and Mike concluded their conversation by deciding to let Alex deal with Guardini, but they both were uncomfortable with the secrecy concerning the modified set of drawings.

Mike returned to his office and called home. When Marion answered, he said, "How's your mother?"

"She's just sad since Dad died and needed a little comforting."

"I'm sorry to have to ask you this, but could you meet me in Riverside Park? it's important." Although Marion protested that she was tired after her trip, Mike finally convinced her. Since his confrontation with the FBI, he had become increasingly concerned that Marion would find out about his secret. Actually it was no longer such a secret, since he had revealed it to Sam. But now, with a possible investigation into his background by the FBI, he no longer felt he could avoid telling Marion.

"What's up?" she asked as she approached him on the park bench facing the river. "Couldn't you wait to talk to me until you came home? I know that we used to meet here in the old days at the beginning of a romantic evening, but that was usually in the warmer weather. It's a little cold and uncomfortable today for a chat."

He handed her a cup of coffee that he had bought on the way, and put his free arm around her shoulder pulling her close. For a moment they sat silently staring at the moving river. "There's something I have to tell you. A story I should have told you long ago but one that I don't want overheard."

"You're frightening me," she answered. "Do you think our home has ears?" She gripped the coffee cup, slightly crumpling the cardboard.

"Don't be upset, but I had a visit from the FBI today and..."

Pulling away from him she shouted, "What do you mean, don't be upset? Of course, I'm upset. What's going on?"

"You don't have to scream at me. It had to do with the murder at the site."

"What's that got to do with you? You don't have any responsibility for that, do you?"

"No, of course not. But, they brought up a question about my past and that's what I want to talk to you about." As Mike revealed the story he had recounted to Sam weeks earlier, Marion was at first shocked when hearing about those first days of Mike's passage from Cambodia to Seattle.

As Mike described the issue with his citizenship, she became agitated and pushed further away from him. "I've felt for a long time that you were hiding something from me. How could you have kept this to yourself all these years? This hurts me deeply. I'm your wife and I thought you would have had enough faith in me to believe that I would understand and support you. Maybe you've forgotten how I stood up for you against my family when we decided to get married. That wasn't easy for me and you should have told me then what you've just told me now. It wouldn't have made any difference in how I felt about you but now..."

Mike reached out to her and tried to pull her toward him. "I'm so sorry. You're right, of course, I shouldn't have kept this to myself but I was afraid. I thought you might not marry me if you knew, and I loved you so….and…I still love as much today as the day we met. Please," he pleaded. "Please forgive me. I need to know that we will face whatever happens together."

"Oh Mike, of course I still love you as well, but…I need time. This has been like a betrayal of trust that I thought we had in each other. I may feel differently in time, but…." They embraced gently as they walked to Riverside Drive where Mike hailed a taxi to take them to the Port Authority, where they caught a bus home. There was nothing else to be said that afternoon.

AFTER LEAVING HIS MEETING WITH Patrick and Mike, Alex tried to call Claire at home and when there was no answer there, he dialed her cell phone. "Yes," she answered coolly, "who is this?"

"It's Alex. I'm sorry to disturb you."

"I'm in the middle of a meeting. Can this wait?"

"It's rather urgent. Can you call me back when you have a break?"

"All right," she answered in a sharp voice. When she did call back an hour later, Alex asked her, "Are you mad at me? You sounded so dismissive when I called."

"Alex, you have to understand that I have a business to run and can't be immediately available whenever you decide to contact me. So, what is so urgent?"

This is not the same woman that I have leaned on for the last few years, thought Alex. Her voice was so clipped and lacked the lyrical quality he had come to cherish. She seemed so cool. But, this was not the time for him to try to understand what was happening to their relationship, so he suppressed any personal thoughts. Instead, he told her about the JPA and the suspicion on the part of the construction team that Guardini was somehow involved in the murder and other problems at the site. He then explained that his contacts in the police department appeared to have a cozy relationship with the JPA and that he suspected that there might be some collusion involved. "Look, I know that you and the mayor have been pretty close lately, so would you mind trying to find out what the deal is?"

"My relationship with the mayor is strictly business. I'm working on the passage of a new real estate bill."

Alex thought, sure, like our relationship was strictly business, but said, "I don't expect you to compromise your position but it would be helpful to me to know the city's position with regard to the JPA."

"I'll do what I can," she said. "Give me a few days." Alex did not see the frown of concern as she spoke. Since their last meeting in February, Claire knew that they needed to spend time apart. She no longer felt that their pleasurable moments of intimacy were emotionally satisfying enough to continue the relationship. In the beginning, Claire was drawn to Alex because of his reputation as a powerful developer. She craved a strong partner and had become disillusioned at his indecisiveness in choosing between her and his marriage.

First with her ex-husband, Greg, and now with Alex, she could not accept how fragile these men were in their relationships. For her part, she had to be tough and in complete control as a leader in successfully shepherding difficult projects through the political and regulatory morass of the city. And in her personal life she needed—and wanted—a supportive partner. Early in their relationship, she thought that Alex could fulfill that role. He was, after all, a developer who had proposed the most dramatic project to be seen in New York since the Lincoln Center, a project that transformed a blighted urban landscape into America's premier artistic center. But now Alex had proved to be no more supportive than Greg. She needed a more fulfilling relationship.

BEFORE LEAVING FOR HIS OFFICE that same morning, Philip sat in his kitchen having a cup of tea with Diane. He rarely had more than his English tea and an occasional muffin for breakfast.

"Why don't you have some eggs this morning to put a little more flesh on your bones?" asked Diane.

"I couldn't possibly eat anything this morning."

"What's wrong, dear?"

"I don't know. I can't seem to shake a bad feeling about the project. When Alex first approached me, I wasn't really prepared to secure a major project so late in my career. So at the time, I thought it was too good to be true."

Diane leaned down to embrace him, folding her arms in front of his chest to pull him close, or was it to comfort him? She thought back to the time a quarter of a century earlier when she got to know this fragile man, the second time that they had met.

It was at a meeting of the Society of Architects in New York where Philip presented his views on the need to integrate organic forms in the design of buildings. He had just completed his first year teaching at Columbia and stumbled through what was his first public lecture, periodically apologizing for his inept presentation. Diane had attended because she had just returned from visiting Paolo Soleri's Arcosanti in the Arizona desert, a visionary fusion of architecture and ecology, and wanted to hear how Corta planned to use organic forms in design.

After the lecture, as Philip was removing his slides from a carousel, Diane walked up to him and introduced herself. Philip looked up and saw a young woman with light brown hair gathered in a bun on top of her oval face to make her appear taller than her diminutive height. She had a pretty face, not conventionally beautiful except for her intense, wide-open, seductive gray eyes. There was something familiar about that face.

Diane spoke first. "I enjoyed your lecture and wanted to know more about your ideas of how to use desert forms in design. I just returned from Arizona and…."

Philip interrupted, "You saw it then. I mean Arcosanti. Isn't it amazing?" He seemed taken aback by the question as he felt his talk was a failure, but this woman fired him with enthusiasm and he craved exploring her insights from the trip to the desert. "Would you join me for a cup of coffee so you could tell me what you thought of it? I'm sorry, I don't even know your name." Of course she had already told him, but he forgot.

She smiled and answered, "Diane Sherwood. We actually met last year in Low Library. I was an art student at that time and, yes…I'd love to tell you what I thought about Soleri's work and get your views as well."

"I thought there was something familiar about you. You can remind me as we talk over coffee." There were many subsequent encounters over the next year as Diane and Philip met over coffee or dinner or sometimes a visit to a museum or a movie. When leaving Diane in front of her building, Philip would usually kiss her peremptorily until one day, Diane pushed him gently away and asked, "Do you always treat your women so dismissively?"

Surprised by the question, Philip raised his eyebrows and said, "I don't know what you mean by 'my women.' I may be a bit awkward in my approach but I thought of our relationship as being somewhat special."

"We've been seeing each other for over a year and I am beginning to wonder where this relationship is going."

"Well!" Taking her hand, he said, "Actually, I have been thinking, we seem to get along so well and I was wondering if you would consider marrying me?"

Diane tried to pull away. "Isn't that a bit premature since you have never even told me how you feel about me?"

"I…I believe I love you."

"You believe?"

"I'm sorry." Philip now took both her hands in his, "I know I love you. I think about you all the time when we are away from each other."

Diane put her arms around Philip's neck and kissed him, causing him to stumble backward for an instant before he took her in his arms. "I don't know what took you so long to tell me," she said.

They married two weeks later and had been inseparable ever since, but Diane recognized over the intervening years that Philip needed her support as he encountered problems in his professional career. She had married a husband who also became the child she could never have.

"This is the project you always wanted, and from what I can see, the construction is moving ahead nicely."

"Yes, but remember the problem with the budget and those mock drawings Ricardo prepared for Alex. There's so much uncertainty… and then there was the accident."

"I wouldn't call a worker being stabbed to death an accident," said Diane. "It is much more serious and senseless. The man undoubtedly had a family that had lost a husband or a father. But you said yourself, after the accident on your first office-building design, that construction is an inherently dangerous profession.

"I don't mean to minimize it but it doesn't mean that your monument will not be completed or that you will not be honored for having designed a brilliant and beautiful structure. You know that's true." Although she was not totally convinced that all would turn out for the best, she knew how desperately Philip needed to believe that Eden would be his finest achievement.

Philip sighed and rose to embrace his wife. "You're right. There's no reason to be pessimistic." Nevertheless, he still felt a sense of unease as he left the apartment.

Soon after he arrived at his office, Philip was surprised when Alex suddenly showed up.

"I just returned from the field and…"

Philip, determined to be positive after his talk with Diane, interjected enthusiastically, "It's amazing the way the buildings are suddenly blossoming, rising up ever higher. I was just telling Diane what a thrill it is to see my drawings, those frail black lines on paper, developing skin and bones that you can get your hands around. It's actually beginning to look just as I had envisioned it."

"Before you burst apart with enthusiasm, sit down a minute. I'll be honest with you, there are still some problems."

Phil's face sagged painfully, his hands began to fidget nervously, and he started to pace back and forth in what little floor space there was between his desk and the closed door. "I knew it. It's the money, isn't it?"

Alex was not about to discuss the fact that he had not yet received the signed commitment from the bank and replied confidently. "It's got nothing to do with money. By the way, thank you again for agreeing to prepare those modified drawings. I'm convinced they will help me get the financial matter straightened out. It's the killing and the other problems we've had at the site that I now feel are more serious than I first thought. Look! I think I can trust you to be discreet, which is why I'm talking to you now. We've known each other long enough and we've worked together before, although admittedly on a small project compared to Eden. The question is, can I trust you?"

"You know you can. I've always supported you even back to the time you were dealing with your father."

"God, I get so angry when I think back to those days. My father was such a bastard at times. I couldn't take it."

"He had your best interest at heart although I admit he could be thoughtless."

"That's all in the past. Right now, I could use a little advice in dealing with the problems we've had at the site. You know about Guardini and his protection racket."

"Actually, no one has told me much about this Guardini fellow. I've only heard rumors and innuendos from Sam."

Alex continued, "From what I've learned, I believe that Guardini is responsible for the murder and the other problems we've had at the site. It also appears that the police aren't aggressively investigating him, and I suspect that there may be collusion involved. So, I've decided to confront him and see if we can avoid any more so called 'accidents' at the site. The truth is, I'm so angry that I don't know if I can do it without losing my temper and...."

"Do you want me to go with you?"

"No, no! What I want to know is how do you keep yourself in check with all the problems we've had… the design changes you've had to accept and the change in finishes to keep within the budget and that last issue with the mock drawings?"

Pausing and looking at his friend who seemed visibly nervous, Philip said, "Believe me, it's not always easy and if you ask my staff, they will tell you I've been intemperate at times but…perhaps it's my English Public School upbringing, and of course, I have Diane, who knows just how to step back and deal with problems as normal, everyday events. When I get upset, she is able to put me back on track and I can't tell you how many times she's had to do that in the last few tortuous months."

"You're lucky. I don't have that kind of support. Lila isn't exactly mother earth."

"If you don't mind my asking, what about Claire?"

"That's another story and not one I'm prepared to talk about now."

Phillip sensed that this was not a direction to pursue. "If you have to meet this fellow, just try to remember that the dispute between the two of you can be reduced to a financial one and I have seen you manage those types of problems with aplomb and stealth. As long as you can control the discussion without losing your temper, I'm convinced that you can resolve this situation."

"You make it sound easy but you know I'm not the most patient person in the world and I'm not sure I can carry it out."

Putting his arm around Alex's shoulder, Philip replied, "No question in my mind that you can do it as long as you keep your goal in mind."

The two friends talked for another half hour until there was nothing more to say. In all that time, Alex never said another word about the financing issue and the lack of commitment from the bank.

ENTRACTE

As construction continued, the Eden Center began to rise above the height of the river's edge structures and became clearly visible from New Jersey—three wings, not yet fully formed but rapidly maturing. The lower floors of the towers were now fully enclosed and the cores of the three towers were being wrapped with multiple layers of drywall, more to provide fire safety than strength.

Installation of interior stairways lagged no more than three floors below the erection of the buildings' steel frames, and concrete was being poured on the floors as fast as the metal decking was completed. Tee-shaped rails were being attached on each side of elevator shafts to provide guides for the ascent and descent of elevator cabs, and to provide a surface for the brakes to grab onto in case of emergency.

The first of two mechanical floors, the one located on the second level, was being crammed with electrical switching gear and communications terminals as well as air conditioning compressors and fans and pumps for water distribution. From there, ductwork, pipes, and wiring snaked into shafts where they were to be distributed to individual floors. The second mechanical floor, below the tower roof, awaited the completion of the structure.

Garlands of bare light bulbs hung from the ceiling of each floor of the buildings, providing barely minimal illumination for the workers erecting partitions, hanging ductwork and a grid of aluminum bars, into which would be placed future ceilings and light fixtures. With so much work proceeding simultaneously, floors were often littered with pieces of aluminum, sections of ductwork, and snippets of multicolored electric wire, causing the workers to step gingerly and without haste to avoid painful falls.

ELEVEN
The Savior
June 2001

THE FUTURE NATURE WALK WAS now clearly defined with a ribbon of concrete girdling the three towers that were destined to be the apartment building, the hotel and the office building. Under this upward-sloping concrete ribbon, a cavernous empty space would soon be filled with a pool and an interior public plaza dedicated to contemplative interaction of visitors.

For the present it was a dark and forbidding space with no sign of life and little activity, awaiting the development of commercial facilities to help finance that part of the project. This was not the only area of the project that had yet to be assigned to an operator. A signed agreement from a hotel operator had not yet been finalized and Alex needed one to improve the financial outlook for the project. Furthermore, he had not yet received the revised commitment letter from the bank and had begun to infuse the empty coffers of the project with what was left of his own funds; a practice he knew was dangerous.

He kept delaying contacting the bank to let them know that if he did not receive the commitment letter he would institute changes to the project based on the mock set of drawings he gave Mike that would result in cost reductions. This would cheapen the project and consequently reduce its attractiveness, causing the bank's investment to lose value. Yet, he hesitated confronting Chip without being able to announce a new positive development such as the assignment of an operator for the hotel or plaza facilities. The reality was that he did not want to make any changes to the project, and felt beholden to Philip and the promise he had made to him.

While this financial problem weighed on his mind, he had followed Phil's advice and called Bruno Guardini, arranging to have the JPA boss come to his office. Guardini hesitated at first, preferring to meet in a more neutral environment but Alex insisted that it was best to keep any meeting on a business level and, by way of concession, agreed to meet on a Saturday when the office would be free of other personnel. For his part, Alex felt more confident having the meeting in his own office, and as the date approached, he prepared endlessly both physically and emotionally.

On the morning Guardini was to arrive, Alex paced nervously around his office. He was not ready. It wasn't enough to follow Phil's advice. He needed help from an old friend one more time. From his desk drawer, he retrieved an envelope and spread its contents on the polished granite surface of his desk. Gathering the white powder into two rows, he used a straw to inhale the magic power source, leaving no grain behind. "Now," he exclaimed to the empty office, "now, I'm ready!"

At the appointed hour, Guardini, wearing a blue-striped business suit with open-collared white shirt, arrived at the Grant headquarters and was escorted to Alex's office by a guard. Alex, dressed in a sport shirt and blue jeans, greeted him at the door and extended his hand saying, "Good of you to come. But on such a warm June afternoon, you didn't have to wear a jacket. Just drop it on the back of the chair. How about an iced coffee?"

Somewhat taken aback by Alex's seeming deference, Bruno nodded, "Thanks, that'll be fine."

As they both sat down, Alex leaned back in his chair, laced his arms behind his head and said, "Bruno, I appreciate your coming here on a weekend. By the way, you don't mind my calling you Bruno, do you?"

"No, Alex! And frankly, a weekday or weekend, its the same thing to me. I'm used to working twenty four seven."

"Let's get down to business. I hear you've been pressuring my contractor for protection money."

Bruno stood and stepped away from his chair. "If you're gonna to start with accusations, this meeting's over."

"Sit down! I'm merely telling you right off what I think. And I expect you to be just as frank with me."

For an instant, Bruno turned as if to leave and slowly turned back and sat in his chair, his back straight and feet squarely on the floor. "I don't understand your approach but I'll listen as long as it's clear that I'm not here to be insulted."

"I'm sorry you took my directness as an insult but… never mind! What I really want to talk to you about has to do with the problems we've had at the site. First, the bad concrete and then the killing of one of our supers."

"I hope you're not implying that we had anything to do with these incidents."

"I'm just trying to find out if you know anything about these 'incidents' as you call them, and to see if you can help me avoid them in the future. By the way, from my discussions with the police, they seem to think you're clean and that you can help them in connection with the murder."

Bruno looked directly at Alex and raised his eyebrows in surprise at this last statement. "I do have some friends in the department and I have helped them in the past but as far as your super is concerned, I don't think I can be of any help. All I know is what I read in the papers."

Alex stood and walked around the desk to sit, with one leg on the floor, on the corner nearest Bruno's chair, forcing Bruno to lean back to look up at him. Looking down, Alex said in a syrupy voice, "A man in your business sometimes hears things that he may not want to share with the police. Perhaps you've heard something that could help me here."

"Look, Alex, we've just met and I don't really know you, so why should I share with you information that is part of my business?"

Alex's free leg swung perilously close to Bruno's groin. "What could I offer you to provide me with such information?"

Bruno tried to push back his chair that would not budge on the carpeted floor, so the chair just tilted backward. "I told you before that I don't have any information about your super's death but…and I'm not making any promises… I may be able to tap into my sources… if we can come to an understanding."

"What do you mean by an understanding. Until you bring me something I can use, I won't know what it's worth to me."

"Suppose I get back to you in a few days and see what I can dig up. Then you can decide what it's worth."

The two men stood facing each other as Alex extended his hand. "In the meantime, I want your assurance that there will be no more unexplained problems at the site."

Bruno reluctantly shook Alex's hand and turned to leave, saying, "You have my word."

When Bruno left, Alex smiled to himself, feeling that he had not only controlled the discussion but also gained an important concession in that last promise.

However, not knowing what Bruno would eventually reveal, he also felt apprehensive about his ability to control the future outcome of this game. The first thing Monday morning, he called Patrick to report the results of his meeting with Bruno and then placed a call to Phil to thank him again for the boost to his confidence level provided by their last get-together.

When Patrick heard from Alex about his conversation with Guardini, he took the opportunity to report on another development. "Boss," he said, "you'll be glad to hear that I have the revised costs based on the mock drawings, and they are virtually identical to the original budget. But you realize that this means cheapening the project. Since the structure is set, all that will be changed are finishes and some of the special spaces."

"Look, I assumed as much and I'm not planning to make these changes. I only need this to pressure the bank. I don't think that they will want to endanger their investment by making the project less successful—and it would be, if we have to reduce the quality based on these revised documents."

"OK! I just wanted you to know."

After hanging up the phone, Patrick walked over to Sam's trailer, passing groups of workers who raised a weak salute as they were leaving for the day. Sam was still at his desk completing paperwork, updating completion charts and setting forth scheduling of the next day's work. When Patrick entered, Sam turned and offered him a beer from a little fridge he kept locked during the workday. "What's up?" he asked.

"I just heard from Alex, who told me he met with Guardini and it looks like he agreed to a truce."

"No way! I wouldn't trust that fucker for a minute. He's got something up his sleeve—you can bet on it."

In his heart, Patrick agreed with this assessment but was concerned that continuing to act defensively, anticipating another problem at the site, was not constructive and would jeopardize the progress of the project. "I know how you feel, but we have to move on because the progress of construction has slowed to a crawl and Alex is pressing me to get back on schedule."

Since late February, when steel erection started, the expectation was for the towers to rise at the rate of a floor per week. In the past twenty weeks, steel was barely up to the 17th floor, which implied that the project was now almost three weeks behind schedule, with no indication of speeding up. "Look at this progress schedule. It's abysmal. You have to do something about it," said Patrick.

"I still have a bad feeling about this Guardini SOB but Alex is the client. Look, I'll let Mike know what's happened and we'll work out a plan to try to accelerate the construction," replied Sam. "But just to be clear, my guys need some assurance that there won't be another killing on this job."

"All I can guarantee is that from the owner's side we've done what we can to prevent further trouble. But before you call Mike, let's lay out a strategy for the future work at the site."

For the next hour, Patrick and Sam reviewed alternatives and concluded that they had to meet with all the job supers and explain the need for improved performance while assuring them that the problems at the site, blamed on outside parties, had been dealt with and would no longer be an issue.

AFTER HIS MEETING WITH GUARDINI, Alex would have habitually have called Claire. However, he had not heard from her since the time he asked for her help in finding out how the administration viewed the JPA. For the past few weeks, he had left numerous messages but had not gotten any response.

Since those calls were unanswered, Alex had spent more time with Lila, trying to deliver on his promise to be more responsive to her and to the children's needs. He also realized that he had missed over a year of the children's development, and needed to reconnect with them before they became strangers to him. He began to look forward to his dinners at home and to a newfound closeness with Lila, who began to allow her past resentments to fade. As he thought about her, he looked at his watch and bemoaned that time moved too slowly and it would be hours before he could return to his family.

THE LIGHT FROM THE LAST rays of the sun barely penetrated the bronze-tinted windows behind Alex's desk, but he felt their heat stroking the back of his neck. For an instant, he closed his eyes and surrendered to the warmth that spread through his body, as images of his newfound intimacy with Lila floated up. Just then, the wild ringing of the telephone almost caused him to fall backward off his chair. He quickly glanced at the clock, 4:30, before picking up the receiver. "Grant!"

The voice on the other end of the line spoke slowly in a high-pitched voice, "Mr. Grant, this is Joshua Golden. I'm the president of the Goldenrod Group."

Alex answered brusquely, "I know who you are. What can I do for you?"

"I've been following your project with great interest. We think it will be a wonderful addition to the city and congratulate you on bringing it this far."

"Thank you very much but I'm sure you're not just calling to wish me luck."

"Quite right! I wonder if you would be willing to meet to discuss the possibility of our providing an investment to help you complete the project?"

"I appreciate your interest in the project but I have all the financing I need at this time so a meeting would be a waste of your time."

Hesitating for a moment, Golden replied, "To be perfectly honest, Mr. Grant, I heard talk in the real estate community that your relationship with your bankers may be, shall we say, a bit shaky."

Alex replied sharply, "I don't know where you heard such a rumor but I can assure you that it is far from the truth, so I don't think we have anything further to talk about."

Golden hesitated before replying. "I appreciate your candor, but my offer stands in case your situation changes in the future. By the way, I understand you're looking for an operator for your hotel. I've worked with Hilton in the past and may be able to provide you with a contact there."

"I might take you up on that if my present negotiations don't succeed."

Before hanging up, Golden added, "In the meantime, all the best of luck with your project."

Once he heard the click signifying that the phone was disconnected, Alex muttered to himself, "Where the hell did this come from?" Real-estate sharks like the Goldenrod Group were always looking for hanging fruit to pluck from a shaky developer's tree, especially if the fruit was tinged with a hint of decay. Yet, Alex was not aware of any questions that were generally known about his issues with the financing of the project. Could it be that someone close to him had contacted the Goldenrod Group? Of course, he had not yet received the increased commitment letter from the bank.

Perhaps Chip was deliberately delaying responding to his request. "If that little fucker thinks he can play games with me, I'll squash him." His face red with anger, Alex could feel the carotid arteries in his neck pulsing madly as he reached for the phone. Of course, there was no answer at the bank, as it was after five o'clock. "What the hell's his cell phone number?" Alex mumbled as he became increasingly frustrated while searching through the contact list on his phone. By the time he punched in the number and heard the periodic ringing he was shaking. After three rings, a voice answered, "Chip Stewart."

Alex took a deep breath before responding. "Chip this is Alex. I'm sorry to disturb you at home but something came up that I need to ask you about."

"If it won't take too long, because Alice and I are about to go out."

"It'll just take a minute. I need to know when I can expect the commitment letter from the bank?"

"I told you the last time we talked that it's in process. In fact, I understand that the investment committee has approved it, and after the executive group passes it, the president of the bank will have it on his desk for signature."

"That's encouraging but…. You haven't by any chance had conversations with Josh Golden recently."

Surprised at the question, Chip took a breath before answering. "You know that Mr. Golden is also a client of the bank but we haven't had any recent contacts. Why do you ask?"

"It's not important now. Can I assume that I will receive the commitment letter within a week or two?"

"Certainly within a few weeks."

"Thanks, Chip. And again, I'm sorry to have bothered you. Have a nice evening and give Alice my regards."

Alex did not know whether to feel relieved or concerned. If it wasn't Chip, then where did Golden get his information?

The following day, Alex received a phone call from Guardini to report that he had heard from his contacts that there is a yet unsubstantiated rumor that the perpetrator responsible for the murder at the site may have fled the country. He was unable to get any other information from his sources other than the fact that the guy disappeared without a trace. What he did not say is that the man had been spotted in Alabama and that an elimination order had been issued. The police wanted him, dead or alive. Guardini just wanted him dead.

"You know, Alex, my friend, that such things happen all the time."

Knowing that the FBI was already involved in the case, Alex asked, "What about the police or the FBI? Can't they get a lead on where he went?"

"I'm afraid that those areas of inquiry are more in your area than mine," said Bruno

After a moment Alex added, "I assume that our agreement still stands that there will be no more problems at the site"

Bruno replied, before hanging up, "Of course I could guarantee it if you hired the JPA but….I will do what's in my power to do."

WHEN ALEX RETURNED HOME THAT evening, he was warmly greeted by Lila, who asked, "Why don't we have a glass of wine before dinner while you tell me about your day." Pleased but surprised, Alex said, "Well, what's got into you?"

"You've changed recently and acted so concerned about us. Anyway, since you were a little late, I put the children to bed and was thinking about what has been happening between us. I don't know what's changed in you, but you have been so much more caring in the last month and I'd really like to know why."

"I'll get the wine if you bring the glasses," said Alex. "It'll be like old times. Remember the cabin?"

"You're going to make me cry," said Lila. "Just pour the wine."

"The cabin's still there. We just haven't used it for years. Remember that big old fireplace? I almost had a hernia when I built it and had to lift those big stones in place. I remember when I lit the first fire, we lay down in front of it and watched the flames and the smoke rise up."

"You were so proud of having built it. We stayed in front of that fireplace the first night until the last embers faded."

The fireplace dominated the cathedral-ceilinged great room that served as living room, dining room and kitchen, with one sidewall of glass overlooking the little mountain lake and the hills in the distance. It was a magical space, both majestic and cozy at the same time. Philip had helped with the design, but the rugged wooden cabin totally reflected Alex's character, from the slate floors to the pine walls to the exposed beams in the ceiling.

Alex responded, "That was long before the kids. We started building the cabin the year before we married. When we went there for our honeymoon, all we had were a couple of wine crates for a table and cushions on the floor. Worst of all was the outhouse we had to use before we had a real toilet."

"It wasn't that bad. Well, maybe it did smell a little! But, we were happy to get away every weekend, away from the tension between you and your father and all the pressures of the city."

Alex leaned over and kissed Lila as he remembered that time. "Yes, we were happy there. Somehow it all changed after we had the kids. There were fewer and fewer weekends there. I don't even know why. It's been years since we've been to the Berkshires. We really should try to go there again now that the kids are older."

"They might like that. I know I would." Lila moved closer to curl into Alex's arms and they sat for a long time without speaking, reveling in the memories of the weekends at the cabin. That night they made love as if for the first time.

TWELVE
Progress
July 2001

IN THE HEAT OF SUMMER, it was not surprising to see shirtless workers, their tanned bodies glistening with sweat, maneuvering heavy steel girders that hung precariously from thin steel cables hundreds of feet above the ground. Standing on the recently placed steel deck on the 24th floor of the central tower, Diane aimed her camera at one of the steelworkers as he stretched his muscular arms up to balance a seemingly weightless steel beam high in the air from the tips of his gloved hands.

For weeks, Diane had been visiting the site to record images of workers at the site performing their ordinary tasks. Because she was on the site for days at a time, the workers became attuned to her presence and virtually ignored her, which allowed her images to be spontaneous rather than posed. She achieved a sense of drama by framing the images without her subjects being conscious of the lens. Often she would allow the sun to backlight a subject, making him or her (and indeed, there were now a few women on the construction site) appear to glow.

Seeing workers hanging precariously from the edge of a floor to bolt a beam in place reminded her of the potential dangers of construction work and the thin line between life and death. It became clearer how Philip had hardened over the years toward his acceptance today of accidents as a routine hazard of construction. It pained her to see him lose a measure of humanity toward the victims as well as the survivors. She pushed such thoughts from her mind as she saw the opportunity for another iconic image of construction in action.

Moving from floor to floor, she stayed on the site for many hours, seeking to illustrate the variety of tasks required to complete the construction of a building such as the Eden Center. As she reached the ground floor and stepped off the rickety construction elevator she was surprised to see her husband waiting to enter. "What are you doing here?" she asked.

"This is my project, after all," Philip answered. "The question is, why are you here?"

"Darling, have you forgotten that I've been photographing the project on and off for months now? This happened to be a gorgeous day so here I am."

For a moment, Philip was unsure whether or not he should enter the elevator but instead, took his wife aside. "It's almost noon. Why don't we drop your equipment in Patrick's trailer and go out for a bite of lunch? There's a wonderful little Italian place nearby and you can tell me all about your impression of the progress of the construction."

"Lovely, we haven't had a date in a long time." She laced her arm into his as they walked to the restaurant.

They ate a light lunch of veal scaloppini, accompanied by a bottle of Montepulciano, while Diane described the images she had been able to record of steelworkers, lathers, plasterers, electricians… all kinds of workers who seemed to take their tasks both seriously and with humor as they bantered among themselves. She was surprised at the intensity and enthusiasm of the workers she talked with.

Philip was equally upbeat as he spoke of his feeling of euphoria at the changes he found at the site since his somewhat depressing meeting with Alex two months earlier. There seemed to be an increased level of energy in the workers as the troubles from last winter faded. He told her how much he looked forward to the topping out of the tallest tower in a few months' time, when the form of his composition will appear completely defined in steel and glass. Of course it would be much more than a year before the project would be truly complete but, he said, "How the various structural elements appear as solid forms rather than lying flat on a two-dimensional drawing, that's what I really look forward to seeing." Stroking his cheek, Diane replied, "You will, my dear, you will!"

"I hope you're right." And then Philip stated with a sudden burst of enthusiasm, "Of course you're right." After a moment he added in a conspiratorial tone, "In fact, I haven't told Alex this, but I invited the critic for the *Times* to meet me and walk through the site."

Hearing this, Diane was concerned, "Don't you think it is too early to do this when there is still so much to be completed?"

"Absolutely not! This is the most important project of my career and I will try to publicize it from now on. It's my last chance at real recognition and I intend to take it."

"I'm certain that they will be just as enthusiastic about the project as you are," Diane answered, worried that any slight criticism, justified or not, could send Philip into a deep depression as he counted so heavily on support from the architectural press. But she sensed that this was not the time to dampen Philip's obvious optimism. Besides, she felt somewhat sleepy from the midday heat, and the effect of the wine, and needed to go home. But first, she insisted on taking photos of Philip walking about the site and observing the construction.

After they separated, Philip resumed his tour of the site, exhilarated by the progress that had been made since his last visit. He passed through a plywood door at the bottom of the future nature walk that slammed behind him, pulled by a spring. He stood in awe at the cavernous area and imagined the day when the gray concrete would be replaced by a brick walk bordered with green shrubs and flowering plants, when the sun passing through the skylight would warm and nourish nature's harvest, and butterflies in bright colors would fly around, giving this space a festive air. His hands flew up as he imagined a butterfly landing on his nose, then absentmindedly brushed it away. Of course, on this day it was only cement dust from the recently poured concrete that blew against him.

Climbing up the slope, he stared at the crystalline skylight above him and the towers that peeked through like distant mountains. *It's just as I imagined it*, he thought. Reaching the top, he stood on the deck that was to be an outlook over the future waterfall. Passing through another temporary plywood door, he crossed a bridge and entered a debris-laden space that was to become a restaurant, and imagined how it would appear when finished, with windows on one side looking out at the waterfall and, on the other side, at the surrounding city.

At this moment, in this magical place, it seemed impossible that anything could go wrong to shatter his dream, but Philip was fearful, as he had been all his life, that he was doomed to fail. *Not this time*, he thought, *not this time*, as he walked confidently to the construction elevator that returned him to the ground.

"Hey Phil," Sam shouted when he saw the elevator gate open, "Have you got a minute?"

Phil answered excitedly, "I was just admiring how much had been accomplished since I was last here only two weeks ago."

"That's what I wanted to talk to you about. We're at the stage when I need to get your approval on some of the finish materials. I have samples in my office and would appreciate if you could come over while you're here and check them out."

Thrilled at the prospect of actually seeing and touching samples of marble, granite and wood that he had only imagined as words on a page of specifications, Philip said, "I'd be more than happy to do that. In fact, I've been looking forward to it."

IN HIS OFFICE ON THE other side of town, Alex stared at the calendar. Had it been two or three weeks since his conversation with Chip? The work at the site was finally moving back on schedule with no further disruptions. Alex assumed that his meeting with Guardini had achieved the desired result of putting him on notice that the Eden Center was a project that was being watched by all the local politicians who were concerned that problems at the site would reflect badly on their reputations to deliver on promises of a trouble-free project. The police had, recently, intensified their nighttime patrols in the vicinity of the site in response to a request from the mayor. Alex expected that this had been at the instigation of Claire following up on the last conversation he had with her. He had heard that she and Mayor Bartlett had been seen together constantly.

It had, in fact been only two weeks since his discussion with Chip, but with so many positive developments, Alex became increasingly frustrated by the absence of a commitment letter. He considered whether this was the right time to use the revised drawings as a threat to move the bank to advance the process.

Since his attempt to find a hotel operator had not yet succeeded, there was still the option of taking up Josh Golden's offer concerning his contacts at Hilton. Yet, Alex was not ready to become enmeshed with the Goldenrod Group. *There was another way,* he thought, and picked up the phone. There was no answer at the number he dialed so he left a message. "Claire, it's Alex! Could you call me back? I have a job for you."

Prior to their romantic involvement, Claire had worked for Alex as a consultant charged with getting all necessary approvals from various governmental agencies needed to start the Eden project. This included arranging deals to permit the project to exceed the size mandated by zoning by proposing to swap developable rights from another site that Alex controlled. She had also introduced Alex to Losey & Sons, the private banking firm that subsequently provided financing for the project. She was clearly the person Alex now needed to help resolve the open financing issue and perhaps even find a hotel operator or a key tenant for the building and thus provide the assurances that the bank needed to issue their commitment letter. But, in view of the change in their personal relationship, Alex wondered if she would be willing to work for him again. When his cell phone rang, Alex assumed it was Claire calling back, so he answered it with, "Hi."

"What's on your mind, Alex?" Claire answered in a cool staccato voice.

"I appreciate that your influence with the mayor has improved the safety at the site. But, I have another problem that I thought you might be able to help me with, strictly business!"

"I'm really quite busy these days. Is it something that can wait?"

"I'm afraid not. Look, could we meet so that I can explain what I need?"

"I don't think that's a good idea. Why don't you tell me a little more of what this is all about?" Alex proceeded to explain his concerns about the delay in receiving a revised commitment letter and his thoughts concerning Claire's being able to exert some influence at the bank and even the possibility of finding a hotel operator and even a tenant for the office building. "I really need you to help me now. I'm not comfortable with the current situation."

"Well, that's quite an assignment. Isn't it a little late in the game to resolve so many key issues? I would have thought that an experienced developer like you would have made deals long ago."

Alex thought he heard a somewhat mocking tone in her voice. "You know perfectly well, Claire, that we've had some unexpected problems at the site that have apparently spooked the bank just when I found I needed an increase in their investment."

"Well, Alex, I was serious when I said that I was quite busy. But..." pausing for ten seconds so that Alex thought the connection had been broken, "I'll try to do what I can but on the condition that you understand that our previous relationship has ended and that, as you said, this is strictly business."

"I understand!" Alex was actually relieved that he would not have to explain his newly rekindled affection for his wife. Claire added, "It will take me some time before I can devote myself fully to your situation but I'll start making some inquiries right away." "There's one other thing you should know," added Alex, "Josh Golden approached me about investing in the project but I turned him down."

"Are you sure that was a good move? You know that he can be quite tenacious and can become a dangerous adversary if he smells blood. In the current situation you can't afford to provoke him."

"I can handle it, and besides, there's still time and if you can't get me what I need, I can still contact him."

"You're playing a dangerous game."

"You should know that's the only way I play."

Claire did not respond to this last remark before hanging up the phone. Alex now felt that he had done all he could to get the Eden Project back on track and was satisfied that he could now relax and fulfill his promise to take Lila and the children to the beach before the start of the new school year.

CLAIRE WAS SECURE IN HER new relationship with Roger Bartlett. As contrasted to her former husband Douglas, as well as her recent involvement with Alex, Bartlett made few demands on her, yet was a warm and affectionate lover while being considerate of her need for independence. It was a new experience for her, although she still felt somewhat conflicted between what she felt in her heart and the dangers of commitment.

Her phone conversation with Alex convinced her that she had ended her relationship with him not one day too soon; for a long time it had been unhealthy and one-sided. In Roger, she had finally found a man with whom she could fully share a life.

Nevertheless, the phone call with Alex had upset her, as she realized that he still commanded her sympathy and still needed her. Yet, she felt sufficiently confident that she could remain objective in what was now merely a business relationship. It troubled her that Alex had not yet received his financing and had not yet signed a major tenant for the office building and had not yet secured an operator for the hotel. It would not be easy, so late in the process, to secure these commitments, especially in view of the problems experienced at the site. Nevertheless this was a challenge that she relished and immediately set to work calling prospects.

It had been many months since she last visited the site and she wanted to see for herself how much progress had been made. She called Patrick to notify him of a visit she planned for the following day. "Come any time," he said. "I'm always glad to help you in any way I can."

She said she needed to be brought up to date in connection with an assignment she would undertake for Alex. "You can explain it to me in the morning," he answered. Patrick wondered what that could possibly mean, but decided to wait until the planned meeting, as he was too busy to even speculate.

Claire arrived at the site at nine the following morning dressed, she thought, for a construction visit, in tan slacks and practical sneakers but with a white blouse seductively open at the collar.

"Mrs. Fletcher," Patrick greeted her, "in that getup you'll create quite a stir with the boys."

"Remember, it's Claire," she responded, "and you may have gathered when we last met that I'm not used to being on a construction site and it's certainly not my intention to upset anyone."

Leading her to the door of the trailer, Patrick said, "You don't upset me in the least and we've now got a few women on the crews who'll keep the wolves at bay. Now, what can I do for you?"

Taking seats facing each other in the trailer, Claire stared at the construction progress chart behind Patrick and said, "I'm trying to understand why the bank is giving Alex such a hard time when I see that progress at the site seems to be on schedule."

"Well, Claire, you see, we've had these problems over the last eight months that have bedeviled the site. First there was an issue with bad concrete and then, of course, there was the murder. That, more than anything else, caused a serious disruption, not so much with the schedule, because we've been pushing like hell, but with the perception that there is something wrong with the project.

"You know, I'm sure, that we believe these problems were caused by the JPA. That bunch seems to have a special relationship with the guys in the city, although nothing has been proved. As a result, Alex tells me the bank has been nervous and can't seem to get off their fat behinds to move forward."

"I've been in touch with the mayor." *I'll bet you have,* thought Patrick. "And he's been told that the JPA has been quite helpful in providing jobs to people who've come from poverty or bad early home situations. I also understand that the police department has been monitoring those employees and found them to be generally reliable and to stay out of trouble."

"That may be, but their boss, Mr. Guardini is a shady character who has pressured the contractor to accept protection services that are not needed."

"I'll mention that to Roger." *Roger, is it*, thought Patrick. "On another subject, you mentioned that progress has been good in spite of the bank's reluctance to complete the financing package. Why is that?"

"Well," Patrick turned away for a moment, unsure how much he should reveal of his suspicions. "I hesitate to say this, but I believe Alex has been using his own funds to keep the job moving."

"I see." Claire did not want to delve further into the project finances, as she did not want to get further involved with Alex's business dealings. "Thank you. I think I understand, but, since I am here, can we walk around the site so I can get a better picture of the project? It looks great from a distance but I've not seen it up close."

"Of course. I'll give you a quick tour," said Patrick.

They started with a walk around the site and entered the unfinished garden area before taking the construction elevator to the highest completed floor. Claire admired the view and tried to imagine how the project would look when completed. She made a mental note to call Philip and tell him how impressed she was with the design, even in its incomplete stage.

After her walk around, she thanked Patrick for his help and left the site. In her mind there was no great sense of urgency to investigate possible tenants or hotel operators. It could wait for her planned week's vacation with Roger In Montauk. When she returned later in August, there would be time enough to complete her promised task for Alex.

THIRTEEN
Doldrums
August 2001

THE SUMMER MONTHS ARE THE best of times for construction, even though the extreme heat often bedevils a project. Workers are often absent, taking a day off to spend time at the beach or by a mountain lake to take advantage of the warm weather. Managing this game of absenteeism, which is often supported by a bogus medical excuse, was difficult. Mike and Sam arranged to stagger their vacations so one of them would always be on site to manage the project.

Since he had no family and spent his free time with his pub comrades, it mattered little to Patrick that he was not able to be away for an extended period. He had no backup and instead took random days off whenever he felt that his presence was not critical.

Lila decided that a family vacation at the Grant house on the Cape was needed after such a difficult year. In spite of his concerns about the project, Alex agreed, but suggested that they invite the Cortas for a week in August when the children would be away at camp. Philip was not enthusiastic about the idea. "It means we'll be with them all the time," he told Diane. "I'm not certain I can take that."

"For heaven's sake, if it makes you uncomfortable you can get away and take a walk on the beach or read a book. I think it would be wonderful to get away from the city for a while and relax. Beside, you deserve the rest, and I know how much you like that house," said Diane. Philip remembered when he first saw the house with its graying shingles, white trimmed windows and wind-worn look. It was a charming, classically simple design; typical of the New England region that reminded him of the cottages he had seen in the English countryside. When Alex commented sarcastically, "It's a throwback to the twenties, typical of the old man's views," Philip rebuked him saying, "You should have learned one thing from taking my course. This style is well suited and fits quietly into its environment." Alex was never won over by this argument.

Philip, of course, was happy to return to the Cape and the Grant cottage but insisted that they rent a car so that they would not be totally dependent on the Grants and would be able to explore other parts of the Cape on their own.

Philip had let his drivers's license expire, so, on a beautiful Saturday in the middle of the month, Diana was at the wheel when the Cortas drove to Truro. Once they arrived at the approaches to the Sagamore Bridge, the crush of summer visitors slowed their drive. It took them two hours to reach Truro after crossing the bridge, by which time they were both exhausted.

"Welcome," shouted Lila when she heard the car grinding on the gravel driveway. "It's late and you must be tired after your long drive. Come in and relax. I've prepared a light supper for you so you can quickly get to bed. After a good night's sleep, we can talk about what you want to do for the next few days."

During their time on the Cape, the Eden Center receded into the background and was never brought up in any conversation. The four friends had picnics on the beach and went out to restaurants, gorging on fresh Wellfleet oysters and lobsters. They spent time walking the streets of Provincetown and climbing the Pilgrim Monument to enjoy the breathtaking view of the bay and ocean. Warmed by the sun and the salty sea air, Philip and Alex became more comfortable with each other. They began to confide in each other as friends, exploring previously taboo subjects.

"Philip, how come you're so uptight much of the time?" They were walking along the beach, shoes off; pants legs rolled up, letting the surf lick the bottoms of their feet. "Diane tells me that it's because I'm insecure, as a result of many disappointments in my life. Of course, I don't really think that's the case. It's that my feelings are always intense, whether it's about architecture or about people."

Philip continued, "After all, I never gave up on you when you didn't live up to your father's expectations. I felt there was something in you that would, in time, come to the fore. When you were my student, I thought that your talent for dealing with development was frankly stronger than your efforts with architectural design. Also, when you and Lila married, I thought it brought out your caring side that you had tried so hard to suppress. She's a wonderful woman and a perfect balance to your sometimes irritatingly gruff personality."

For these three days, cell phones were turned off, severing contact with all possible problems. On the fourth day, the landline at the Grant house rang insistently. Alex was in no hurry to answer it but on the sixth ring he picked it up.

"Alex, this is Chip Stewart. I've been trying to call you for days and I finally got your secretary to give me this number."

"What's wrong?" Alex was brusquely shaken out of his relaxed, vacation mode.

"No, no. Nothing's wrong. I've been trying to get in touch with you to give you the good news that the bank has agreed to increase the construction loan that you requested. I just thought you should know right away."

Relieved, Alex answered, "It's about time! When can I start to draw on the new line?"

"You can sign the note when you get back to the city," said Chip. "It's just a formality and as soon as you sign, you can initiate a draw," adding, in his most formal Connecticut voice, "and as you know it's based on the level of completion of the work."

"Yes, yes, I understand," answered Alex, impatiently pleased by the good news, "and, thank you."

"Philip," he called out. As there was no answer, he ran outside and looked down to the beach where he spotted Lila and the Cortas lounging under an umbrella. He ran down the two-story wooden steps leading from the top of the dune to the beach and tripped at one point, catching himself on the handrail before almost falling. When he reached the bottom, his loafers dug into the sand before he had a chance to remove them.

Hearing her name called out, Lila turned to see her husband, in a tee shirt and striped shorts snaking his way toward the umbrella. "For heaven's sake, Alex, take off those ridiculous shoes. You look like a drunken hippo trying to run."

Alex stopped for a second to slip off his shoes and ran to fall at the feet of his wife and friends. Breathlessly, he said, "You'll never guess who just called." After explaining what had just happened, he added, "Get yourselves together. We're going out to the best restaurant on the Cape for a celebratory lunch....on me!"

Two days later the Cortas left to return to the city, and Alex spent the rest of his vacation on the Cape, relaxed in a way he had rarely experienced. The pressure of getting the commitment letter no longer weighed him down. Even when the Cortas left and his children returned from camp, he felt no sense of urgency to return to the City just to sign the commitment letter, and instead took the time to enjoy his children, more than he had done in a long time. For once, he could play, play, play.

FOURTEEN
The Fall
September 11, 2001

PATRICK AND SAM ARRIVED AT the site at 7:30 on a bright, blue, September morning for their regular Tuesday meeting. There was not a cloud in the sky; the air smelled fresh, and, as Sam noted, was free of pollen, allowing him to breathe without wheezing. After a tedious hour-long review of the status of the construction, Patrick donned his hard hat with the swirling Eden Center logo and suggested to Sam that they take the lift to review the progress of the work on the topmost-framed floor that had reached 30 levels above the ground.

The Eden Center now dominated the low-rise neighborhood of nineteenth century red brick industrial buildings that were interspersed with the occasional walkup apartment building and a few vacant lots owned by speculative developers hoping to cash in on the hoped-for success of Eden.

The lower floors of the office tower, which they passed as the lift rose upward, were now clad in alternating bands of brilliant bronze-tinted glass and insulated bronze panels. The nature complex was similarly enclosed in matching bronze panels. The other two towers were still partly naked with their steel skeletal framework, the bones and muscles, exposed and the beginnings of the circulatory and nervous systems, the ducts, wires and pipes, stepping upward.

As they exited the lift, they both donned dark glasses to shield their eyes from the intense morning sun that hung above most of the buildings in the southeast. The long arm of a crane mounted near the center of the tower was slowly turning, revealing a steel beam hanging from its hook.

Following the progress of the beam as it approached the north face of the building, both men saw an airplane, which seemed to be flying lower than usual, turning toward them in the distance. "What's the fucker doing up there?" said Sam. "Probably lost," said Patrick, chuckling as both men resumed watching the steel beam being jockeyed into position on the floor. As the jet came closer it became difficult to talk until the sound became a screaming wail as the plane roared past them overhead. *Well, that's worth a call to the FAA*, thought Patrick.

Two dozen blocks farther south, Jules Naudet, a French videographer, aimed his camera at a group of New York firefighters as they were examining a reported gas leak in the street, when he heard the high whine of speeding jet engines and raised his camera to point at the sound. What he saw in his lens was a passenger jet heading directly toward the North Tower of the World Trade Center that, within seconds, hit it and disappeared in a ball of fire and smoke. It was 8:46 on an otherwise beautiful morning of September 11th.

Patrick and Sam stared in disbelief at the expanding crimson and gray cloud that enveloped the top of the Trade Tower and both exclaimed in virtual unison, "Oh, my God." The sound from the crash arrived within a fraction of a second, followed by a pressure wave that gently shook the naked steel frame of the Eden Towers.

Patrick exclaimed, as he turned toward Sam, "What the hell is going on, here? This is crazy! We've got to do something." Sam pulled off his glasses but could not move. He stood, as if hypnotized by the disaster he was witnessing. Heavy plumes of smoke were pouring out of smashed windows near the top of the tower and orange flames licked at the aluminum skin of the building.

"Sam, pull yourself together," yelled Patrick. "There must be people trapped in that tower. Get down to the ground and clear the site and send our guys downtown to see if they can help with any rescue efforts."

With tears in his eyes, Sam slowly headed for the lift while Patrick took his phone out to call Alex.

Alex slept soundly, as he had ever since returning from the vacation in Truro, but was up early as he planned to see Chip later that day to sign the commitment letter. Lila had stayed up late the night before and asked him to get the children their breakfast and prepare their school lunch before putting them on the school bus. He was now lying on the couch in his study with a cup of coffee in his hand when the buzzing of his cell phone shook him out of a daydream he would later not remember. "What?" he moaned into the mouthpiece.

"It's Patrick. Have you heard what's happening down here?"

"Another problem? Is the building OK?"

"Not our building… It's the Trade Center! A plane just smashed into one of the towers and it looks serious so I've sent Sam and some of the crew to see if we can be of help."

"We can't get involved in someone else's problem. We have enough of our own," said Alex.

"For Christ's sake, this is not just some little problem. From the extent of the damage that I see, there is a good chance the Trade Tower may collapse. You've been notified!" Patrick angrily smashed down the cover of his flip-phone muttering, "I can't believe the selfishness of the guy."

Alex threw off the blanket in which he was wrapped, sat up on the couch, and turned on the TV. Before the image came into focus, the voice of the reporter spoke of an as-yet-unidentified plane hitting one of the twin towers of the World Trade Center. Authorities were not certain what kind of plane was involved and reminded the audience that in 1945, a small military plane had smashed into the Empire State Building on a foggy morning. But, of course, this was a bright clear morning.

Alex was not able to focus on the tragic aspects of this incident but instead became concerned that if potential tenants for the Eden Center feared tall buildings, it could affect the value of his project. The more he thought about this, the more anxious he became, and by the time he returned from the kitchen with a fresh cup of coffee he was faced with a news flash that told of the second tower of the Trade Center being hit by another plane. It was now 9:06 and on the screen he saw people running away from the damaged towers and occasionally glancing back, incredulous at the scene of horror that was unfolding.

Placing his coffee on the table, he now sat transfixed, staring at the images on the television and hearing the dire analysis of the commentators. Two planes smashing into the two towers of the World Trade Center was clearly not an accident, and government officials came on the air to warn listeners to stay away from downtown New York.

There were also announcements of another two planes that were flying toward the nation's capital, out of contact with air controllers. "Oh my God, what's happening," Alex pleaded as he cupped his hands over his face, scraping the stubble of a nascent beard. He was about to call up to Lila when she burst into the study. "Do you see what is going on? What does it mean? The children are in school. I should go and pick them up and bring them home."

Alex looked up at her and reassured her, "I'm sure if there were a problem at the school we would be contacted. They are perfectly safe there." In a pleading voice he added, "Sit with me. I don't know what all this means except that..." This was not the time to involve Lila in his business, his dream. "We can watch together. Perhaps it will become clearer."

Alex reached for her hand and gently pulled her down next to him. She tensed at first but allowed her arm to relax before her whole body stiffened as the image of the south tower suddenly filled the TV screen shrouded in a cloud of dust as it crumpled to the ground entombing hundreds of victims.

It was now 9:59. She was reminded of an image she had seen in school, of the flaming dirigible, Hindenburg, falling to the ground in 1937 while a radio newsman wailed, "Oh, the humanity, all those passengers...." At the time, it was a tragedy of unimaginable proportions, yet was a minor event compared to what she now saw unfolding on the television screen in front of her eyes. Debris flew in all directions, shards of steel, gray dust from crushed Sheetrock, a butterfly cloud of torn sheets of paper. "Those poor people," was all that Lila kept repeating, "those poor people." Alex was frozen, leaning forward, cradling his face in his hands, and could not speak while the disembodied voice from the screen attempted to describe in detail the scene of devastation that was unfolding with gruesome images of bodies falling from the still-standing tower until thirty minutes later, that tower too fell, leaving no sign of its earlier majesty. Lila began to gently rub Alex's neck. "What's going to happen?" she asked.

Alex turned toward his wife, a woman he had kept so distant for so long, and softly replied, "I don't know, honestly, I don't know."

"Look at me! Shouldn't you call the site to see what is happening there?" she said in a confident voice, a voice free of pity and sarcasm, a voice Alex recalled from so many years ago, all the while taking both of his hands into hers.

"You're right. I don't know what's wrong with me. Patrick called me earlier and I was somewhat short with him. I had better call him back to see what I can do to help." Getting off the couch, he added, "Don't move, I'll be right back. We'll watch together."

THE CONSTRUCTION TRAILER WAS CROWDED with dozens of workers looking for guidance from Patrick. "Guys, we're doing what we can with the crew I've sent down to the Trade Center site. The cops are worried since one of the towers collapsed, and told me not to send any more people down there, so I don't think there is any reason for any of you to stay here. Go home to your families. I'm sure they'll be happy to see you."

As the trailer emptied, Patrick sat at his desk, wondering how this catastrophe would affect the project. The Eden site was within a mile of the collapsed Trade Center Tower, and with the recovery effort that was anticipated, it would be weeks before any sense of normalcy could return to the area. In the meantime, the fate of the Eden Center would be in limbo. When he received a call from Alex, although he was still angry following their earlier conversation, he explained what was happening at the site and that there was nothing Alex could do at this time.

THE CORTAS WERE HAVING BREAKFAST in their apartment when the urgent ringing of the phone interrupted them. "Turn on your television set!" shouted the caller. Diane switched on the television in the living room and watched transfixed when she saw the special bulletin and immediately called to Philip to join her.

The announcer spoke of a plane hitting one of the 110-story World Trade Center towers, possibly an accident but no comments yet from the authorities. On the screen was the image of the wounded north tower with flames and smoke rising from every orifice of the damaged upper floors. As they watched, unable to speak, another airplane was shown flying past the Statue of Liberty headed directly toward the south tower at an incredible speed that would later be determined to be 560 mph. It appeared to be turning and descending at the same time and hit near the southeast corner of the second tower, setting off a massive fireball and hurtling debris into the streets below.

As the fireball subsided, a great gash, which covered almost a half the width of the tower, was clearly visible on its face, as if a giant monster had taken a big bite out of it. It was shortly past nine and all mention of an accident disappeared from the television commentators' observations and was replaced by talk of a terrorist attack. Philip nervously walked to the door of the apartment and said, "Oh, my God! I've got to go to the site."

"Please don't," pleaded Diane. "There's nothing you can do there. Why don't you call first and see if anyone is there."

"You don't understand. The Eden site is so close to the catastrophe and if there's a problem, I've got to be there. There's surely something I can do!"

"If you insist on going, I'm going with you. Let me grab my cameras and brush my hair." Phil knew better than to argue, and waited impatiently as Diane put together what she needed, changed into a pair of slacks, brushed her hair, applied a quick stroke of lipstick and joined Philip at the door. They stepped out of their Greenwich Village brownstone, and as they reached the street, were met by a scene of utter confusion, with people running in all directions amid the wails of police cars and other emergency vehicles filling the air.

"Come on," Philip yelled as he pulled Diane westward toward the Eden site and the river. There was an acrid smell in the air coming from dust and smoke that spread from the smoldering tower. As they reached the next main north-south street, they could see the Trade Center Towers. Diane insisted they stop as she took pictures.

Just at that moment, a great puff of smoke rose from the south tower and they watched in awe as the great megalith, a symbol of commercial power, quickly crumbled to the ground, releasing a shower of flaming debris and gray dust. In the distance, firefighters in full uniform ran toward the fallen tower, yelling to bystanders, "Get off the street. Go home."

The Cortas stood immobilized in shock as the cloud of dust rapidly advanced toward them. Phil was immediately reminded of the people of Pompeii who were unearthed looking like living statuary, having been enveloped by a pyroclastic cloud that choked the life from their bodies before they even had a chance to move.

"We can't stay here a minute longer!" yelled Philip.

"Just one more shot," said Diane as Philip tried to drag her across the street and westward toward the relative safety of the Eden site. Diane saw this moment as an opportunity to record a major historical event and kept shooting pictures of the reaction of the people who passed her, and of the destroyed tower, framed by a street lined with ocher-colored nineteenth-century buildings.

Far ahead of them were firefighters with their distinctive emblazoned helmets and slicker-clad police carrying stretchers with wounded people away from the devastation. Diane was too far away to record the pained expressions on their faces. Other firefighters were hauling hoses with nowhere to hook them up, passing hydrants where water no longer flowed, as the pipes feeding them had been severed by the falling tower.

The nearby streets were littered with shards of glass and steel, paper of all colors and shape, and the gray broken pieces of gypsum panels that once enclosed elegant offices. The wail of sirens from police cars and the blaring of horns from fire engines filled the air. It was a scene of utter chaos and confusion, a picture out of Dante's Inferno.

"Please, Philip, let me go. There are people down there whose stories I need to record." At that moment, the North Tower suddenly crumpled to the ground. It was now 10:28. Diane ran ahead and sliced southward through a crowd of people fleeing the scene of the devastation, men and women staring back in disbelief at the unfolding catastrophe, some with hands covering their mouths and noses to keep out the stench of the dust cloud, a look of fear and confusion on their faces. She aimed her camera, trying to capture their pain, and as she turned toward the fallen towers, all she saw through her lens was a cloud of dust and a broken piece of the grid-like exterior frame of a tower projecting up from the debris at a drunken angle. For a moment, it made her feel dizzy.

"Diane?" Philip called after her. "I can't see you. Please wait for me."

Philip was surrounded by the unbearable noise with the cacophony of sounds from the scream of ambulances and police and insistent blaring of fire trucks, all heading downtown. Before he could find Diane, a dust cloud enveloped him and he began to cough uncontrollably, causing him to become disoriented. He failed to notice that the passing crowd fleeing northward melted away, leaving only an occasional stray person running past him with a masked face, bleached by the wet dust.

Meanwhile, Diane, who was already closer to the fallen Trade Towers, became confused by the sounds of the emergency vehicles and dust cloud that also enveloped her. She suddenly found herself alone on the street as a man emerged from the haze and walked quickly toward her. He appeared menacing, with his clothes disheveled, unruly hair and a week's growth of beard. As he approached, he held out his hand and was trying to say something above the general noise.

Diane sought to steady herself and reached out to grab the hand that was offered her. However, the man attempted to pull her toward him and, fearing danger, Diane wriggled away from his grip and staggered backward just as an ambulance appeared out of the mist and struck her, twisting her up in the air. She tumbled backward and violently fell to the ground, striking her head on the curb. Her camera flew out of her hand and smashed on the ground, ejecting shards of glass and plastic. The ambulance stopped as the man who had tried to pull her out of the way, leaned down and tried to talk to her but, as blood oozed from the wound on the back of her head and spread over the curb onto the street, it was clear that she was seriously hurt.

Philip was more than two blocks away when he heard the screeching of the ambulance stopping, and began to run toward the sound. As he reached the next corner, he saw, through the haze, an ambulance and people hovering over a figure lying on the ground.

"Oh my god," he uttered as he ran closer and saw that it was Diane. The ambulance attendants were preparing to put her on a stretcher and he turned to them pleading, "Is she all right?"

"Do you know this woman?" one of the attendants asked.

"She's my wife." Philip had tears in his eyes and was flaying about uncontrollably.

"You had better come with us," the paramedic said. "I'm afraid your wife has been badly injured. She jumped right in front of the ambulance and we couldn't avoid hitting her."

"I'm sorry, mister," said the bearded man. "I tried to pull her out of the way when I saw the ambulance heading toward her, but she pulled away from me."

The attendants put the stretcher with Diane in the ambulance and Philip picked up the broken camera and stepped in as well, sitting on a bench facing his injured wife. As the ambulance drove toward St Vincent's Hospital, Philip watched helplessly as the paramedic placed an oxygen tube in Diane's nose and injected her with—he did not know what. The streets leading to the hospital were jammed with people who were still walking and running uptown to escape the turmoil in the area surrounding the Trade Center, slowing the progress of the trip.

During the ride, Diane's body stiffened. She vomited and almost choked before falling into unconsciousness. As the attendant cleaned her, her body started to shake rapidly and uncontrollably before falling still once more.

Philip became more and more frantic, calling out her name as the paramedics attempted to stabilize her and noted that the whites of her eyeballs reddened, a sign of internal bleeding. At the hospital she was quickly diagnosed as suffering from a compound skull fracture and a serious concussion that resulted in subarachnoid bleeding.

When Philip was allowed to see her, Diane's face appeared pale and barely visible behind the tube taped to her nose and the many wires connecting her to monitors above her bed. The only sound in the room was a steady beep – beep – beep. The attending physician arrived and advised Philip that the bleeding, caused by a torn blood vessel, was causing pressure to be applied to the brain. He warned that her blood pressure was rising and because she was still in a comatose state the outlook for recovery was poor.

Philip was lost and asked, "What can I do, what can I do? Please tell me! Oh, my god. Can I stay with her?" "Of course," the physician answered. "Is there anyone I should call for you?"

"No! …I don't know…Yes, there is someone." Philip went to the nurse's station and called Alex at home.

"That's horrible," Alex said, "after everything that's happened today. I'll come right down to the hospital."

"Thank you. I don't think I can go on alone."

Philip returned to Diane's bedside and kneeled down, burying his head in the sheets as he began to weep, all the while whispering, "Please, Diane, please come back to me." He remembered the day he first met her and relived memories of their life together. But, the thought that kept constantly going through his mind was: Why didn't I stop her? Why didn't I stay with her? It's my fault that she was hurt. Over and over again he relived the moments before the accident.

As the night wore on, the hospital became very quiet with only the occasional visit by a nurse to check on the condition of her patients. Philip fell asleep in the chair by Diane's bed, his body stretched out and his head leaning to one side. For the first time since the accident, he was overwhelmed by fatigue.

As the sun began to shine through the window on the other side of Diane's bed, there was a sudden, insistent high-pitched ringing that caused Philip to wake with a start and look at the monitor that, instead of a periodic curve now indicated a flat white line etched on the black screen. A nurse, followed by a doctor pulling a cart with an electrical instrument enveloped by cables, burst into the room and told Philip that he had to wait outside.

"What's happening?" he asked. "You have to leave now." The nurse repeated insistently.

Outside the room Philip saw Alex walking down the hallway toward him. "Thank God, you're here," Philip pleaded. "Something's happened to Diane."

For the next fifteen minutes Alex tried to find out what was going on, but received no information from medical personnel passing in the hallway until suddenly the door to Diane's room opened. The doctor stepped out, faced Alex and said, "Mr. Corta ?"

"I'm Corta," Philip mumbled.

The doctor turned toward him and said, "I'm sorry, Mr. Corta. We did everything we could, but your wife died five minutes ago."

On hearing this Philip's legs buckled and Alex moved quickly to support him and lead him to a chair. "I'm so very sorry," the doctor said.

Philip leaned forward, cupped his head in his hands, and quietly wept, whispering, "Why did you leave me? Why? I need you. Why? I can't go on without you. Why?"

Alex was unable to comfort Philip, as he could not truly understand the depth of his friend's loss. When his father had died, Alex sensed only relief. At the loss of his mother, he was saddened but could not even shed a tear. What his friend was now living through was a foreign emotion, beyond sad, in fact, beyond anything that Alex had ever experienced.

Suddenly standing, Philip said, in a trembling voice, addressing no one in particular, "I have to see her. Please let me see her."

The doctor who was standing nearby said, "Of course. You can have as much time as you need to say goodbye."

Philip entered the room where his wife had recently died and closed the door behind him. As he approached Diane he was surprised to see her face so calm and smooth, free of wrinkles, free of worldly cares and free of the tubes and monitoring cables that had so recently obscured her face and body. He touched her hand that was still warm and supple and stood for a long time looking at her silently. "My darling," he finally said, "you look so beautiful even with your eyes closed. Those sweet lips that I've kissed so often; your delicate celestial nose that I've rubbed back and forth with mine; that dimpled chin of yours full of strength; your broad brow hiding so much understanding. Oh, Diane, what am I to do without you?"

For the next hour Philip talked to his wife as if she were still living. He talked until his trembling heart calmed and he could sense her spirit entering his being. When he left the room, Alex was waiting for him. "Thank you for waiting. I'm ready to leave now, unless...."

"Don't worry," said Alex, "I've taken care of all the necessary arrangements. We can talk about it later."

They left the hospital and Philip turned to Alex and said, "Alex, you're a good friend. I know you have your own worries and I really appreciate your being with me at this time."

The depth of empathy he felt for his friend surprised Alex. He could not remember another person with whom he had felt such a connection. Although the Eden Center needed his attention, Alex spent time consoling Philip and contacted Patrick to apprise him of Diane's death. He would later make arrangements for a memorial service since Philip had told him that, in accordance with Diane's wishes, her body would be cremated instead of buried.

FIFTEEN
Aftermath
Day 1

AFTER LEAVING THE HOSPITAL, ALEX convinced Philip to come to the Grants' townhouse instead of going directly to his apartment. Lila met them at the door and hugged Philip tenderly. "I can't tell you how deeply sad I am. There are really no words that can express my sorrow for such a senseless tragedy. Please, come in and sit down for a while."

"Thank you! I do feel a bit weak in the knees."

"Of course, I understand, considering what you've gone through. Let me get you a drink."

Going to the bar, Alex spoke up. "A jigger of scotch might be just what you need."

"Thank you both. I'm not sure what would have become of me if Alex had not met me at the hospital."

"Why don't you stay with us for a few days?" Lila asked Philip. "We have a bed in Alex's office and you shouldn't be alone."

"That's very kind of you," said Philip, his eyes looking nervously around at the photographs on the walls of the Grant living room, "but I really think that I'd be better off in my own apartment. There's so much I need to do."

He was not comfortable in this room with its furnishings representing the eclectic taste of the Grants with Victorian overstuffed chairs facing an Adirondack coffee table supported by spindly branches for legs. The voices of the children also made him nervous and he vowed to leave as soon as possible and return to the peaceful environment of his own apartment.

At the same time he dreaded the constant reminders of Diane's presence... her darkroom in that blacked-out closet, her clothes on hooks behind the door that she had not had the time to hang in the closet, the sweet smell of her perfume that hung like a cloud in the air of their apartment. It was time to face the fact that she is gone, but how was he to do it? The pain of his loss was too great. After an hour he said, "I really think I should go home."

"If you're determined," said Alex, "I'll drive you to your apartment. I have to go near there anyway to check on the project."

"I'm sorry that I've taken so much of your time. I can imagine that you have rather much to deal with since work at the project stopped."

"Don't be ridiculous, your loss is more important than the damn project. So don't even think that way. You're our friend, and friends help each other out during difficult times."

"It's not that I don't appreciate your concern but..." at this point, Philip felt his chest tighten and his eyes began to tear. "I need time alone."

The city was still in turmoil with most of southern Manhattan cordoned off. Every government building throughout the city suddenly sprouted concrete blocks to keep vehicles from approaching as the fear of further terrorist attacks coming on the heels of both the WTC disaster and the damage to the Pentagon by another terrorist-commandeered plane.

There was a sense of paranoia as people gazed suspiciously at every passing person who looked even faintly middle-eastern. Driving around the city was a nightmare as many streets were blocked. It took Alex a long time to drive Philip to his apartment and he offered to take him to the door but Philip said he preferred to go in alone. Alex waited in the car and watched as Philip slowly walked up the stoop and took keys out of his pocket to open the carved wooden front door of his building before disappearing behind the closing door.

As he entered his apartment, Philip switched on the light and instinctively began to call out, "Dia…" before hesitating and placing a hand over his mouth to silence himself. For a long moment he stood in the living room absorbing the silence, then removed his glasses and wiped them with the hem of his jacket before hooking them back over his ears. No change, he noted. Still nothing. He went to the bedroom and lay down on the unmade bed, reached over to take Diane's pillow and placed it over his head, then breathed deeply, absorbing the faint remnant of her odor. He slowly let sleep overcome his resistance.

AFTER DROPPING OFF PHILIP AT his apartment, Alex headed toward his office. The city appeared paralyzed as police in riot gear guarded every government building and private guards were deployed in front of all major banks and commercial buildings. The area of Manhattan below 14th Street was still, with subways, buses and the bridges and tunnels leading to the city still closed, making the island a virtual prison. Only workers and equipment essential to the recovery effort at the Trade Center site were permitted to move about unrestricted.

Alex realized that it would serve no purpose to go to his office since it was late and there would be no one there. He turned the car around and drove home to spend time with Lila and evaluate with her the impact of the double tragedy of the past two days. Her empathy toward Philip led him to realize that she was the wife he remembered from their early marriage years; someone with whom he could be free to discuss his deepest thoughts and fears. This warm intimacy was always missing from his relationship with Claire, from whom he received relief with their brief encounters but who always remained aloof and judgmental.

"Lila," he called out when he entered his townhouse.

"Sshh, the children just fell asleep. Come to the kitchen. You must be tired and you didn't have dinner. Would you like a bite to eat?"

"That would be great." They went into the kitchen and Alex sat at the counter while Lila prepared a snack and said, "I'm glad we have a chance to talk alone after all that's happened, with the towers falling and then Diane's senseless death. That was just terrible. I'm really concerned about

Philip. He seemed so lost. I worry that he will not be able to deal with this tragedy. I hope you were sensitive to that when you took him home."

"You're right," said Alex, ignoring the undercurrent of worry in his wife's voice. "I'm not sure that Philip can handle this. He's more than just broken up. On top of that, I don't know what's going to happen to the project. I'm afraid that the bank will see all this as a reason to pull the loan."

Lila placed a small plate of cut sandwiches on the counter and leaned down to place two fingers in front of Alex's mouth saying, "Please don't bring up the project now. Too much has happened in the last forty-eight hours that has turned our world upside down but nothing can be done about it right this minute. Maybe after a good night's sleep you will be better equipped to consider your options. Then, we could discuss them together and see what we need to do for Philip and also see if we can find a way to make certain that the project doesn't fall apart. I love you and know how much Eden means to you. I will do whatever is necessary to help."

Alex stood and took his wife in his arms and kissed her. "Do you know that this is the first time in a long time that you've said you love me?"

"That's because for so long you made me so angry and had moved so far away from me. Now, I feel we're closer than we've been in a long time.

Alex felt his fatigue fall away as he led his wife to their bedroom.

Day 6

The ghosts of the thousands of souls lost in the fall of the towers cast a pall over the city as the identities of the terrorists who perpetrated this tragedy were revealed and the organization of the conspiracy led by Al-Qaeda leader Osama bin Laden became clear. This prompted fears of further terrorist actions and calls for revenge, causing suspicions between workers at the site, who no longer trusted some of their coworkers with Arabic names and, irrationally, turbaned Sikhs as well. The death of Diane Corta, compounding the tragedy of 9/11, cast a pall over the project. Furthermore, the constant presence of police around the site added to a feeling of vulnerability and unease among the workers. The Eden site had been shut down for the week following 9/11 with only essential workers remaining, as all available manpower was diverted toward a recovery effort and debris removal to facilitate finding possible survivors at the site of the former towers.

On the Monday following the fall of the Trade Center Towers, the city awoke from its fretful slumber. With the dawn came an understanding of the depth of the tragedy while work at the site of the former towers moved from a rescue and recovery effort to an investigation phase as the chance of finding more survivors dimmed.

While this event dominated the news and would do so for many weeks and months, a level of normalcy returned to the areas of the city away from the immediate vicinity of the fallen towers, yet the consequences of the attack would forever change people's sense of balance and security. Few workers were at the Eden Center site as Mike had sent most to participate in the recovery effort at the WTC site. When Sam arrived late that morning, he walked directly to Patrick's trailer. "Sorry, I'm so late but driving into town was a real bitch, the police were still checking cars at the entrance to the tunnel, slowing traffic to a crawl."

"I can imagine," said Patrick. "I walked, and even though I left very early, it took me almost an hour."

"Well, where do we go from here?"

'You know," Patrick began, "This business of the death of Corta's wife coming on top of the Trade Center tragedy has really hurt our project. I don't mean to be cold blooded about this but who the hell is going to want to live and work in a tower after what's happened? I talked to Alex this weekend and he seems worried that the bank may reconsider their loan."

"We're so far along. You don't really think that they would stop the project, do you?" asked Sam.

"I wouldn't put it past those greedy bastards," said Patrick. "They're happy to lend you money when everything looks rosy. But if there's a problem—bang! They cut you off. Anyway, we've got a more immediate problem. Alex wants to hold the memorial service at the site, using the unfinished interior public plaza. It's going to be held next Sunday, so we're going to have to get the place cleaned up. It seems that Diane Corta would have wanted Philip to scatter her ashes over his greatest project.

"That's a bit weird," said Sam. "It's like having a cemetery in the middle of the site."

"It's only ashes," said Patrick. There's no stone or anything like that. Beside, there's plenty of dust and ashes already all over the site. No one will know the difference."

"I still think it's a hell of a way to remember someone you love."

Reluctantly, Sam called Mike to arrange for a crew to prepare the space for the memorial service.

Day 8

THE DAYS PASSED UNDIFFERENTIATED FOR Philip. He would wake late in the morning, make himself a cup of tea, and butter a piece of toast topped with marmalade. On the third day the milk smelled a bit sour and on the fourth day there was no more bread. He thought about shopping to fill the empty cupboards but could not bring himself to act on it.

To pass the time and avoid thinking of the terrible loss he had suffered, he watched the unfolding news on television. At first, he had not been aware that in addition to the two planes that hit the World Trade Center, there were two other hijacked planes, one of which crashed into the Pentagon and the other that fell in a field in Pennsylvania. More and more information was revealed about the origin of the hijackers and the route they followed from their homes in the Middle East to their deaths in the crumpled and fallen aircraft.

There were stories of survivors who talked about their co-workers, trapped in the fallen towers and unable to make their way out, and of families who had lost husbands, wives, children, fathers and mothers.

Philip found it difficult to sympathize with all these sad people who had suffered their own tragedies, since the daily memory of his own wife's death completely consumed his thoughts. Other times of the day, he spent at his table overlooking the garden, absent-mindedly moving papers around and unable to let his mind complete a thought.

As it had done every day, the dreaded phone call came in the early afternoon. Lila invited Philip to dinner and said that Alex would pick him up at six. Every day, Lila found a reason for their needing to get together. Most often she said that details of the memorial service needed to be arranged. At other times, she insisted that Philip needed nourishment, as he was not eating properly while dealing with his grief. Finally, she said that she needed Philip's help in going through Diane's photos for an eventual exhibit that had not yet been scheduled but for which she was negotiating a venue. Philip responded to each invitation with, "It's sweet of you but I need some time to be by myself and,…" This was not acceptable to Lila who would argue strenuously until Philip acceded to her wishes, but every evening after dinner, Alex would drive Philip back to his apartment where, once again, he would collapse on his bed under the weight of his loss.

On Friday before the scheduled memorial service, Philip ventured out by himself for the first time and walked the streets leading to the Eden site, undisturbed by a light rain. When he arrived at the site he was accosted by a burly steelworker who walked up to him and hugged him tightly, saying, "I'm sorry, man. She was a beautiful woman and we all loved her." Throughout his wanderings around the site, one worker after another would greet him with a warm handshake or a hug expressing sympathy for someone they seemed to consider a colleague, and for whom they felt great respect. "It shouldn't have happened," said one carpenter foreman.

Since Diane's death, Philip had not really focused on the fact that it was an accident that could have been avoided. This suddenly made him angry, pulling him out of his lassitude. Why didn't he stay at Diane's side when she walked down that street? Didn't she hear the ambulance coming out of the mist? What caused her to pull away from the man who could have saved her? Couldn't the ambulance have avoided hitting her? However, it seemed that the answers to these questions had melted into the fog of the general confusion that existed on that fateful day. Philip left the site and walked home to wait for Alex to pick him up for dinner.

At the appointed time, Alex was surprised to see Philip waiting for him, sitting on the stoop in front of his brownstone, and even more so when he was immediately bombarded with questions about the accident.

"Get in the car and we'll go over it again," Alex ordered.

Reluctantly, Philip squeezed into the right seat of the Porsche and sat silently with his hands in his lap waiting for some revelation from Alex. He was met by a veil of silence until, as they approached the Grant townhouse, he finally said, "Well?"

"Well what? I told you that you're going to have to accept the fact that Diane's death was an unfortunate accident. The street was clouded with debris and there was almost no visibility. It's no one's fault. Not yours, not the ambulance driver's, not the Good Samaritan's who tried to save her."

"You don't understand. My Diane died pointlessly. Whom should I blame? God?"

"I understand how you must feel but..."

"You can't possibly know how I feel."

"Please, Phil, before we go in, try to calm down. You'll upset Lila if you keep talking like this. Why don't we just have a nice dinner together and think about what still needs to be done for the memorial service. I know, for instance, that Lila is trying to decide what music would be appropriate."

Exasperated, Philip blurted out, "All right! I don't want to burden Lila with more of my problems. She's been such a wonderful help to me already."

"Believe me, Lila has been more than anxious to help out. She loved Diane and loves you and wants to relieve you of any extra worry."

Lila greeted Philip with a long, strong hug that momentarily unburdened him of his grief and reminded him of Diane's warm embraces. Over a glass of scotch before dinner, the conversation centered on the question of music with Philip explaining that Diane preferred the classics and was therefore not a great lover of popular music but that she did love *Annie's Song* by John Denver. "That's so appropriate," said Lila, "as that song celebrates love and mirrors the bond between the two of you."

"That's settled, then," said Alex brusquely. "So, can we have dinner? I'm starved."

Lila turned toward her husband and looked annoyed at this sharp utterance that broke the mood of her concern toward Philip's feelings. Later, when they were alone, she would reprove him for his insensitive remark.

Day 12 (Sunday)

Less than two weeks after the tragedy of 9/11, traveling in the city was still difficult, with police checking cars driving through the many bridges and tunnels that guarded access to Manhattan Island and an enhanced police presence evident in subway stations and the bus terminal. The site of the collapsed towers reminded Philip of scenes of bombed-out sections of London he had seen as a young child after the war, with crews working to remove massive amount of debris.

Thousands of workers were engaged day and night to clean up the site in anticipation of building it anew. It was a process that would eventually take eight months, with trucks carting the detritus of the fallen towers to dumpsites on Staten Island and in New Jersey. These trucks could be seen and heard roaring past the Eden site.

Warding off a steady rain, a sea of umbrellas sheltered the mourners arriving on this Sunday morning at Eden Center for the memorial service for Diane Corta. The cavernous space that was to house the eventual public plaza and pool had been cleaned for the occasion and fitted with folding chairs facing an altar, in reality just a tall, square wooden table, on which sat a simple terra cotta urn and a photograph of Diane. Next to the altar was a lectern fitted with a microphone connected to a speaker that sat on the floor. In keeping with Philip's wishes, there were no flowers other than a single red rose in front of the portrait of Diane. Playing softly in the background was *Annie's Song*, looped to play over and over again.

> *You fill up my senses, like a night in a forest*
> *Like a mountain in springtime,*
> *Like a walk in the rain*
> *Like a storm in the desert,*
> *Like a sleepy blue ocean*
> *You fill up my senses,*
> *Come fill me again*

Behind the altar, the huge wall that was eventually to be glazed was framed temporarily with a wooden grid to which were tacked sheets of translucent plastic that made whooshing noises as they flapped whenever light wind gusts passed over them, just as if they were sails.

The first arrivals for the memorial were a group of workers who wanted to pay their respects toward the little lady with a camera dangling from her neck, for whom they had developed a warm affection. Since the front two rows of seats were cordoned off with a thin yellow tape, they were ushered toward seats further back, causing one of the men to grumble, "Ain't good enough to sit in the front, eh!" He was quickly told to stop crabbing by one of the women in the group.

Mike, Marion, Sam and Jan arrived together, followed soon thereafter by Patrick. Other early arrivals included the Stewarts and Claire Fletcher, who was accompanied by Mayor Bartlett. The space filled slowly, while waiting for the arrival of Philip and the Grants.

Alex and Lila had promised to pick up Philip to take him to the service but when they arrived at his building and rang his bell, there was, at first, no answer. Becoming concerned, Alex rang the bell more insistently. "What's the matter now! He knew we were going to pick him up…. The man will be late for his own funeral!"

"Give him a minute," said Lila, "and don't be so nervous. After all, the man lost his wife and he is having a difficult time dealing with it."

After what seemed to Alex to be an interminable time, the buzzer to open the downstairs door sounded. "Wait in the car," Alex called out to his wife. "I'll get him!"

The door to the Cortas' apartment was unlocked and Alex pushed it open. The apartment was in disarray with clothes dangling from the lounge chair in the living room and one shoe lying in the middle of the room while another waited in front of the bedroom.

Philip called out from the bedroom, "Please sit down for a minute while I finish dressing. I couldn't get to sleep until three in the morning and I'm afraid I overslept."

Alex did not respond immediately as he tried to control his frustration but finally said, "Lila thought that's what might have happened but listen old buddy, we're going to have to move along since we're already late."

It took another ten minutes before Philip appeared in his usual black jacket over a black turtleneck shirt and black pants. His glasses could not hide the redness of his eyes and his hair appeared barely combed as Alex hustled him to the car.

When they arrived at the Eden site and entered the place reserved for the memorial service, they saw, in the aisles, clusters of chatting people, who quickly scattered back to their seats. While Philip and Lila took their seats in the front row, Alex stood at the lectern and asked, "Before we begin, can I ask that we observe a moment of silence." After a minute, he continued, "My wife, Lila has asked to begin this celebration of the life of Diane Corta."

Lila, in a black dress that clung to her ample curves, stood up, and, gathering some papers from her purse, walked over to the lectern. Taking a moment to gather her thoughts, she said, "You'll have to forgive me if I seem hesitant. I'm not used to speaking in public. I usually leave that to my husband. However, on this sad occasion I felt that it was important." She looked around the room and put both hands on the lectern to steady herself and began speaking in a halting voice.

"On this day in this month and this year, this memorial service for Diane Corta is one of so many going on in cities and towns all over this country and in fact in other countries as well. They are being held to remember each of the thousand of our friends, neighbors, mothers, fathers and children lost in such a horrendous attack on our way of life. Many of you here have already attended other memorial services or soon will do so. I lost a dear friend in a senseless accident on September 11, an accident that would not have happened had the Towers not been attacked."

Lila took out her handkerchief and, turning away from the audience, wiped her eyes as she stared at the picture of Diane that was placed against the urn containing her ashes. Composing herself, she turned back and, looking directly at Philip, began, "Philip, during her life, I had too few opportunities to know Diane but I cherished every one of those times we did meet and talk together. You may remember that the four of us first had dinner together almost ten years ago. Since then I've had the pleasure of getting to know Diane better. Only six weeks ago we spent a glorious week together on the Cape. I'm so glad that the four of us had that last time together."

"She was my life," interrupted Philip.

Lila took a deep breath and continued, "She was a wonderful person, warm, kind, caring and always involved as a listener. I can't tell you how many times I came to her with my problems. If she could have charged me for these therapy sessions, she would have been rich. It is tragic that her life was cut so short and in such a senseless manner, but yet in her 51 years she was able to accomplish what most of us never complete in a lifetime.

"She used to tell me that whatever she achieved in life, she owed first of all to her parents. From her father, who was a professor of history, she learned the value of forever being inquisitive, as the family used to sit at the dinner table discussing issues of the day and world events. Her mother provided stability, compassion for others, and an understanding of the value of patience. Growing up outside of Boston, she could have become a spoiled only child, but her parents constantly challenged her to discover new ideas and to listen to others.

"By the time she entered Smith College, she was far ahead of her classmates in having a balanced worldview as well as a considerate and respectful way of dealing with her peers. Steering away from her father's discipline, she decided to explore the world of art. I've seen some of her drawings and they're good, but they were not good enough to satisfy her sense of excellence, so she concentrated on learning what makes good art. That's what drew her to you, Philip, and I heard all about how the two of you met. It was so romantic…"

She stopped to wipe away a tear and after a pause began again. "In college, she developed an eye for what constitutes a good photograph, but through you, she discovered that architecture and construction could become her canvas. I'm not talking about mute images of things but rather dynamic portraits of the act of building. Those portraits she created were her children and will be her legacy.

"Then, of course, there was the love the two of you had for each other. That can never die, even if she is no longer here in person. It is her spirit that lives on and that will comfort you every day. I don't know what else to say except that I miss her, as I know you do. We all miss her."

When she finished, Lila walked over to Philip, who had removed his glasses and was wiping his eyes with his handkerchief, and embraced him. They held each other for a long time before separating, as he thanked her for having given such a caring eulogy.

There was a long moment of silence after Lila took her seat. Alex then stood and invited others to speak; Mayor Bartlett and one of the iron-workers spoke of Diane's spirit and contribution to a better understanding of the gritty nature of the construction process. Sam spoke for the construction team, recalling her special relationship with the workers on the site and the respect they developed for her. All of Philip's architectural team then stood to honor her, as Ricardo Vegas, his chief architect, turned to face the participants.

"Philip, we have not worked for you that long, but in that time we had the honor of getting to know Mrs. Corta. I speak for the whole architectural team when I say that she was a jewel and that without her mediating influence on you we might have had difficulty staying with you. You are a demanding boss and…" The architect next to him pulled at his sleeve to get him to stop. "Mrs. Corta always reminded us that you were under great pressure and that we should not take your impatience as a sign of disapproval. Anyway, because of Mrs. Corta, we will honor her memory and stay with you as long as you want us to and need us." He sat down quickly as a murmur rose in the crowd with smiles on the faces of some of the participants.

Alex then thanked all for coming.

As the mourners filed out of the service, they either hugged or shook hands with Philip while expressing their condolences. When Ricardo extended his hand, Philip smiled and reached out to hug him. "Thank you. I didn't know," he said.

As Claire left, she briefly looked at Alex but they did not speak. When all had left, Philip asked Alex to carry the urn and walk with him to a far corner of the site where he uncovered the urn and let the contents spill to the ground saying, "You'll always be here for me." As the ashes reached the wet ground, they mostly dissolved into a gray mud.

SIXTEEN
Betrayal

Day 20 (Monday)

ALMOST THREE WEEKS AFTER THE collapse of the trade towers and the death of Diane Corta, the appearance of normalcy was returning to the Eden site. Workers wearing light parkas to protect them from a cool morning mist streamed past the front gate and disappeared into the bowels of the towers, each heading to the site of an assigned task.

Sam met with the foremen for the various subcontractors, urging them to accelerate their normal pace of work in order to make up for some of the lost time. In the office of the Urbanland Corporation, Mike was busy reviewing a stack of accumulated papers when he noted that he had not received payment on his last monthly invoice. Although he attributed this to the recent tragic events, he was concerned that he would soon be pressured to pay his subcontractors so he placed a call to Alex to find out what was holding up payments.

The timing of payments on a construction project is often part of an elaborate dance between the parties, with developers and contractors each trying to delay in order to gain a few more days of interest on the floating money. At the bottom of the pyramid, the subcontractors had no float since they were obliged to pay workers weekly, even if they had to borrow the funds.

When Alex received a call from Mike, he tried to stall, claiming that the delay was caused by a banking slowdown resulting from the interruption of electronic transmissions at the Trade Center site. "And, by the way, I received a call from Jim Hammersmith last Friday that concerns you."

Instinctively, Mike tightened the grip on his phone. "What about?"

"You'll be happy to know that the FBI has decided to drop the inquiry into your immigration status. It seems they're too busy with their terrorist investigation and also cannot find sufficient evidence to continue with your case."

Relieved, Mike took a deep breath, releasing the tension in his chest. "I told you there was no problem, just a bureaucratic snafu." Unconvinced, Alex let his doubts slip away as he had more immediate concerns and tried to call Chip at the bank. He was told that Mr. Stewart was in a meeting and could not be disturbed. "Have him call me the minute he is out of his meeting."

A SECTIONALIZED MAHOGANY CONFERENCE TABLE that dated from the founding of the firm in the early twentieth century dominated the boardroom of Losey & Sons. Surrounding the table were fourteen high-backed leather chairs, six on either side and one at each end.

The bank president, Arthur Griswold, had called an emergency meeting of the investment committee to review outstanding loans that may be impacted by the Trade Center disaster. Among the loans being discussed was the one to Grant Development Co. for the Eden project. Mr. Griswold sat at one end of the table with a recording secretary next to him and three members of the committee on each long side of the table.

"Stewart," said Mr. Griswold, "could you walk us through the numbers on this loan?" All eyes turned to Chip, whose face, on hearing his name, flushed even though the room was cool. He licked his dry lips while deliberately opening a folder and began,

"You will note that we recently approved an increase in the construction loan, but of course, that was before the events of 9/11. At that time, the numbers clearly showed that this was a well-balanced project with a high estimated return. In fact, I was going to recommend that we make a commitment to a 30-year balloon mortgage. In view of recent events, I've had second thoughts. The projected income stream is dependent on a minimum 85% occupancy for the project as a whole. Also, the two public facilities produce no income other than from concession stands. Although the needed occupancy may develop over time, it now seems that it will take at least five years or more to regain the confidence of the public willing to work and live in this part of the city. Regretfully, I now no longer believe that we should provide a long-term mortgage."

"What about the construction loan?" asked one of the committee members.

"I've given that some thought," said Chip, "and believe we should call the loan but give Mr. Grant time to allow him the opportunity to secure alternate financing."

Before reaching a decision, there ensued a heated discussion started by one of the newest members of the committee of the wisdom of providing such a risky loan in the first place. Since Griswold was instrumental in originally approving the loan, he squelched this as being a hindsight look at a *fait accompli* and closed further discussion.

When he returned to his office, Chip drafted a letter summarizing the decisions reached at the board meeting.

October 1, 2001
Dear Mr. Grant:

At a meeting of the loan committee on this date, it was decided, in view of recent events, to deny your request for a mortgage for the Eden project. Furthermore, the changed economic climate forces us to call for a repayment of the original loan extended to you on the 10th of March 2000 as modified on August 8, 2001. Therefore, the president of Losey & Sons has directed me to request repayment of this construction loan. You are hereby notified that the total capital and interest in the gross amount of $84,659,000 is payable in full on or before the 31st of December 2001.

We regret the necessity of taking this action but a review of the financial projections for the Eden project resulting from a reevaluation of the market in downtown New York bring into question the future financial viability of the project.

Sincerely yours,

/ss/

Charles Stewart

Vice President

Alex was in his office when a messenger delivered this letter. His secretary placed it on his desk and turned to leave as Alex looked down at it, jumped up and exclaimed, "Son of a Bitch, these bastards can't do this to me!" Walking around his desk as his secretary reached the door, he yelled out, "Close the door behind you!"

If there was one thing that Alex learned from his father it was that development is a risky business in which you can be on top of the world one day and bankrupt the next. But he was also told "Don't play with your own money" because if an investment fails you risk losing everything that you have built up over time. This was the situation that Alex now faced, as he had already invested a considerable portion of his personal wealth in the Eden project and could not afford to lose it in the threatened foreclosure.

He considered his options. He could try to approach another bank, but in the current atmosphere of fear and uncertainty about future development in downtown Manhattan, local banks would hesitate to provide loans until a degree of clarity returned. This was unlikely to occur in the near future and he had less than two months to refinance his project. Perhaps he could explore offshore options. Foreign investors had been actively seeking opportunities for investments in the US, but again, it seemed unlikely that such a deal could be achieved in such a tight time schedule. However, there was another option!

Day 22

FROM THE OFFICES OF THE Goldenrod Group on the 45th floor of a black-clad tower in midtown, the landscape of high and low, stone and steel buildings could be seen scattered in every direction. Joshua Golden, a man in his late middle years with an oval face topped by a thin crown of receding grayish hair neatly parted on the left side, sat behind a glass-topped desk on which was placed a computer monitor he used to keep track of his properties.

The desk was centered between a sheer glass outside wall and an interior partition that was interrupted by a door that led to his secretary's station and the rest of the firm. This arrangement allowed Golden to look out at the panorama of the city while entertaining visitors who would sit facing him and a white wall on which hung a large Brice Marden painting in brooding colors.

Golden had not been surprised by the telephone call he received from Alex Grant asking for a meeting. He recalled his last conversation two months earlier in which Grant appeared supremely confident, compared to the respectful tone he projected on the telephone last evening. Always impeccably dressed, Golden pulled down the French cuffs of his oxford shirt on which were embroidered the initials JAG, adjusted his paisley blue tie, and buttoned his double-breasted pinstripe suit as he stood to welcome his guest.

As he approached the desk, Alex stretched out his hand. "It's good of you to see me, Mr. Golden, especially on such short notice."

"Please, call me Josh and I'll call you Alex. We don't have to be formal in our dealings at this time. Please sit down."

"That's an interesting painting behind you. With its vertical bars in brown, blue and yellow it reminds me of the Trade Towers…. A real tragedy!"

Turning to look at the painting, Josh replied, "I see what you mean, but, why don't we get down to business. I can guess why you're here. You've reconsidered my offer. Of course, you understand that I've been advised of your problems with the bank, so anything I can offer must acknowledge the changed conditions resulting from the collapse of the Trade Towers."

Alex sat forward in his chair. "Mr...Josh, I'm not here as a beggar. You understand that the property I'm developing has great value as evidenced by the interest of everyone who has seen it. You should also know that a group of foreign investors who have an interest in helping finance its completion have approached me. What I'm looking for is a short-term bridge loan."

"Alex, let's not dance around the real issue. You have less than sixty days to come up with a large sum of money or the bank will foreclose on your construction loan, and you know perfectly well that foreign investors cannot, and do not, act fast enough to prevent such a foreclosure. So, as far as I can see, unless you have another local developer willing to take a chance on this risky project, I'm your only hope. Can we agree on that?"

Alex stretched his arms across the desk, clenched his fists and let them fall to the top of the desk. "I don't know," he said. "You may be right but you have to understand that I've put my life into this project and a healthy part of my wealth, so failure is not an option for me. Here," and he took a stack of papers from his briefcase and handed them to Golden. "Look at these stats. I'm sharing with you all the financial and construction information on the project. Take a couple of days to review it, and then let's talk about what you can do and what I can accept."

Golden leafed through the papers Alex had handed him and after a moment said, "These seem quite complete. OK, give me a couple of days and I'll get back to you and see if I can do anything to pull you out of the fire."

New York developers often acted like a club, helping each other out, because the failure of any single project could hurt the chances of other projects being concurrently planned or built. It was, therefore, in Golden's interest to find a way of preventing the foreclosure of the Eden Center. Of course, the price he would impose for this munificent act on his part would be quite steep.

Alex left the meeting feeling that his dream project could fall apart.

He wished he could talk to Philip, but decided that it would be an unfair added burden for his friend to bear. He had asked Claire to help him with the financing of the project, but that was before the events of 9/11. Clearly, Claire could no longer provide any help once the bank issued its foreclosure letter. Instead, he drove home and asked Lila to join him in the study as he unburdened himself of his fears.

"Sweetheart," he said.

"It must be serious because you haven't called me sweetheart in a long-time."

"I'm afraid it is. You know that the project financing was always on the razor's edge. Foolishly, I've used a great deal of our money to carry the project forward, and now, the events of the past few weeks have caused the bank to reconsider their loan. We could lose almost everything we had built up over the years of our marriage."

Lila listened intently and held out her hands, "I love what we have here, but it's not the material things that I ever cared about. Remember that the most wonderful, loving years we had together were when we lived frugally and worked on the Berkshire camp together. Now, we have two wonderful children and have recently renewed our love for each other. Those are what matter to me. I don't need fancy things when we love each other."

On hearing her soft, confident and loving voice express thoughts that he had forgotten about, Alex took her in his arms and allowed tears to blind him, saying, "I love you and I promise that I'll do anything necessary to keep our family together even if I have to give up the project." It was a promise he was not certain he could keep.

AFTER POSTPONING IT FOR SEVERAL days, Alex met with Patrick to advise him of the possibility that a partner may be brought into the project to assist with financing. "Will it affect the design of the project?" asked Patrick.

"Let me worry about that. For now, that's not your concern," answered Alex.

"Well, I am concerned about how it could affect the construction. We're well advanced and any changes could set back completion of the project."

Becoming impatient with Patrick's argumentative attitude, Alex raised his voice. "I don't need any damn new issues brought up right now. I've got enough to deal with just to get the project back on track. And, by the way, lets just keep this between us. I don't want the crew or even Phil hearing about this."

"OK, boss!"

When Alex left, Patrick sat for a long time looking out at the site, at a project that was the most dramatic he had ever undertaken, which was now in trouble. Finally, he said out loud, "Well, if that's the way it's going to be...." He picked up the phone and placed a call to a friend in Chicago.

SINCE HE HAD NOT RECEIVED payment on his last invoice, Mike advised Sam to delay the introduction of subcontractors needed to finish the project. "Keep working, but don't rush," he said.

As a contractor, he relied on a bank loan to allow him to pay his workers and subcontractors prior to receiving payment from the developer. He was not eager to incur additional interest payments on that loan, since it would simply cut into his potential profit. Furthermore, Urbanland Construction Co. was close to reaching the limit of its line of credit from the bank. The time had arrived to confront Alex, so he dialed his number.

"This is Mike," he said when Alex answered. "I thought you were going to get back to me after our last conversation. I don't see a check and I'm going to have to shut down the site unless I receive payment by the end of the week."

"Hold your fucking horses," said Alex. I don't like to be threatened. I told you I'm working on it. After everything that's happened in the past month, you just have to be a little more patient."

"I've been patient, and I'm not threatening you. This is business and I need a check on my desk by Friday morning. Please, no more excuses!"

After hanging up the phone, Alex realized that he was running out of time and decided that he needed to place a call to Golden who, it turns out, was out of his office. "Please tell Mr. Golden that it is important that I speak to him today. He can call me back on my cell phone."

Golden did not return the call until after five in the afternoon. "What's so urgent that could not wait until morning?"

"A situation has come up and I need to know if you are still interested in the project."

"I've given it some thought and I would be quite interested under certain conditions."

"What do you have in mind?" asked Alex.

"This is really not a conversation we should be having over the phone. Why don't you meet me at seven at the grill in the Four Seasons? I'll reserve a quiet table where we can have a nice chat."

Upon his arrival at the restaurant, Alex was ushered to a table sufficiently separate from others to afford a sense of privacy being set against a golden wall. *That's an appropriate coincidence*, he thought.

Without arising from his chair, Josh pointed to the opposite chair and said, "Sit! I've taken the liberty of ordering some small dishes so we won't be disturbed during our conversation. Hendrick's martinis OK with you?"

Somewhat flustered, Alex answered, "Fine."

Golden, in a clear, autocratic tone, turned to the waiter standing by the table and placed the order for the drinks. "And when you bring the food, just put it in the middle of the table and leave us be." Turning to face Alex after the waiter had left, he said, "Yes, it is a beautiful project and you should be proud of it."

Somewhat taken aback, Alex answered, "Thank you. I certainly am proud of it and consider Eden to be the best project not just from my personal viewpoint but the best new project in the city. Look around town! There is nothing else like it. It's possibly the most important addition to the cityscape since Rockefeller Center."

"I'm not sure I would go quite that far but we can agree that it has potential. So, where do we go from here?"

The martinis arrived; Alex pulled his glass closer and rolled the stem between his fingers. "As you know, the bank is playing games with me and I need to develop a bridge until this situation can be straightened out."

Josh took a sip from his glass and responded, "This situation, as you call it, is simply that you've run out of money and need a partner. We've looked at your financials and are prepared to offer you a proposal."

Alex suddenly felt he was being put in a defensive position, took a quick sip of his drink and sought to turn the conversation around. "Of course, it depends on what you have in mind."

"Alex, my friend, as I said, it's a beautiful project and I salute your architect. But—and I say this after having carefully looked at the details of the project—it does not completely make financial sense. The office tower, residential tower, and hotel all are eminently developed. But, the nature walk, plaza and pool make no economic sense. Consider the large volume of the building that these two elements occupy and look at the potential return on investment, and you have to agree that they are financial losers."

"Maybe, but these give the project its character and if they have to be subsidized by the other parts of the project, so be it."

"I'm sorry Alex, but any project I invest in has to be economically sound and no part should rely on another for its financial viability. No Alex, if I am to invest with you, those two elements must change. I realize that the structure is already built so we have to live with it, but the functions have to change to introduce profit-making ventures, or possibly non-profits that will, with reduced rents, afford us a tax advantage."

The food was brought to the table: popcorn shrimp, crispy oysters, and Chinese dumplings placed in the center of the table. Josh took samples from each dish and placed them on his plate.

Alex continued nursing his martini. "Those 'losing elements,' as you call them, are the heart of the project and you're proposing to cut them out. It would emasculate the project."

"Don't be so emotional about it," interjected Josh, "I've had my people look into alternatives and they've come up with what I consider real gems."

"I'm listening," said Alex as he absentmindedly picked up a shrimp.

"Have you ever been skiing in the Alps or even out West?"

"Yes! What's the point?"

"In those alpine villages there's always a street climbing up toward the entrance to the lift, and it's lined with shops to entice you to buy the latest fashions or gadgets. Well, your nature walk would make a perfect Alpine Shopping Street. And unlike your garden, the rents would make the venture profitable."

"My architect will never go for that."

"Let me remind you that you provide your architect with a program and he has to develop it. If he won't do it, get another one!"

"You don't understand. Phil's my friend and he had as much to do in creating this project as I did. His vision is the reason I was able to get it approved by the local community, which had been vociferously against any development in the area."

Waving a finger in Alex's face and raising his voice, Josh said, "And now, if you go bankrupt, then there will be nothing left of the project. Is that what you want? At least hear me out."

"OK, OK, and what else did your whiz kids come up with?" said Alex sarcastically.

Looking up to signal to a passing waiter, Josh asked, "Bring my friend and me another round please." Turning back to face Alex, he said, "If you didn't like the Alpine Street idea, I can imagine what you'll say about the other concept we've developed. Anyway, that space below the nature walk is ideal for a large hall. Have you ever heard of the Rev. Stephen Devereau Honeycutt?"

"Can't say I have."

"He happens to be one of the most charismatic television preachers in this area and he is looking for a space where he could install a mega-church. I've heard him, and he's got real flamboyance and sex appeal, with a message that almost leads me to convert, so I can see why he draws in such a large congregation. He reminds me of the Rev. Schuller and his Crystal Cathedral in Los Angeles."

"And you know what happened to that group. They went bankrupt."

"If you're not going to hear me out without so much sarcasm then this conversation's over."

"Sorry! But, you must understand how frustrating this is for me."

"And you had better open your mind to other possibilities or you won't have a project."

For the next half hour Josh described all the changes that needed to be made as a condition for him to invest in the project. He concluded by defining a proposed partnership whereby he would provide the financing in exchange for a majority ownership position. In addition, if Corta were unwilling to make the proposed changes, he would bring in his own architect.

Before the meeting, Alex had resigned himself to having to give up some control of the project, but the conditions that Josh proposed were so onerous that he delayed responding while weighing his options. The more he thought about it, the more he realized that he had run out of options and that if he were not to agree, he would be forced into foreclosure. Then, the bank would take over his project and he would lose his substantial investment.

He considered his promise to Lila that he was willing to give up the project to keep the family together, but nevertheless said, "You've got me against the wall but at least give me credit for what I've accomplished by making us equal partners."

Josh sat upright and leaned across the table. "You don't understand. It's 55/45 or no deal!"

Feeling defeated, Alex stood up and slowly extended his hand. "But this does not mean we have to be friends. As you pointed out before, this is business."

Josh stood and the two men shook hands. "I'll have the papers drawn up, and when you sign, the bank will get their check." Ever the shrewd negotiator, Golden did not reveal that before arriving at this deal, he had obtained commitments for substantial tax incentives and even a cash subsidy from city and state officials. These funds had become available in the aftermath of 9/11 as the government sought to encourage investment in construction in lower Manhattan. Since the Eden project was already underway, the Mayor convinced the federal government to provide funds that would guarantee its completion as a beacon of rebirth for the area.

As it turned out, the financial incentives meant that Golden did not have to provide any of his own money to complete the project. Alex realized that such incentives were available, but his financial needs were immediate and, knowing how slowly the government works, he did not think there was enough time to prevent a default. He wished he had been in a better position to negotiate a more equitable participation with Golden.

But now, as he turned and left this meeting, Alex was at least assured that although he had lost a large measure of his dream, his project would be completed and he was still involved, although he now lacked the leverage to control its destiny. *Lila would understand*, he thought, but as he walked out of the restaurant, he tried to imagine how to tell Philip to make the changes that had been imposed as a condition of Goldenrod's involvement. Philip, whose own life had been turned upside down with the loss of his wife, his anchor, would now be faced with the prospect of being asked to compromise the artistic and social integrity of his masterpiece. How could he be asked to do it when it was all he had left that gave meaning to his life?

Alex decided not to confront Philip with such a painful choice when he was so vulnerable. He decided instead to first let Patrick know what had just taken place so that preparations for the disruption that was likely to follow could be started. However, after he went home and spent the next morning with his family he thought it best to wait for the contract to arrive and sign it to conclude the deal before involving anyone at the site.

Day 24

WHEN ALEX FINALLY WENT TO the Eden site on Friday, he was surprised at the silence: no hammering, no machines rumbling, no sputtering pumps, no whirring motors. He asked the guard at the gate what was happening and was told that the general contractor had suspended work.

Furious, Alex walked rapidly to the construction office and yanked open the door, causing it to slam against the side of the trailer. As it banged, Patrick and Sam turned to face the open door.

"What the fuck is going on here. Who gave the order to shut down this job?" yelled Alex.

Sam answered first. "Mike called first thing this morning and told me to send everyone home. Apparently he had not received his last payment and could no longer carry the project."

Alex's face reddened and the veins in his neck stood like Greek columns supporting his head. "That son of a bitch. I signed a contract last night that will give him his goddamned money today. He had no right to stop the work. I'll have his ass for this. It's a violation of our contract. Just tell him that… never mind! Get him on the phone."

Patrick dialed the number for the Urbanland home office and when Mike answered, handed the phone to Alex, who immediately screamed, "You had no fucking right, no right at all to stop the work. I promised you payment and you'll get it today. Now get the crew back to work."

In a voice that flowed like molasses, Mike answered, "Before you give me any orders, you had better talk to your partner. He called me first thing this morning and said the site would be closed until changes could be made to the plans. "

"What?" Alex was stunned and momentarily held the phone away from his ears and looked at it in puzzlement. "What partner?"

"Mr. Golden also told me that you and he had made a deal that, from now on, would require me to work with him on financial issues. "

Alex dropped the phone and walked out onto the site and, leaning against the side of the trailer for support, stood stunned by the news. When he regained his composure, he walked further away from the construction trailer to give him the privacy he sought and took out his mobile phone to call Golden. As he waited for the phone to be answered, he wondered what had led to this confrontation. Only weeks before, Eden had been his project alone and now he had to share control—not only control, but he also was being treated like an employee of Goldenrod rather than a partner. A voice over the cellphone broke his reverie. "Hello, this is Josh."

"This is Alex and I don't know what kind of rules you're playing under but I really resent the way you've taken over this project." He spoke calmly and in full control of his emotions.

Golden would not let him finish before interrupting him. "When you signed our agreement, you gave up financial control of the project. I hope that was clear! You didn't think that when I provided the needed funding to finish the project that I would just let you continue along the same losing path you were on, did you?

"In case you didn't read it, our agreement puts me in charge of money matters and you are responsible for the development, which, by the way, means you have to make the necessary changes to plans in accordance with our discussions. So, either your friend Corta will change the silly nature walk to a commercial street and the plaza and pool to a mega-church or you had better find someone else to do it. And, until those changes are made, the job will remain closed."

For a moment, Alex was frozen in place but when he regained his composure, he replied, "You should have checked with me before shutting down the job. As you say, I'm in charge of development and I could easily have shifted construction to those areas of the project that are not affected by your proposed changes. It makes no sense at all to simply stop everything and, even from your viewpoint, no financial sense, because

205

you will be paying overhead while no productive work takes place. With your experience in development I would think that you would know that." Alex felt a sense of renewed confidence as he waited for Josh's reply.

"Well, I wanted to make a point."

"You've made your point. Now let me get on with my work and tell Mike to open the site. I'll get your goddamned changes made."

"Maybe you're right," Josh replied and after a pause, added, "OK, I'll give you ten days to get new plans ready because I'm planning a reception right after that to introduce our partnership to the folks at the City. One last matter; I'm bringing in one of my own managers to work with your man Connolly. I want my own eyes and ears on the site. He'll start in two weeks."

Alex was mildly disturbed with this last statement but realized he had won a major concession and walked back to the construction trailer to announce triumphantly that the work would restart. As he presented a summary of the changes that will take place on the project and the need to concentrate on the completion of the towers while new plans are being developed, Alex did not mention that the site office would have a new occupant, a representative of the Goldenrod Group.

It was now urgent that he tell Philip of the needed changes to the plans, and called him to meet later at the architect's office.

Corta's office consisted of a large drafting room with eight desks, on which sat large computer monitors and keyboards. Each desk had a side table holding stacks of drawings. Drawings of the Eden project were pinned along one sidewall, showing elevations of the buildings from four sides as well as a bird's-eye rendering of the project. Along the opposite wall were three large windows from which the Eden site could be seen behind nearby brownstones.

Philip's working space was in a separate room furnished with a drafting table facing a window and a small conference table with six chairs, more than he ever thought would be needed. Philip had not come back to the office since Diane's death and in the interim his architectural team carried on the work.

When Philip received a call from Alex, he was at home and was not prepared to return to work, but Alex insisted that it was vitally important that they meet. "Can't you tell me what this is about?" asked Philip. "No! We have to meet in your office."

It took almost an hour for Philip to shave, dress, and walk to his office where Alex was already waiting impatiently. "What took you so long?"

"I'm sorry but I was not prepared to go out. Now, what was so important that you could not discuss it over the phone?"

Alex waved his hand in the direction of the conference table. "Let's sit down." After a moment, when the two men took seats on opposite sides of the table, he continued, "I didn't want you to hear this from anyone else but I've had to make a deal with the Goldenrod Group that will affect part of the project."

Philip interrupted, "I don't understand."

"Please let me finish. You know that the bank recently extended their credit line. But in view of what happened on 9/11, they decided instead to call the loan. You realize that, of course, I had to find another source of financing and the opportunity came up with Goldenrod. Josh Golden offered to provide the financing for a share of the project. Now, here's the part that affects you. Golden insisted on increasing the future project revenues by converting the nature walk to a commercial street and the pool and plaza to a megachurch."

Philip stood, causing his chair to topple backward. "I don't believe this. You know, Alex, that those were the only functions that gave the project its unique character. How could you agree to this? It's a violation of everything I've tried to accomplish. You've betrayed me."

Angrily, Alex replied, "You don't realize, I was up against the wall and could have lost everything so I had to take the deal."

"I can't be part of this. I just won't do it!"

"I'm sorry Phil, but you have to or I'll get someone else to do it. At this time, your prima donna attitude just won't fly."

Philip walked toward the door. "I can't! I just can't." As he walked out he turned for a moment and said, "Talk to Ricardo," and walked out.

Ricardo, who months earlier had helped to create mock drawings to further the cause of seeking the increase in financing, was a pragmatist. He would recognize the necessity of making the changes that were demanded while exerting enough aesthetic control to keep the final appearance of the Eden project as close as possible to Corta's dream. It seemed to Alex that assigning the task to Ricardo, whose loyalty to Philip's vision was clear, was better than trying to find another architect to make the required changes.

So, after Philip left, Alex called Ricardo into the office and described the extent of the plan changes that were required, and explained that the work would have to be completed in less than two weeks. Ricardo, who was used to working on design charettes, requiring an architectural design to be completed by working day and night, accepted the challenge as long as he was not placed in the position of violating Corta's design aesthetic.

"I understand that perfectly and I want you to keep the outward appearance of the design as close as possible to the current one." Of course, Alex did not reveal the reason behind the changes and saw no necessity for doing so, as Ricardo asked only for the details of the programmatic aspects of the new design requirements.

For the next week the architectural team worked diligently to prepare a set of drawings that could be presented to the contractor reflecting the changes that had been dictated by Golden.

After several days had passed, Alex came to Corta's office to view the progress of the work and to provide encouragement to the young architects who had been working diligently to meet the imposed deadline. When he saw the incomplete state of the drawings, he began to worry that the work would not be finished in time, and pressed Ricardo for an explanation.

"This is not an easy change," Ricardo said. We have to deal with the fact that much of the structural work is complete and try to minimize the amount of demolition that will be needed to fit the new uses into these existing spaces."

Alex explained that money was not an issue, speed of completion was! If the plans could be delivered in time, Josh would then have to deal with the financial consequences.

By the ninth day, an exhausted Ricardo delivered a completed set of modified drawings to Alex and the construction team. A copy was also sent to Golden who, after looking them over, smiled in a self-satisfied way, knowing that his presentation to the business community could go forward. But first, he asked an artist in his office to prepare a colored perspective of the interior of the church and another of the shopping street. "And, give it a little pizzazz," he ordered.

Day 40

The Reception

ALEX AND LILA ARRIVED EARLY at the Eden Center on the day of the reception. Where five weeks earlier the interior plaza was used to host a memorial service for Diane Corta and had been decorated in muted colors, now there were hanging banners in bright yellows, reds, and oranges covering the gray concrete walls.

A screen with the faintest outline of a figure on a cross hung over the immense glass facade, and colored renderings rested on a-frames around the room showing the proposed transformation of this space into a bright cathedral. One illustration showed the great glass façade with a giant cross and a Christ-like figure in stained glass illuminated by lights, both on the inside for night-time views and on the outside for daytime emphasis. Another illustration showed a balcony behind this crystalline wall that was to provide needed additional seating and seemed to float between the two sidewalls. The altar in front of the narrow back wall was shown as a marble slab supported by two marble piers. On the side walls of this proposed cathedral were indicated colorful banners with printed images of biblical scenes.

The press would label this as "the ultimate kitsch" and an "irreverent monstrosity," but some people would embrace it for its dramatic imagery and cathedral-like quality, with its nave illuminated in multiple colors by sunlight streaming through the stained-glass wall during the days and electric lighting at night.

Along the back wall, other renderings illustrated the developer's vision of the alpine shopping street with its cobble-stoned walk and colorful boutiques in faux half-timbered frames lining each side. A moving side-walk in the center of the walk was shown to lead customers to drop-off points along the slope.

Where the altar with Diane's photo had stood only weeks earlier, there was now a sturdy podium with chairs for honored guests and a lectern fitted with a microphone. It reminded Alex of the day well over a year ago, when he first introduced the project to the world, standing on a shaky platform on the edge of a muddy field. He was now within one of the buildings he had then only visualized. As they walked around the room looking at the various renderings, Alex became visibly uncomfort-able, nervously looking around to see if anyone was watching him, but it was Lila who first spoke up.

"I thought you wouldn't accept such a tragic mangling of the project. Have you forgotten what you said a few weeks ago? Does Philip know what is happening? I can't believe he would agree to this… this cheapen-ing of his ideas."

Alex took Lila brusquely by the arm and led her to the back of the space and opened a plywood door, into an unfinished room. "I really can't talk about this now. We have to get up to the podium in a few minutes, but I know you're right and I'm sorry. Philip will die when he sees this but you have to understand, I had no control over this change. Once I made the deal with Golden, I lost control of the project but if I had not made a deal, we would have lost everything and I just couldn't let that happen. So, please let's try to live through this day. I only asked Ricardo to change the use of the spaces. These pictures are only artists' renderings. It may not be as bad once we see these illustrations developed into finished spaces. Besides, I doubt Philip will be here because he was not personally involved in the design change."

"You could have refused and I would have understood. Now I don't know what to say. I feel that you haven't kept your promise."

"Look, I'm sorry, but I can't undo the deal. There's no time now to discuss this further because the reception will start and we have to go to the podium."

Lila felt the blood draining from her cheeks. Her eyes exploded with horror as she was suddenly struck by the realization that the man to whom she had been married all these years, the man for whom she gave up dreams, that man was so selfish that she could no longer believe that he cared for her.

Taking a deep breath to compose herself, she said, "You go alone. I'm not going to stand on the same platform with your Mr. Golden." Holding back tears, she added, "I could never face Philip after that. I told you before that I was willing to give up some of our material possessions but not my self-respect. You told me that you felt the same way, but now I don't know what to believe and I'm not sure how I now feel about you."

Lila turned away from what she now realized was his betrayal. "I'm leaving."

Shocked and annoyed and in a sharp voice Alex said, as she walked away, "Fine, have it your own way, but at least wait for me outside," and made his way through the gathering crowd toward the podium. He passed Patrick, Sam and Mike who were standing together and waved to them without properly greeting them. Mike turned to Patrick and said, "I guess your boss doesn't want to talk to us. He seems upset but I don't know why. He should be happy that he found someone willing to put up new financing and with only minor consequences to the design."

Just then they saw Lila coming out of the back room and standing against the back wall of the hall with her arms folded and a pained expression on her face before moving toward the exit.

"Trouble in paradise! Maybe that's why Alex looked so glum," said Patrick.

Sam turned to Mike and said, "By the way, those minor changes you talked about are not so simple. For instance we have to add a balcony in the back of the 'church' to provide additional seating. That's a major structural change and as far as the shopping street, we will need to introduce a stepping scheme for the stores and also that moving sidewalk. I've looked at these in a preliminary manner and my guess is that we're talking about at least $30 million more."

Mike was not unhappy to hear this, as he had been looking for ways to increase his fees and saw this as a great opportunity. "Don't worry about this now. I'll have a detailed estimate prepared and I'll negotiate with my new 'financial' boss, Mr. Golden."

Patrick spoke up, "Good luck, and I hear he's a tough negotiator."

With a smile on his face, Mike answered, "Maybe, but he hasn't yet dealt with someone from the inscrutable east."

"Anyway," Patrick said, "It will be someone else's problem because in less than two weeks I'm out of here."

Both Mike and Sam turned in surprise and said almost in unison, "What do you mean?

"Well, Golden is bringing in his own man representing him and I'm not one to share responsibility with anyone. Anyway I've only got a few years before I retire and I want to enjoy them, so I decided to leave. I've have already notified Alex of my intention. I'll be going to Chicago to work with an old friend as a partner in a new development company."

"We'll sure miss you," said Sam. "I considered you a real friend as well as a guy that I could work with and after what we've been through on this job, I don't know if I can develop the same relationship with the new guy."

Mike said, "Good luck! I know that working for Alex hasn't been the easiest but you've been great to work with."

"Thanks guys. I'll miss you too."

"The hell you will," said Mike with a smile.

Sam turned to look at the door opening beneath the glass wall and exclaimed, "There's Ms. Fletcher in the arms of the mayor. She does get around, doesn't she?" Since her breakup with Alex, Claire had been seen in the company of a number of different men in business and government, all of whom were in the category of "movers and shakers." However, for the past few months her constant companion had been Roger Bartlett, serving his second term as New York's mayor. Bartlett was a charismatic man in his early fifties, twice divorced, used to being the center of attention and proud to be seen with beautiful, younger women whom he could subjugate.

Claire, after deciding to end her relationship with Alex, sought a greater degree of influence in future relationships with men. Her pairing with Bartlett, therefore, seemed unlikely were it not for the fact that her intelligence attracted him in ways he hadn't expected. No longer did she stand behind the man in power but she now stood next to him. Bartlett, for his part, not only accepted this equal relationship, but also became reliant on it and looked forward to their time together, so much so that he was prepared to marry this extraordinary woman. However, Claire was not ready to move that quickly. She preferred to keep their relationship close but not yet totally intertwined.

When Alex, who had arrived at the edge of the podium, saw Claire, he stepped forward to greet her and Bartlett and invited them to take their seats. "Where is Mrs. Grant?" asked Claire. "She prefers to stay out of the limelight," answered Alex and quickly turned away to greet other guests.

As the hour of the presentation approached, the hall filled quickly. In the front row reporters from the major municipal news outlets occupied the seats closest to the lectern. Behind them were representatives of the municipal government and the bank.

Chip Stewart sat nervously fidgeting with papers in his hands. Since sending Alex the default notice on the construction loan, Chip had been actively working with Josh Golden to transfer the loan to Goldenrod and to establish a new loan limit. Golden was one of the best customers of Losey & Sons, which carried a number of his mortgages, so Chip was careful not to offend him or cross him in any way.

Unlike Alex, who operated on the edge of fiscal responsibility, Golden had a substantial portfolio of profitable properties and was a good risk. However, even with the changes that Golden was making to the Eden project, Chip was uncomfortable with the level of return that was projected. It was simply too much money being spent to build such a visionary project with only marginal returns from rents. Furthermore, Chip considered the Church idea to be a risky venture, since he remembered the Crystal Cathedral's bankruptcy and so many other radio and TV preachers who ran into either moral or financial difficulties with their ministries. Once the space has been configured for a mega-church, it would be costly to reconfigure it for a more commercial use.

These questions weighed on Chip's thinking as he considered whether to communicate his doubts to the bank president. But the bank had a long history with the Goldenrod Group and Mr. Griswold, the bank's president, had often expressed his confidence in the judgment of Josh Golden. After the debacle with the Grant loan, Chip feared that his position at the bank might be in jeopardy should he say anything. Also, as it now stood, it was the bank president and the loan committee, not Chip, that had made the commitment to Golden for the Eden project. In fact, Chip was no longer directly connected to the project. So, he felt a little more secure and relaxed as he tore the letter he had prepared expressing his doubts to the bank president, and put the torn pieces in his pocket.

Philip arrived without being observed, as he wore a navy pea jacket and had a cap pulled down over his eyes. He made his way slowly around the room.

The assembled crowd was becoming a bit restless when, accompanied by the Rev. Honeycutt, Josh Golden climbed to the podium and went directly to the lectern.

"Good afternoon, ladies and gentlemen I'm Joshua Golden and I'm sorry I'm late but I had to pick up a little surprise for you. The Rev. R.D. Honeycutt, whom many of you may know from his television ministry, has graciously agreed to accompany me today for his first visit to this magnificent space that is to become his church, his new home, the anchor of his ministry. Before I ask him to speak to you, let me first tell you what is happening to this great project that my friend, Alex Grant, has had the daring to develop.

"As with all great enterprises, there came a time when Alex needed a partner to help him in reaching his goal. I'm grateful that he had the confidence in me to let me be that partner. When I first saw the plans for Eden Center I was awestruck by its imaginative blending of different elements and I said so to Alex.

However, upon closer examination I concluded that two of the elements were incompatible with such a commercial venture and with the neighborhood in which it stood. I approached Alex with two suggestions that he enthusiastically supported, well; maybe he was not totally enthusiastic. What I suggested was that this space in which you are now seated become a church to serve a nationwide audience, including some who will be lucky enough to be right here when the Rev. Honeycutt delivers his sermons. In reality, this space has the grandeur to be more like a cathedral than a simple church.

Now, moving upstairs, I have always been in love with those lovely alpine ski villages and their cobblestone streets lined with little boutiques selling everything under the sun. Well, here I have the chance to create just such a village street. In fact, we have already negotiated with a number of major retailers to develop these shops. They see this as an incredible opportunity to get away from the blandness of a typical shopping mall. Look around this room and you will see illustrations of both of these new ideas that will make the Eden center even more dramatic than it originally was. Now, let me..."

Philip had been listening to this introduction and had become more and more agitated as he walked around the hall and looked at the renderings hung on the walls. Finally, he could no longer contain himself, and as he reached the edge of the platform, yelled out, "What about the joy that a nature walk and public plaza and pool would bring to the people of this city. What you propose is purely crass commercialism and a betrayal of this community." He jumped up onto the platform and grabbed the microphone from Alex's hand and continued shouting, his voice breaking from tension and his free arm flailing about, "I've been betrayed, and more that that, this community has been deceived."

Taking control of his anger, he added, "This is not the project that they approved and I can't believe that they will stand for such a vulgar change." Turning to face the podium guests, he continued, "Claire, you know, what I mean, you were there. ...." And left in disgust. Claire was visibly shaken by this outburst and turned to whisper something in Mayor Bartlett's ear.

Golden stared at the departing figure and said, "Sorry for this interruption folks," and turning to Alex, whispered, "If that was your architect, he's finished."

"We'll talk about this later," answered Alex.

Gathering his thoughts, Josh said, "As I was about to say, perhaps Alex Grant, the developer of this project would like to say a few words."

Shaken by the outburst from his friend, Alex walked up to the lectern and, looking around the room, sought out Lila, who was long gone. He hesitated before speaking, "Many of you around this room know me and know that I would not agree to make any substantive changes to this magnificent project that my friend, and the architect of this building, Philip Corta designed. Philip, who just walked out, is understandably upset that any changes to his vision should be undertaken, but you can be assured that I would not allow the commercial needs of the venture to diminish that vision. What Josh Golden just described to you represents a modification of only a small portion of the project and one that will not materially change its appearance. In effect, it changes the interior use only..."

"What about the glass face of the church with its cross, Isn't that a major change?" one of the newsmen shouted out.

"Nothing is etched in stone yet and there will be further studies and community board input before the final design is ready."

Another reporter asked, "If that was your architect who just walked out, was he consulted about these design changes?"

Somewhat flustered, Alex blurted out, "All these questions will be answered after the conclusion of the presentation, so please hold off until then! Josh, would you like to continue?"

Alex stepped back as Josh moved to stand in front of the microphone. "It gives me great pleasure at this time to introduce the Rev. Honeycutt who has asked to say a few words."

Honeycutt jumped up from his seat and strode confidently to the lectern with his arms stretched out like a bird and a smile on his pear-shaped face. In a high pitched voice, he said, "Bless you, bless you all."

A tall man with a sturdy build, Honeycutt didn't just occupy the stage, he commanded it. His eyes shone like lightning bolts landing on all members of his audience. With his bear-like hands he possessed the air around him. Wearing a loosely fitted rust-colored suit, he stood apart from the other guests on the stage. "I'm rarely at a loss for words but being here today in this magnificent space humbles me. Ever since Josh Golden first suggested that this place might become the seat of my ministry, I have prayed to the Good Lord that it might come to pass. Now, as I look around this room, I can't wait for the day that I can stand on a podium that will be located on the far end of what will be the nave of our church and can consecrate it in the name of Jesus Christ, our Lord. So now, I urge you to pray with me."

Bowing his head and intertwining his fingers close to his chest, he continued, "I am your servant, Lord, and will do your bidding in all things. Give us the strength and the means of accomplishing the great task that is before us, to transform this heavenly space into a great cathedral to serve you and allow your flocks to worship you. Amen."

There was absolute silence in the room as people didn't know whether this signaled the end of the proceedings or whether there were other speakers until Josh stepped forward and, taking the microphone from Honeycutt's hand, said, "Thank you Reverend for these uplifting words. Before we break up I would ask our mayor to say a few words."

Mayor Bartlett turned toward Claire before stepping up to the lectern. "There is nothing more that I can add to what has already been said. I do want to remind the developers that there will be further review before this change can be finalized. Nevertheless, I still believe that the Eden Center represents a giant step forward for a city in recovery from the tragedy of 9/11." He thanked the two partners on the development side for their willingness to move dramatically forward when so many others had hesitated. At the conclusion of his speech, reporters moved toward the podium to question the mayor, the pastor, and the two developers while the crowd slowly exited the room.

One man waited in the back of the room until the group in front of the podium began to thin out. Under his arm he clenched a copy of today's *Post*. As he moved away from the back wall, he smiled and let the newspaper fall to the floor. It opened to a page with an advertisement for a sale at a local department store and a column of national news. In the top right corner, a paragraph had been circled. It read:

> Early Friday morning a car was discovered abandoned on the side of the road outside Waterboro, South Carolina. Two men in the front seat of the car had both been shot at close range. The local sheriff determined that one of the men was a fugitive wanted in connection to a murder earlier in the year at a construction site in New York. He was identified as, Justin Cameron. The other man carried no identification. The sheriff is asking local residents for information to help in identifying the assailants.

When he saw his chance, Bruno Guardini moved quickly to intercept Josh Golden before the latter had a chance to leave the room. Bruno introduced himself and explained that since there were still many months of construction left before this project would be finished, he offered to guarantee protection of the site and its occupants for a reasonable fee. Josh agreed that this was desirable but said that the details should be worked out with his field representative who was now in charge of the site. Within a week, Bruno managed to extract a contract for protective services without the knowledge of Mike and Sam, who were now powerless to change it.

As the reception was coming to an end, Alex looked for Lila, who he found standing at the corner of the site, where a temporary wooden plaque was nailed to a post that marked the spot where Diane's ashes had been deposited. As he reached her side, he said, "What are you doing here?"

"I even heard Philip's outburst out here but I couldn't face him. He was right in saying that what's happened was a betrayal. I just don't understand how you could have agreed to such a tasteless change to the design."

"Be reasonable," Alex exclaimed. "First of all, I never saw the renderings before. They don't necessarily reflect how things are going to look. Those are just Golden's jazzed up illustrations and I know that even if Philip won't work on them, Ricardo is talented enough to turn them into something more acceptable....even to you."

"I don't know. You can't imagine how sad this is for me, especially standing here, when I think back to Diane and the friendship we had together. Alex, we have to do something for him. You can't let him feel that you don't care. You have to go see him and explain and convince him that you will do what is needed to return the design to something closer to his vision."

"I don't know. His ideas about the garden and all that, well, it's gone and I can't bring it back."

"But," Lila interrupted, "you can assure him that what's now planned for those spaces will be more tasteful. Please, you need to do this."

Exasperated, Alex responded, "OK, I'll see him tomorrow."

"No!" said Lila, "That's too late. We'll both go to see him now. You owe him that."

"We don't even know where he is."

"Then we'll look for him at his apartment."

Alex knew better than to continue arguing and took her by the arm to lead her to his car.

When Philip left the reception, he was angry. Angry at Alex for agreeing to change his design, angry at Ricardo for changing the drawings, angry at himself for being helpless to prevent these changes to what he felt was a perfect balance between commercial needs and public good. He feared the reaction of critics to what had been previously hailed as a brilliant addition to the urban landscape. How could he face his peers, who would judge him a failure, having capitulated to a developer's greed?

Diane. What would she have said? If only she had been here, she might have advised him how to deal with this. But she was gone and he felt frightfully alone. For the next few hours, he walked along the river, watching the flow, dreaming that it could carry him out to the Atlantic, perhaps all the way back to England where his career had begun.

A new beginning...but that was foolish. There could be no new beginning as this time represented the end of his career. He turned away from the river that beckoned him and before nightfall, he approached his brownstone and was surprised to see Alex's car parked in front. "What are you two doing here?" he asked when he saw both Alex and Lila sitting in the car.

Lila answered, "We had to see you to try to clear up what happened at the reception. Can we go to your apartment to talk?"

"I don't know what you could possibly say," said Philip, "that those images around that room did not make perfectly clear."

"Look Phil, I think I can convince you that what you saw is not the way it will turn out, I promise you we'll get it back on track. Please, let's talk."

So many broken promises, thought Philip, but at Lila's insistence, he reluctantly agreed to have the Grants come to his apartment. For the next hour, Alex tried desperately to convince Philip that the proposed changes can be made in such a way that the overall aesthetic image of the project is not destroyed. "You don't understand," said Philip. "The public spaces were intended to give the project a human quality to balance the utilitarian parts of the project."

"What's more human than a church?" replied Alex.

"I didn't see anything uplifting in those gaudy illustrations. We're not talking about a classic Gothic church but more like a cartoon version."

"Alex assures me that these were only illustrations and that Ricardo had nothing to do with them," interjected Lila. "If you trust Ricardo, I'm sure he can turn it into a more classic and aesthetically acceptable form."

"You have to understand, Philip, that my arrangement with Golden keeps me in control of the development as long as I stick to certain financial guidelines" said Alex. "Well, the change in the use of the spaces was his idea but how it is done is my responsibility. Believe me, I want this part of the project to reflect your vision to the greatest extent possible. After all, a negative response from the press and the public would reflect badly on me as well."

"I know you're trying to make me feel better but..."

"I'm not trying to make you feel better, I want you to see that I'm on your side," said Alex.

"I know you both are trying, but I don't know. Let me sleep on it. And Lila, thank you for being so understanding. Without your understanding, I know the two of you wouldn't have come to see me tonight."

Alex was about to speak when Lila gently pushed him toward the door and said, "That's a good idea. Sleep on it and we can talk again tomorrow or whenever you want."

Once the Grants had left, Philip looked around the room that held so many memories of Diane, and thought, *I don't know what to think. It's possible that Ricardo could develop a design for that church that was not so god-awful. I trust him but do I trust Alex to keep his word? I want to believe, but I've been disappointed so often that I don't know if I still can. Dear Lila, she is such a sweet person and was so close to Diane. I know that she will do whatever she can to see that Alex keeps his word. So many questions! I don't know if I can deal with them any more. If you were only here, Diane, you would know how to guide me. You were always able to clear up my muddled head.* He lay down on the bed, as he had every day since her passing, and breathed in the last whiff of her perfume.

WHEN THEY RETURNED HOME, LILA turned to Alex and said, "I want you to sleep in the study. I really can't be with you any more tonight."

"You're taking this Philip thing totally our of proportion. It's got nothing to do with us, with our relationship."

"It has everything to do with the way I feel about you. And, if you can't understand that, then I don't think we can stay together. Perhaps you should leave tonight."

"This is crazy." Grabbing Lila roughly and shaking her, he added, "This is my goddamned house and I'm not going to be kicked out by you."

Lila pulled free and stepped back. "First of all, it's our house, not yours, and I'm not afraid of you any more, and I want you to leave now."

Alex moved toward her, raising his hand to strike her, when he saw his daughter coming down the stairs. He stopped and turned to leave, his voice shaking with rage. "This is not over. I'll be back."

The daughter ran to her mother, who took her in her arms as both sobbed.

WHEN CLAIRE WAS DROPPED OFF at her apartment she went over in her mind how she must proceed, since she had made clear to Roger that the current proposal must not be permitted to proceed as illustrated. Philip's outburst at the reception clarified what she must do. Since she was responsible for helping to obtain the necessary variances from the community board that made the Eden project feasible, it was now important that the conditions imposed at that time must be enforced.

At the reception she had already convinced Bartlett to remove an unconditional endorsement of the changed project in his prepared remarks. Now she must contact the community board and ask them to review and hopefully reject the proposed changes. She was mad. Mad that Alex had used her, mad that Alex could so easily bypass a review. After all, Golden was not privy to the history of the project, but Alex knew full well that this proposed change could not be made without a further review by the community board. Now, she was not going to allow this review to take place without her presence and input.

The next day, Alex was notified to attend a community board meeting to discuss the outstanding changes to the project. Golden did not attend but made clear to Alex that he was to make certain that the changes be approved.

The meeting was held in a boardroom with a long table accommodating the twelve board members with chairs along the walls for guests and observers. Alex sat in a chair on one side of the room while Claire, as a consultant, sat at one end of the table. A discussion ensued at which Alex was asked to describe the changes made to the approved project. "It doesn't really materially change anything except some of the interiors of the project," Alex said. There was much questioning concerning the loss of community facilities and the substitution of commercial elements. "You have to understand that the project has to be financially feasible and we could not keep all these non-paying elements in the project," Alex explained.

"What do you have to say to that, Ms. Fletcher?" the board chairman asked.

"Mr. Grant knows that he was granted an increase in the buildable area of the project in exchange for having public facilities within the project, which should have been sufficient to provide a strong financial base."

Alex stood and glared at Claire. *That bitch is trying to torpedo me*, he thought.

A heated discussion ensued with some board members vehemently opposed to the proposed changes and some willing to consider at least some of them. Late in the evening, Claire suggested a compromise. Let the developer keep the commercial use of the "alpine walk" but return the church to its public use as a garden and pool with maintenance provided by the developer.

"That's impossible," shouted Alex, as he did not want to endanger his contract with Golden. After almost an hour, he was finally convinced to think it over and discuss it with his partner. Reluctantly, he promised to do so, and left the meeting without acknowledging Claire.

When Josh Golden heard from Alex that they had to eliminate the church, he was furious. "I thought the project that you shared with me did not have restrictions on it. This is not only irritating but it is a personal embarrassment for me. How do I tell the Reverend Honeycutt that he won't get his church? I'm frankly disappointed in you."

"For Christ sake, Josh, you said yourself that the church is not a moneymaker. So, you have to eat a little crow. So what! A few pennies difference in rents and we can easily make up the small income we would have gotten from the church. Let's just move forward." After a long pause while Josh walked over to the window and looked out at the city landscape, he said, without turning to face Alex, "All right, but, I'll remember this." A public announcement of this change would not become public until the following Monday.

Alex left the room sheepishly and picked up his cell phone to call the community board chairman to announce the acceptance of the terms of the compromise. He thought of calling Philip to make him aware that the most distasteful part of the changed plan was gone, and returned to a public garden. "No, that wouldn't accomplish anything." He thought of going home but home was now a midtown hotel room and that was not what he wanted. Instead, he headed for his favorite restaurant and immediately ordered a double scotch on the rocks.

Day 50

Acceptance

FOR MANY DAYS, PHILIP WEIGHED the arguments that the Grants had made in favor of trusting Ricardo's aesthetic judgment in translating the now program into a respectable design, against the cartoonish images shown at the inception. After all, it was not the architect's responsibility to define a program but rather to make it work within the context of an overall design concept.

I couldn't make those changes, thought Philip, *but surely I could rely on Ricardo.* He remembered what Ricardo said at Diane's memorial pledging his loyalty to Philip and the project. But he could no longer trust Alex, whose morals were clouded and whose motives had been shown to be strictly centered on protecting his own financial interests. Philip lay back in his lounge chair day after day, contemplating alternatives but unable to focus on a clear direction.

On the Sunday following the reception, Philip had come to a decision. He shaved and showered before leaving his apartment to slowly walk to the site of the Eden Center. Along the way, he absorbed the now familiar streetscapes, avoiding the street corner where Diane was killed.

When the full scope of the Eden Towers came into view, he stared upward at the unfinished office tower, the centerpiece of his masterpiece, soaring high above a neighborhood that still contained mostly abandoned warehouses and a few seedy walk-up apartment buildings.

"Magnificent, yet..." he said out loud, but there was no one to hear him. He continued walking toward the main gate where the single guard recognized him and greeted him with a weak salute. "Good morning, Mr. Corta. I was so sorry about your wife. Isn't it a shame what's happened to this project? I hear that they're going to change it in a big way."

"Thank you. I thought I would take a quiet walk around to see how the project has progressed, if that's OK."

"Of course. Just be careful where you step, as there is a lot of debris that hasn't been cleaned up since they slowed the project down. And, don't be surprised by the guards we have walking around to make sure nothing leaves the site."

"Don't worry. I'll be careful." Saying this, Philip walked toward the towers with the lower-level façade sporting alternating bands of bronze cladding and bronze-colored glass, *like candy canes.* Looking up, the unfinished upper levels of the towers sprouted naked spike-like columns pointing to: *It can't be heaven, not after what had happened.* Carefully stepping around loosely thrown debris of drywall and empty paint cans, he reached the construction elevator, a rickety box enclosed with wire mesh, and switched on the power. He stepped into the cab, closed and locked the plywood gate, and pushed the controller to the "up" position.

As the small cab rose higher, Philip watched the changing vista through the grill, his face devoid of feeling but his mouth open in awe at the revealed cityscape, with towers of all heights and forms that appeared across the expanding horizon. *It's so beautiful, yet it hides such ugliness.* All was silent except for the slow grinding noise of the elevator as it moved higher. *I have to get off. I feel weak and can't stop shaking! If this dizziness would just stop!*

The cab stopped with a jolt when it reached the highest floor and Philip stepped out onto a steel deck that had not yet been finished with concrete. Philip's hand brushed against a rough concrete wall as he calmly walked toward the edge, protected by two tightly stretched cables anchored to the building columns and adorned with yellow banners warning, *Don't come any closer.*

There's so much left to do, he thought. *I've spent a lifetime learning and struggling and now that I've mastered my profession, life is over, and someone else will repeat this same cycle. It's not fair!* He looked down and observed. *The towers will be as I designed them. It's only the base that's been changed. Surely I can still influence what will be built there. But my vision of the complete project is being undermined. It's not possible to subdivide it and be satisfied with one part and discard another. Is it really too late to glue it all back together? Alex, you made me believe in paradise and now you've betrayed me. How can I forgive you and how can I forget?*

For the longest time he looked out at the site, dreaming of an uncertain future as he heard the slow grinding of the elevator in the background. He ducked under the upper cable while holding it firmly with one hand and stood precariously on the outer edge of the floor, looked down at the skylight above what was to be his entertainment complex, and said, "It could have been magnificent."

Looking toward the corner of the site where he had placed her ashes, he added, "Please forgive me, Diane, but I just can't accept what has happened and I cannot start over again without you." Remembering a poem by Emily Dickinson, *'Tis not that Dying hurts us so- 'Tis Living- hurts us more-*, he released his hold on the cable just as a hand clenched around his arm, pulling him back. He heard, "Not on my watch."

Philip tried to twist away. "Let me go." But the man holding him was too strong and wrestled him to the ground, saying, "You don't want to do this." He imagined himself falling soundlessly, as he sailed with his arms outstretched and his eyes wide open, relishing in the thoughts of his visionary project during his last moments until crashing through the skylight of the nature walk he had envisioned. He imagined hitting the hard surface, his breath and life crushed. He felt a hard object pressing him to the ground just before losing consciousness.

THE TELEPHONE RANG IN THE Grant house and Lila came in from the garden to answer it. Since she had told Alex to leave, she felt her life opening again, and spent time in the garden that had been neglected, braving the cold while removing dead plants so that she could start anew in the spring. When she picked up the phone, the voice on the other end asked for Mr. Grant. "I'm Mrs. Grant, can I take a message?"

"It's Artie at the site. I'm afraid something's happened to Mr. Corta."

Lila raised her voice in shock. "Oh my God, is he all right?"

"He ain't hurt but he ain't right in the head and they've taken him to Bellevue."

"When, how?…Thank you. I'll go there right away." Lila had so many questions in her mind, but no time now to ask them, so she quickly prepared to leave.

When she arrived at the hospital, it took her a long time navigating the many long corridors before finding Philip's room. It was in a minimum-security area as Philip was not considered to be a danger either to himself or others. When she reached the room she ran into the attending physician and immediately asked, "Mr. Corta, what's wrong with him?

Is he all right?"

The physician explained that Philip was slightly bruised and unconscious when he arrived but as he awoke, he became excitable and confused and was given a sedative to calm him. "He's awake now, and if you want, you can see him for a short time. But don't say anything to upset him."

When Lila entered the room she saw Philip lying still in his bed. He had a bruise on his nose and brow but seemed otherwise fine. "Philip," she said. "How are you feeling?"

Philip turned his head to look at her when he heard her voice. His eyes moistened. "Lila, I'm so sorry to have troubled you. I wanted to get closer to Diane but I'm afraid I've made a bloody mess of it. I don't know what I thought I was doing."

"Don't think about it now. Just let the doctors help you get well and when you are better, I want you to come and live with us."

"I couldn't do that. Alex….I couldn't"

"First of all, Alex will not be there and…"

"Oh no! I hope that's not because of me!"

"No, no. we've separated for reasons that have nothing to do with you. He's changed over time and I've changed, so don't worry about it. You can use Alex's study. There's a good bed there and you can be very comfortable. We'll bring your books and anything else you need."

"That's very kind of you, but I don't know…"

"You don't have to decide now. Just think about it. Now just get some rest and get well."

When Lila returned home, she called Alex to tell him what happened to Philip.

"He tried to do what?" Alex yelled into the phone. "What's wrong with the guy? What's he trying to do to me? I was even going to call him to say that his goddamn waterfall is back."

"Is that all you can say? You had better look into yourself. If you did, you would see that you had a lot to do with his trying to end his life."

"Look, I feel badly but don't try to put that on me," said Alex. "He couldn't deal with the reality of life and the fact that sometimes you have to make compromises. That was his problem, not mine. I kept trying to make him understand."

"How could you be so heartless?" said Lila "Of course, Philip was upset. When Diane was killed on 9/11 his life was turned upside down. It was such a cruel ending to a day on which we were all shaken by an unimaginable tragedy. Thousands of our neighbors being killed for what, for some crazy beliefs of a few demented terrorists? I knew one of the women who died in the collapsed towers. At least I was sympathetic to her family.

"I never heard you say one word about any of the people who died. All you moaned about was how it would affect Eden. And then the way you were so cavalier about making changes to Philip's design. On top of Diane's death, of course that made him more depressed."

Taking a moment to compose herself, Lila added, "Frankly It's becoming clear to me that we no longer have anything to say to each other." And she hung up.

The next morning Lila called Bellevue and arranged to have Philip transferred to a private clinic where she felt he would recover more quickly with more personalized care. For the next six weeks Philip began to deal with his insecurities and with the tragedy of Diane's death. Lila would visit often. He began to look forward to these visits. "I don't really recognize you as the woman I saw with Alex. You seem so different, so confident, so self-assured."

"I feel different. Sometimes it scares me… and the children are more relaxed, not so clingy." Beaming, she added, "In fact, I feel great."

After three weeks, the doctors announced that Philip was ready for a transition. Lila was told that he should not live alone for some time. This fit in perfectly with her plans, and she told Philip again of her offer to have him live in her house. After she explained the details of the living arrangements, Philip was not as reluctant to accept this offer as he first had been, and in fact relished the idea of being with her family.

"You remember that Diane and I very much wanted children and it was her great regret that we were unable to have them. I admit that I've always been somewhat awkward around most children but I always felt comfortable around yours." Smiling, he added, "Of course your children are no longer babies. I'm not sure I could have survived the crying and whining. At 9 and 11 you have real little people and I think I will enjoy getting to know them."

On the taxi ride home, Lila emphasized that Philip was not to worry about the progress of the project. She had talked to Ricardo, who had risen to the occasion and taken charge of completing the architectural work in accordance with the compromise agreed to by Alex. Of course, Ricardo would always consult with Philip before releasing the final documents.

When the taxi arrived at the Grant house, Philip hesitated for a moment before getting out. He had visibly aged since his hospital stay, with new lines crossing his brow and his gait had slowed as his movements became more measured. "How lovely," he said as they reached the study. "You've put out flowers for me."

"Not only that but I took the liberty to have some of your clothes brought over so you would not have to go back too soon."

"That's really considerate of you. If you don't mind, I'd like a little time to settle in and become familiar with my new surroundings." As he looked around the room, he wondered if Lila would mind if he brought over some of his own furnishings.

"Take as much time as you need. When you're ready, come upstairs for a little lunch. The children won't be home until four o'clock."

Lila had filed for divorce shortly after she told Alex to move out, as she realized that the man she had known at the beginning of their marriage was now buried inside the body of an inconsiderate and insensitive monster. Within a month of their initial separation, Alex had begun a relationship with a model he met at one of Josh Golden's parties and, shortly thereafter, he moved into his new girlfriend's apartment. To her amazement, Lila was relieved. And she was surprised to find that her children were perfectly happy to see their father every two weeks and no more.

Philip was charmed by his new family, as the children enjoyed "Uncle Phil," who taught them how to draw pictures of their cat, Cici. Alex Jr. watched as his older sister, Susan, drew a cat-like image. He was frustrated as his first drawings were more of an abstract impression of a cat. Philip patiently showed him how to begin with a sketch of the overall shape before trying to fill in details. In time, they developed an easy camaraderie, which amazed Lila, as she had never thought of Philip as a patient teacher.

Where in the past Lila would have retreated into herself, she now sought new friends and started to explore taking courses in art, as she had been encouraged to do by Diane before her death. She also began to consider what to do with the house in Truro that sat empty for most of the year. Alex was not interested in it, and an idea occurred to her that she would share with Philip once he was completely comfortable in his new surroundings.

As THE TOWERS ROSE EVER higher, twisting into the clouds, the construction team moved quickly to adapt to the resolution of the design change. Mike and Sam had been deeply affected by Philip's attempted suicide, and blamed Alex, whom they viewed as a heartless, insensitive boor. They avoided contact with him as much as possible.

Of course, Alex was a participant in the weekly site-coordination meetings, but since Golden's site representative, Jack Stein, had taken over as the leader of the development team, Alex's role had been pushed into the background. Also, Mike generally dealt only with Golden on financial issues, further diminishing Alex's role. Since his position on site had been so constrained, Alex became increasingly frustrated and would often absent himself from the weekly meetings. Sam, whose loyalties had been to Patrick, reluctantly accepted his replacement, as he found Stein to be a good manager.

Within a month, a topping-off ceremony would be held at the site, representing the installation of the last piece of steel at the top of the towers that would be memorialized with the attachment of a flag at the peak.

Mike asked Sam to meet to discuss their future. Sam suggested they meet in the bar where he and Patrick had spent a memorable evening cementing their friendship. "Not exactly the kind of place I had in mind," answered Mike, "but if that's what you want, OK."

They met the following day after work and when the regular patrons saw Sam, they asked, "Heard from Patrick lately? Hear he's a bigwig in Chicago now."

"No, but glad you reminded me and I'll be in touch with him." Turning to Mike, he asked, "What'll you have?"

"Scotch'll be fine."

"Make it two," said Sam to the bartender. Settling into the same booth that Sam remembered, he asked, "So, what do you have in mind?"

"This project is going to end in the near future and I wanted to talk to you about that. We've been working together for many years now and we've also become friends. But more than that, I've come to respect your work."

"Thanks, and I have really appreciated the opportunity you gave me and…"

"Let me finish," interrupted Mike. "I've been giving this some thought and would very much like to have you become my partner."

"That's a relief! Quite honestly, if you hadn't offered it to me, I was going to ask you for a promotion at the end of the project. Of course I accept! And thanks."

"I should have known, since you're a real self promoter. But anyway, welcome aboard! There is something else I wanted to mention. I've been giving a lot of thought about the future direction of the firm. I've come to the conclusion that from now on we should take only projects that have a humanitarian purpose. I'm not talking about totally restricting our clients, but to favor projects such as medical facilities, social housing, and so on."

"Well," said Sam, "if I'm to be your partner, shouldn't I have something to say about it?"

"So, what do you think?"

"I think it's a great idea and I know that Jan would be crazy about it."

"Then it's settled, partner." They shook hands across the table and each finished off their scotch.

PHILIP SETTLED INTO A ROUTINE, spending mornings at his office reviewing the final details of the design. These visits became more infrequent as the project moved toward completion. He discussed with Ricardo the future of the office as he let him assume more and more responsibility for the work. "I've been considering this for some time. After this project, I plan to close the office to devote myself to writing."

"But," exclaimed Ricardo, "this project will make you famous. You will be offered many new projects."

"You may be right but I find I don't have the urge nor the stamina to start new projects. Beside, Lila has offered me a dream. I can occupy her house in Truro for the rest of my life. It is a wonderful place to work and to be close to nature. You know that I've always felt that architecture derives from natural forms. This will give me time to explore this further and to write about it. It will be a complete exploration well beyond D'Arcy Thompson's classic work, *On Growth and Forms,* and that of contemporary organic form architects. I'm genuinely excited to start."

"What will happen to the office?"

"I will close it but—and I've given this much thought—I propose that you take over the office. I would recommend you to any clients that approach me. I have all the confidence in the world that you can manage. I've seen some of your design work and seen how you have executed and improved my design and know that you will make a brilliant architect."

"It's been an honor to learn from you and I hope your confidence in me is not misplaced."

"Actually, Diane used to tell me, 'That Ricardo is a gem.' As always, she was right."

Epilogue
March 2003

BALLOONS FLOATED UP TOWARD THE ceiling of the Eden Grand Hotel above the crowd of invited guests to the grand opening of the Center. On the stage, Josh Golden greeted the guests and invited Alex Grant to stand beside him as photographers memorialized the event in flashes of light. Alex was not comfortable being in the limelight, especially since his breakup with his girlfriend and the news stories that followed. "Noted developer caught cheating on his girlfriend and ends up in court after assaulting her for trying to kick him out of her apartment."

Claire sat on the stage next to Mayor Bartlett. She was visibly pregnant. When she first found out, she was very upset, but when Roger told her how delighted he was, she wanted this baby at all costs. She and Bartlett married three months ago and she moved into the mayor's mansion. Lila called to congratulate her and the two became friends, sharing dinners, with Lila often accompanied by Philip, who came down from the Cape. Philip thoroughly enjoyed his life in the house in Truro. He would spend his days taking long walks, sketching a plant or flower or seashell that he wanted to use as an illustration in the book he was writing.

The Longs and Ruths attended the opening, but stood disconnected from the audience of politicians and business leaders, some of whom they recognized from seeing their pictures in newspaper articles but who were strangers to them. Since the completion of construction, the two families had become even closer, especially after Sam was made a partner in Urbanland Construction Co. Mike and Sam sought new opportunities, but vowed never again to work for Alex. They had each received an identical email message from Patrick. "Congratulations on surviving your experience with Mr. Bigmouth. If you ever come to Chicago, there's a great little Irish bar that I think you would both enjoy. My treat! Pat."

Breaking away from the crowd, Jan and Marion headed to the corridor leading to the alpine shopping street. Along the wall were a series of images in crisp black and white that Diane Corta had taken to capture the story of the construction from the perspective of the workers in all their strength, sweat and grit. The two women stood and admired each of the photographs that illustrated a different aspect of the work. The last photo was an image of Philip, looking straight at the camera, a blank expression on his face and, reflected on his glasses, the naked frame of the Eden Center.

ABOUT THE AUTHOR

Matthys Levy is a founding principal and chairman emeritus of Weidlinger Associates. His credits as structural designer include the Rose Center for Earth and Space at the American Museum of Natural History, the Javits Convention Center, and the Marriott Marquis Hotel, all in New York City; and the La Plata Stadium in Argentina, which features his patented Tenstar Dome.

Levy is co-author of *Why Buildings Fall Down; Structural Design in Architecture; Why the Earth Quakes, Earthquakes, Volcanoes & Tsunamis;* and *Engineering the City.* He is also the author of *Why the Wind Blows: a History of Weather and Global Warming,* published in 2007.

He is a founding director of the Salvadori Center, which teaches New York City youngsters mathematics and science through hands-on learning about the built environment. He was born in Switzerland and holds a BSCE degree from City College of New York and Master's and CE degrees from Columbia University.